# in the
# *Shenandoah*
# VALLEY

# My Heart Belongs

## in the
# Shenandoah
# VALLEY

*Lily's*
*Dilemma*

## Andrea Boeshaar

## BARBOUR BOOKS
An Imprint of Barbour Publishing, Inc.

ISBN 978-1-68322-222-4

Adobe Digital Edition (.epub) 978-1-68322-224-8
Kindle and MobiPocket Edition (.prc) 978-1-68322-223-1

Series Design: Kirk DouPonce, DogEared Design
Model Photograph: Ildiko Neer/ Trevillion Images

Published by Barbour Books, an imprint of Barbour Publishing, Inc., P.O. Box 719, Uhrichsville, Ohio 44683, www.barbourbooks.com.

*Our mission is to publish and distribute inspirational products offering exceptional value and biblical encouragement to the masses.*

Member of the
Evangelical Christian
Publishers Association

Printed in the United States of America.

# Dedication

For Daniel, my real-life hero.


Special thanks to my critique partner Stephenia McGee
and my friend Susan Beganz.
You both helped me rediscover my love of writing.

# Chapter One

*Middletown, Virginia, 1816*

So what do you think, Cap'n?"

McAlister Albright, "Mac" to most everyone except his sea-weathered former first mate, bit into one of the few ripe apples dangling on fruit-laden branches. The perfect mix of tart and sweet exploded in his mouth, tempting him to take a second bite. "I say, I've never eaten a better apple."

"Ha!" John Blake guffawed and clapped him on the back hard enough that Mac stumbled forward. "It's 'cuz ya own this here orchard now. You're a reg'lar landlubber; 'tis what you are."

"True enough, old man." Mac had parted ways with the sea—ever since the Second War of Independence, which had commenced four years ago.

But last year was the worst—a bitter war with those he loved in Alexandria.

A light breeze cooled the sudden perspiration on Mac's brow. The war was over. Besides, Father was counting on him to make something of himself—prove the gossips wrong—in this new land in the Shenandoah Valley.

Truth to tell, Blake suggested the same thing. *Prove them wrong.*

Mac took another bite of the apple and forced his thoughts to the sunshine-dappled lane flanked by fruit trees. But the treasure didn't end with the apples. His orchards included peach and cherry trees. To the east lay a sprawling wheat field and acres of corn. It had been a marvelous investment—and Mac hadn't even gotten to explore the southern part of his property on the other side of Cedar Creek.

"So where do ya plan ta build your house?"

"Not sure." Mac finished his apple and pitched the core just as a strange sound flitted to his ears. He halted. "Hear that, Blake?"

"Hear what?"

"A song. Someone's singing." The sound sailed to his ears on a soft, moist wind, drawing him like a siren's call.

"All I hear is these birds cacklin' overhead."

"No, not them." Mac continued following the melodious notes to the creek's bank.

*"Know ye that the Lord he is God: it is he that hath made us, and not we ourselves..."*

Mac made out the words to the rich mezzo-soprano's song. He wasn't unfamiliar with opera, and his many years in religious schools allowed him to identify the song's words as coming from the Holy Scriptures.

*"We are his people, and the sheep of his pasture."*

The singer ended on a superbly pitched high note.

Mac moved aside a low-hanging tree branch, expecting to see a woman washing clothes or fishing. Instead, he got an eyeful of a bathing female—a shapely woman with golden hair. She stood beneath a canopy of trees in waist-high water with her back to him. Her damp, ivory skin glistened beneath filtered sunlight.

He swallowed hard. He should turn around immediately and make his presence known. That's what any gentleman would do—

And then Mac recalled that Alexandria's affluent society would deny that he was a gentleman. Only Mary had believed the best of him.

And she was gone.

The woman in the creek disappeared underwater then resurfaced seconds later. Her wet hair clung to her bare shoulders. Finding her footing, she wrung out her golden tresses. He hadn't noticed the soap in her hand until now when she lathered up while continuing to sing. Her voice both drew and enveloped Mac. He couldn't recall ever hearing a voice so pure.

The nymph dove under the shallow water then glided through the creek with such grace and ease that he was tempted to believe all those mermaid tales sailors never tired of sharing.

Blake's footfalls crunched behind him. "What is it, Cap'n?"

He tore his gaze from the enchantress. "Nothing. Go back up to the orchard." He wasn't about to share his vision of loveliness, not even with his best friend.

"Nothin', you say?" Blake stared at him from beneath arched brows. "It's somethin'. I can tell by that look of longing on your face." He craned his neck. "It's a woman, I'd wager."

"Yes, and show some respect." Mac's conscience bellowed at his hypocrisy. But, alas, he'd done enough peeping for one day. "Madam, you are not alone in this orchard," he called over his shoulder.

His words were met with a startled little cry. "Sir, you are trespassing."

"So it is a woman, eh?" Blake snickered.

Mac gave his former first mate a shove toward the orchard.

"I demand you get off my property at once!" came the woman's voice.

"She demands, Cap'n." Blake snorted.

Wearing a grin of his own, Mac wondered if he'd heard a slight German accent in the woman's angry tone. "Madam, this is my property. I have the deed with me."

"You're a liar and a knave. Now please remove yourself from my land or I shall summon the authorities."

Blake broke into a chuckle, and Mac had to admit, the image of her fetching the authorities was amusing, especially given the state of her undress. He spotted her brown and beige print gown and the rest of her frippery slung over a low-hanging branch of a giant willow. A slight wind blew through the leaves and the wise old tree seemed to whisper a warning against any teasing.

Mac wondered at his prick of conscience, but he trusted his instincts. They'd helped him survive the war, after all. And perhaps the woman's jealous husband lurked nearby. The last thing Mac wanted to do was anger his neighbors.

"Sir, if you would please step away and allow me a bit of privacy. . ."

"Of course, madam."

"I'm not a madam. I'm a miss. . .Miss Lilyanna Laughlin, and you're trespassing."

"So you've said." Mac thought her name sounded as mellifluous as her song. "I am Captain McAlister Albright. My friend and I shall await your presence some distance from the creek bank."

"Do not tarry on my account, sir. I would prefer that you return from whence you came. This is Laughlin land—land that my grandparents purchased decades ago and presented to my parents as a wedding gift."

Mac wasn't about to continue the shouting match. He'd wait until Miss Laughlin dressed.

"The lass has pluck," Blake said. "I'll give her that much."

Mac bit down on his back teeth. The matter no longer amused him. Did she really believe this was *her land*? As if in reply, he heard the rustle of nearby foliage, accompanied by angry mutters.

Blake plopped down beneath a tree and stretched out his burly but amazingly nimble frame. "We'll be waitin' here for some time, Cap'n. I feel it in m' bones, and you know my bones don' lie."

Mac plucked another apple and tossed it to Blake. "Gnaw on that for a while to help pass the time."

Blake grumbled, and Mac folded his arms across his chest. The old man had his faults, as Father aptly pointed out, but Blake had been the finest, most loyal first mate and friend Mac had ever known. And it wasn't as though Blake cheated at cards or stole another man's property. He simply enjoyed the rougher parts of Alexandria—the parts of town respectable folks stayed clear of.

"I hope you are keeping your distance, sir." Miss Laughlin's voice carried above nature's din of twittering birds and buzzing insects. Tree branches waved in a telltale sign of her progress. "I hope you are a man of your word."

"I am, miss." Mac leaned one shoulder against a tree trunk.

"If you can hear me, then you're too close. Move away at once."

Mac smirked. "I cannot see you, so your privacy is ensured."

"Bossy little thing, ain't she?" Bits of apple lodged in the corners of Blake's wide mouth. A spark of amusement lit his blue eyes.

As usual his friend spoke Mac's very thoughts.

Blake snorted a laugh. "Methinks the afternoon just got more interesting, Cap'n. What say you?"

Mac cast a glance toward the swishing green shrubbery. "I say we will have to wait and see."

❤

Lily's hands shook so badly that she fumbled with her shift and her drawers. What was that man doing here, on her property, and just how much of her midafternoon bath had he witnessed? She pulled her petticoat over her head and managed to secure it in the back. Her shoulders ached from her attempt at weeding the wheat field this morning. Some help her younger brothers had been, the scamps.

Despite her damp legs, Lily managed to roll up her thigh-high stockings and secure them. She yanked her simple gown over her head then tied complementing ribbon around its high waist.

She lifted Papa's pistol from the rock on which she'd set it. She readied it just in case she'd need to use it. She knew how to shoot. Papa had taught her when she was just fourteen in case the British tried to possess their lovely *Haus am Bach*—house by the creek.

At last Lily felt ready to greet her trespassers. Except for her hair. Her fingers fumbled through her thick locks as she tried to pin it up, but since she'd forgotten her comb there wasn't much hope for the tangled mass.

Using the worn and familiar rooted path, she easily made her way up the creek bank. She peeked around a willow's wide trunk and spied two men loitering beneath her apple trees. One was plainly attired and seated in the grass, a leather satchel and two straw top hats beside him. Even in repose, he looked as short as he was wide. His shaggy gray hair hung nearly to his shoulders, and he appeared to have the whole world etched on his face.

The other gent looked younger, and Lily guessed he couldn't be more than nine and twenty. His jet-black curls were fashionably short, and neatly trimmed dark whiskers extended from above his ears to halfway down his jaw. Broad shoulders shifted beneath an ivory shirt with its voluminous sleeves and typical necktie. A suede vest stretched across the expanse of his chest. He sported no frockcoat, so his expertly tailored buckskin breeches revealed narrow hips and well-toned legs. On his feet he wore tall black boots. Quite the handsome dandy, although a brooder, judging by the deep set *V* of his swarthy brows.

Slowly, Lily stepped out of the brush. A twig snapped beneath her slipper and both men swung around as if to nab her. She gasped and raised her pistol, aiming at the younger man's midsection. Papa had taught her to aim low so she'd strike high. With any luck, she might hit her present target in the throat.

Both men's eyes widened, the younger man's shining like her brothers' ebony marbles.

"No need for that weapon, Miss Laughlin," the dark-haired man stated.

"And how am I to believe that when you're spying on me and just now scared me half to death?"

"We weren't spyin', lass." The older man sprang to his feet. "We just happened to hear you singin' and got curious, is all."

Lily worked her lower lip between her teeth. She had been singing—and at the top of her lungs. Besides, the pair didn't resemble vagabonds. Their clothes were much too fine.

"It's the truth, Miss Laughlin."

Lily recognized his deep, smooth, and quite sincere-sounding voice. He was, indeed, the captain.

"Lass, we don't mean you any harm," the older man said. "If we did, we could've done it already."

He had a point, but Lily took her time lowering the pistol just in case they weren't truthful. "Why are you on my property, and what must a girl do to make you leave?"

"Shootin' us is one way, I s'pose." The older man snorted and a smile stretched across his leathery face.

"Do not give her ideas, Blake." The captain glowered. "It was I at whom she pointed her weapon. I didn't survive the war only to be felled on my own property."

"But this is not your property, sir. It belongs to my family and me."

His gaze slid back to her. "I'm afraid you're mistaken, miss. I purchased this land weeks ago."

"So you are Captain Albright?"

"I am." He gave her a sweeping bow that, in another place and time, she might have deemed most charming. "And this is my swashbuckling friend, Mr. John Blake."

"A pleasure, miss."

"Likewise." Lily looked from one man to the other.

"If you'll permit me. . ." The captain pointed to the leather pouch. "I will produce the deed and clear up this unfortunate misunderstanding."

"Unfortunate for whom?" Lily narrowed her gaze and thought she saw a hint of a smile curve the captain's lips.

He slowly stepped sideways, extracted folded documents from the satchel, and strode toward her. He stopped only inches away, and his leathery, musky scent wafted to Lily's nose. He unfurled the papers with a snap.

"See here, Miss Laughlin." He pointed to the inked words and then proceeded to read them to her.

"I can read the deed for myself." Lily snatched the documents from his grasp and read the first page. She used her right wrist to assist in turning the page and the two men hit the ground.

Lily glanced at her pistol. "Begging your pardons, sirs. I forgot I was still in possession of my weapon."

Captain Albright stood. "Allow me, Miss Laughlin." He eased the gun from her fingers. After uncocking it, he set it near her feet. If she wasn't mistaken, he exhaled a relieved-sounding sigh before brushing the dried leaves and dirt from his breeches.

Once more, Lily gave the deed her full attention. It was filled with complicated jargon that she didn't completely understand, except for the last page. Captain McAlister Albright's name was printed and titled "Purchaser." His signature was scratched above it. And the seller?

Lily sucked in a breath and coughed when more than just air filled her lungs. "It can't be. . ."

However, there was no mistaking the name. *Silas Everett.*

"It's my signature," the captain said. "I can prove it."

"No, it's not your signature I'm disbelieving. It's Mr. Everett's." Lily stared at the man's name. He'd been Papa's closest friend, and for the past nine months he'd looked after her, her two younger brothers, and Aunt Hilda, just to make certain they wanted for nothing.

So how could he sell their home with nary a word?

He couldn't have!

Lily looked up into the captain's dark eyes. "Mr. Everett doesn't own this property, so he can hardly sell it."

"Pray, who owns it then?" Frown lines creased the captain's sun-bronzed forehead.

"Why, my father owns it, sir."

The captain surveyed the land around him. "Where is he, that we may settle this matter?"

Lily's mouth went dry. Her lips moved, but the words seemed stuck in her throat. Her knees threatened to buckle as reality hit.

"Out with it, lass," Mr. Blake chided. "We haven't got all day. Why, it'll be nightfall—"

The captain silenced his chum by simply lifting one hand. "Miss Laughlin?" His voice sounded less potent. "Where is your father?"

Tears blurred her vision. "He's dead, sir. Died suddenly some nine months ago."

"Leaving only you?"

"My two brothers, my aunt, and me." Lily teetered and the captain cupped her elbow.

"I'm sorry for your loss, Miss Laughlin, truly I am. But I presume that your father named Mr. Everett as executor or guardian and, thus, Mr. Everett had every right to sell the property to me."

"Yes, I suppose he did." Papa had left no will, so the magistrate had appointed Mr. Everett. It only made sense, as Mr. Everett was Papa's trusted friend. "I see that I have been a silly little fool."

"No, no. . .it was a misunderstanding." The captain's voice caressed her.

"How very gracious you are, Captain, considering my rudeness." Lily scooped up her pistol. She wouldn't need it. The captain and his comrade posed no threat. "You will want my family and me to move out of our house immediately, I presume." She licked her lips and tipped her head. "But might you give us time to find somewhere to go?"

"Are you referring to the limestone manor across the meadow?" The captain indicated the northeast corner of the acreage.

"Yes, sir, I am."

"Well, see?" Captain McAlister's countenance brightened at least two shades. "Good fortune is smiling on us both. I don't own the manor. If you'll walk with me, I will show you the property lines."

She gave a nod while relief spiraled down inside of her. *Haus am Bach* remained in their possession.

The question was, for how long?

# Chapter Two

o that's the situation," Lily explained while Aunt Hilda pounded a lump of dough into submission. "We'll have no crops this year."

"And what will we eat? Our shoes?" A streak of flour dusted the older woman's cheek, and Lily gently brushed it away. It seemed like Aunt Hilda had lived here forever, even though she'd moved in only a decade ago, after Uncle Thomas succumbed to his weak heart.

"Speaking of food," Lily began, "I've invited our new neighbor and his comrade to take supper with us."

"You invited strangers?"

"Not strangers, Aunt Hilda. Our new neighbor." *And a very handsome new neighbor at that.*

A gentle breeze blew in through an opened window and reminded Lily of how the wind had tousled the captain's ebony curls. The thought of the cleft in his chin and his shadowed jaw had made it difficult to concentrate on the property particulars. And those eyes. . .so brown they appeared almost black. They seemed to hide a treasure trove of secrets. What girl wouldn't be tempted to try to unlock them?

Lily realized her aunt was staring at her with a peculiar expression.

"Did I mention that the captain has a friend with him? His name is Mr. John Blake."

"I believe you did, but I don't like the sound of this, Lily." Aunt Hilda resumed kneading the bread dough. "Something's fishy, and it's not our supper."

"I might agree, Aunt, but what can I do? Captain Albright's deed looked official, and I don't believe he's a swindler. But rest assured, I will think of something."

"Well, don't go marrying Mr. Everett."

"Aunt, please!" The very thought brought bile to the back of her throat. "The man is Papa's age. Papa's friend."

"He has wanted to wed you for some time, Lily. I can see it in his eyes."

Lily dropped into the closest chair. "I can't. . .won't!"

"Good girl." Aunt Hilda continued with her bread-making. "I don't trust Silas Everett. I fear your father, my dearly departed brother"—she hurled a reverent gaze upward before returning her attention to Lily—"made a terrible mistake by not making a will."

"But I'm sure he did. We simply have to find it."

"We've looked everywhere." Aunt Hilda punched the dough. "It doesn't exist. What's more, Silas Everett is a tyrant when it comes to business matters. Everyone in Middletown knows it. He's a cheat and a liar and—"

"But Papa trusted him." Lily sighed. "And now so must we."

"Your papa was an easy target. He took people at face value, never considering their motives."

Lily groaned.

"Your father also enjoyed the gaming table at the Stony Inn, and he wasn't much good at gambling. Mr. Everett liked that part the best since he has that sinful den of iniquity called a card room in the back of his establishment." Aunt Hilda narrowed her gaze. "And where did he get the money to remodel that inn of his, hmm?"

"Papa's funds?" Lily squeaked out the reply. Truth to tell, she couldn't wrap her mind around the idea that Mr. Everett cheated them. More than likely Papa had gambled his money away. "If Papa's funds are gone and Mr. Everett needed to sell off part of our land, will he also begin to charge us rent?"

Aunt Hilda lifted sturdy shoulders.

"How will we pay it now that our orchards and grain fields belong to another?"

The ripening apples came to mind, a crop they had been readying to pick and harvest, but one they could no longer sell at the market. And Aunt Hilda's sweet apple treats and equally as tasty pear, cherry, and grape jams; peach cobblers—all gone with a stroke of Mr. Everett's pen. Bushels of corn and wheat were no longer theirs for the taking, which meant no bread, cakes, or pies. Middletown folks hailed the Laughlin crops as some of the best in the Shenandoah Valley.

"We'll be indebted to Mr. Everett," Aunt Hilda said, "and that's just the way he likes it. He hopes to force your hand so you'll have no choice but to marry him."

"Never!" Her shoulders sagged. What if the money was truly gone?

With her elbows on the table, Lily held her head in her hands. "There simply must be some mistake." She brought her gaze up to meet Aunt Hilda's. "I, at least, want an explanation. Mr. Everett owes us that much."

"He owes us nothing. He holds the purse strings."

Before a reply could form on Lily's tongue, her two brothers burst through the side door. Aunt Hilda muttered something about wayward youths and waved her flour-encrusted rolling pin, but Lily took action. She stood and caught the pair by the collars of their shirts.

"What on God's footstool makes you think you can gallop into the house like a team of ill-bred horses?" She gave them a shake. "And just where have you been all day? I needed your help weeding." What a waste of time that had been. The field no longer belonged to this family.

"We were in the cornfield, sissy," said Jed. At twelve years old, he was the spitting image of Papa with his dark locks and stormy-gray eyes. Lily's heart ached for her father each time she set eyes on her little brother.

He was also the truth-teller of the two.

"We got lost in the middle of it and had to figure out how to get out."

"We weren't lost." Fourteen-year-old Jonah was as fair as Lily and stood nearly as tall, which gave him a false sense of confidence. He wasn't on the brink of manhood. He was a child. "I knew where we were the entire time."

"And I knew you weren't helping me with the chores." She tweaked her brothers' earlobes, causing them to wince. "Now go out to the well and wash up. We're expecting guests for supper."

"Mr. Everett is coming, same as always," Jonah groused, rubbing his ear. "Why do we gotta wash up for him?"

"Because our new neighbor and his friend will join us for supper. He is the new owner of the orchards, wheat fields, cornfields, and the barn and property across the creek."

"But that's our land!" Jed looked up at Lily with questions shining in his eyes.

She shook her head. "Not anymore, I'm afraid."

"Did Mr. Everett sell it?" Jonah cocked his head and Lily wished her brother weren't quite so astute.

"Yes. But the good news is we have gained a pleasant neighbor and, Jonah, you might be interested to know that he was a sea captain during the war." Lily dangled the bait.

Jonah stared at her with wide, eager eyes. He couldn't get enough of hearing seafaring tales. Even his name evoked images of a tempestuous ocean and desperate sailors.

"He was a patriot, I hope."

"Well, I presume so. He didn't speak like a Brit." Truth was, Lily never asked. His friend, Mr. Blake, on the other hand, sounded as though he was British born.

She guided her brothers out of the kitchen and toward the well room's pump before taking in their dirt-stained shirts and trousers. "You'll both need to put on some clean clothes too."

Both boys groaned and hung their heads back.

"Oh, stop your bellyaching." Lily put her hands on her hips. "You live a hard life, you two, playing in the cornfield all day while I worked until my hands blistered." She lifted her still-stinging palms as proof.

When neither of her brothers came back with a retort, Lily returned to the kitchen.

"You've got your hands full with those two, Lily." Aunt Hilda glanced up from her bread dough. She'd made two fat mounds and set them on the baking stone. "Those boys need to be in school come fall."

Thoughts of her brothers' education—or lack thereof—caused Lily's heart to ache. Mama had wanted her children to be learned people. Her hope had been that Jonah and Jed would master a skill and become successful tradesmen.

With a sigh, Lily reclaimed her chair as Aunt Hilda set aside the dough so it could rise before baking. At the fire, she stirred the contents in the black kettle dangling on its hook above the flames. The tantalizing smell of mutton stew made Lily's mouth water, and she smiled at how dwarfed her aunt seemed by the large oven. It filled an entire wall of the kitchen and stood as high as the ceiling. Every morning it was Jed's responsibility to sweep out the ashes, but time after time he forgot, until Aunt Hilda reminded him with a whack on his rump with her wooden spoon.

"I hope you plan to speak with Mrs. Kasper about adding those boys to her classroom come school time."

"I do, but the boys don't want to go. I fear that if I press the issue, they'll only become more stubborn about it." She met Aunt Hilda's reprimanding frown. "The truth is, whenever the boys act up I find myself reconsidering Mr. Everett's offer of a boarding school."

"I might agree if I trusted that man. . .but I don't."

Lily didn't question her aunt. They had discussed the matter before and Aunt Hilda still maintained that Mr. Everett was a dishonest snake in the grass. Lily, on the other hand, was grateful that the man saw to their needs.

"Those boys need a shove in the right direction, Lily. They come and go as they please and terrorize the good citizens of Middletown."

Lily wanted to defend them, but last week's prank was still fresh in her mind. The boys had climbed trees on either side of the pike and, when Mr. Everett's carriage rolled by, they pelted it with eggs—fresh eggs that could have been enjoyed at the breakfast table. Of course, Mr. Everett was livid and Lily couldn't blame him.

"I suggest you begin by speaking with Mrs. Kasper and then go from there."

"All right, Aunt. Perhaps I can talk to her on Sunday." Mrs. Kasper was, after all, the reverend's wife. "If she's preoccupied, I'll walk over to the parsonage next week."

Aunt Hilda seemed appeased by the plan, but there was still a lot of time to pass between now and then—which meant more opportunities for Jonah and Jed to get into trouble. And what would the captain and Mr. Blake have to say about the boys?

Lily closed her eyes and sent up a prayer that her pesky siblings would behave themselves tonight.

♥

"So you were a patriot during the war, Captain Albright?"

"Yes." Mac resisted the urge to squirm beneath the boy's interrogation. The only reason he suffered it was because he recognized a love and appreciation for the sea burning in the lad's eyes.

Except Mac and the sea had parted ways—for good.

"I began as a privateer," Mac said. "My father, an Alexandrian merchant, owns a shipping company. My older brother Prescott inherited the business and took to all the bookwork while I desired to see the world."

"That's what I desire too." The boy's blue eyes widened. "Did you ever fight the Brits? I'll bet you won, right?"

"Fight I did. . .at first." Why bother lying to the boy? "But my ship was overtaken and Mr. Blake and I were impressed into the Royal British Navy."

The lad's expression dropped like an anchor.

Blake sat silently across the room. He looked lost in the depths of his homemade apple cider.

"Then what happened?" the boy asked, perking up a bit.

"Then—" Mac's chest tightened. "I was forced to work on a frigate, a warship designed and christened to kill Americans." He didn't add that a majority of Alexandrians felt the nobler thing would have been for Mac to fall on his sword or fling himself overboard.

Miss Laughlin entered the room. Mac's mouth went dry as he stood. If he'd been taken by her presence earlier, he was mesmerized now. Her golden hair that had hung past her shoulders in wild abandon only hours earlier had been tamed. Soft ringlets, tied with a headband that matched her gown, now framed her lovely oval face. She smiled and dipped in a curtsy, causing the bodice of her coral-pink gown to give him a hint of what lay beneath all those feminine layers.

"Welcome to our home." Miss Laughlin's gaze fell on her brother. "Jonah, I hope you have not been pestering the captain. He's our guest tonight."

"No, sissy." He swung a guilty look at Mac, who fought the urge to grin.

"I see my brother has given you some refreshment while we wait for our supper."

"Just like you told me, sissy."

She sent him an approving smile.

Mac held up his shiny silver goblet. "Your brother has been a most gracious host, Miss Laughlin."

"And now we're talking about the war and how—"

"No talk of war tonight, please." Miss Laughlin's features tightened. "We must look to the future and forget the past."

"Hear, hear!" Blake raised his goblet.

The lad's shoulders slumped in defeat.

"Perhaps another time, Master Jonah." Mac winked.

Jonah brightened. "My sister never wants to talk about war just 'cuz Oliver Ashton got himself killed in it two years ago."

"Jonah, I'm sure Mr. Blake and Captain Albright do not wish to hear such a woeful tale. They most likely have their own. Everyone does." She arched a delicate brow. "Now, no more talk of war."

"Yes, sissy."

"Forgive my brother, sirs." Her gaze flitted from Mac to Blake. "He is still a child and lacking in the social graces."

Beside him, Mac could almost feel Jonah tense.

"I'm not a child." He looked up at Mac. "I'm old enough to hire on to a ship, aren't I?"

"Why, certainly," Blake spouted. "You'd make a fine cabin boy."

Jonah beamed with momentary triumph. "See?"

"Dismiss thoughts of hiring on a ship this minute, young man." Miss Laughlin pressed her lips together and deep lines appeared on the bridge of her nose. Her gaze slid to Mac. "He's too young, isn't he?"

"Not at all, miss." Blake seemed oblivious to Miss Laughlin's trepidation, but Mac couldn't abide her troubled expression a moment longer. He stared down at Jonah. "But bear in mind that such a position is only offered to boys who know how to take instruction and follow orders."

Noticeable relief spread across Miss Laughlin's face. Then she graced him with a sunny smile that warmed his insides and made him feel as tall as Goliath.

"The cap'n's right, Master Jonah. Rebellious cabin boys walk the plank." Blake closed one eye and scrunched up his face, resembling any number of famously depicted pirates.

But Blake's remark, no matter how flippantly intended, brought back a wave of raw regret and images of Mac's crewmen being forced to jump to their deaths by their British captors. Sometimes Mac still heard their panicked screams in the middle of a sleepless night.

"Do either of you need a refill of cider?" Miss Laughlin's question plucked Mac from the deep.

He glanced into his cup. "Not I. Thank you."

"Me neither, miss," said Blake.

Mac cast aside his horrid memories and took in the sight of Miss Laughlin. She was a vision, all right. Her flawless complexion reminded him of a ripened peach and sweet cream, and her lips, full, ripe, and pink, made him long for a sampling.

She cleared her throat and motioned for them to be reseated before lowering herself into a cane-backed chair. "It's been a hot summer here in the valley."

He arched a brow. *Hence her bath in the creek this afternoon.*

As if she guessed Mac's thoughts, a blush worked its way across her cheeks and down her bare, alabaster neck—a neck that begged for kissing.

"I should tell you that the cider you're enjoying is from our—I mean, your—orchard. My Aunt Hilda makes it. She claims it's good for the stomach." Miss Laughlin sent a nervous glance toward the sitting room's archway. "My aunt will join us shortly."

"Can't say I've tasted a better apple cider, miss." Blake drained his cup.

"Oh, Aunt Hilda makes the best in the county." Enthusiasm lightened her tone. "She'll be pleased to hear you're enjoying it, Mr. Blake." She tossed another glance toward the entryway.

"So it's been a hot summer, eh?" The scamp in Mac surfaced. He couldn't resist teasing her, although he did wonder how the heat affected the crops. "Has there been much rain?"

"Lots of it," Jonah piped in. "Our swimming hole is deep enough that we can jump in off a tree branch without our backsides touching the bottom."

"Yes, I believe your sister showed me your swimming hole."

Her pink blush turned scarlet. "But there will be no more swimming, Jonah. Remember, I told you the orchard now belongs to Captain Albright."

"Yes, sissy." The lad hung his head sadly, plucking something deep inside of Mac.

"I'm sure I can be persuaded to allow you to cross my property to get to the creek."

A smile replaced Jonah's disappointed frown.

Miss Laughlin's gaze slid from her brother to Mac. "And speaking of your orchard, Captain. . ." She sounded eager to change the subject. "You'll find your harvest in excellent condition, although there have been those who predicted doom last spring."

"The world is filled with those who predict doom." Mac had experienced that firsthand when Alexandria society's whispers about his participation in the war became roars that were eventually printed in the newspapers.

"Aunt Hilda!" Miss Laughlin was on her feet in mere moments. She headed to the entryway and took the arm of an older woman.

Mac stood and motioned for Blake to do the same. Too long at sea had made his good friend lax when it came to manners.

"Aunt Hilda, this is Mr. Blake," she said before turning to Mac. "And this is our new neighbor, Captain Albright. Sirs, may I present my aunt, Mrs. Brunhilda Gunther."

"A pleasure, ma'am." Mac gave the woman a polite bow.

"The pleasure's mine, sirs." The woman's cheeks were as round and rosy as the apples in his newly acquired orchard. They appeared pressed into her doughy skin.

Mac lowered his gaze and grinned inwardly. Extraordinary how he saw food in the ladies this evening. Then, again, not so unusual, given the fact he hadn't eaten a solid meal since leaving Alexandria. The Stony Inn's rooms were comfortable enough here in Middletown, but the establishment could not boast of its meals.

"I'm especially pleased to meet you," Mrs. Gunther said, "if you're men who enjoy bowls of hearty mutton stew and thick slices of bread."

"My mouth salivates in anticipation, madam." That was no lie. The smells wafting in from the kitchen had tantalized Mac since he'd walked into the house.

"And I can eat at least twice as much as the cap'n." Blake guffawed.

"Well, then. . ." Mrs. Gunther rubbed her palms together. "Let's get to it, shall we?"

"But Aunt, shouldn't we wait for Mr. Everett to arrive?"

Mac tipped his head. "You invited the innkeeper?" Did she intend to protest the sale of land he'd purchased?

Miss Laughlin's eyes were wide and innocent. . .or so they appeared. But what really lurked behind their sky-blue depths? He'd learned more than a decade ago that women all too often harbored secret motivations.

Except for Mary Hanover. Never was there a sweeter female. Ever since they were children, Mac never had to guess at her intentions.

He probed Miss Laughlin's gaze, but no dubious gleam shone from it. He was certain he'd recognize it if it did.

"Mr. Everett has dined with us every night since my father's passing. He has been very generous with his attention and care of us."

"I see." Mac wondered if the true motive didn't lie with the tasteless food Everett's establishment served. "In that case, Blake and I are more than happy to wait for him, if that's your wish."

"Well, I'm hungry," young Jonah stated.

"Me too." Another boy, this one dark headed, pushed his way into the room.

Miss Laughlin caught his arm. "Sirs, may I present my youngest brother, Jedediah."

"Jed for short," Jonah whispered to Mac.

"I'll remember that," Mac murmured in reply.

Young Jed extended his hand and greeted first Blake then Mac.

"Well, it's not my wish to keep hungry children and guests waiting," Mrs. Gunther said. "I say we eat before our supper gets cold."

The boys cheered.

"Very well, Aunt." Something akin to uncertainty flitted across Miss Laughlin's lovely face. "Lead the way."

# Chapter Three

$\mathcal{L}$ily entered the dining room and realized at once that there was no place set for Mr. Everett. She sent a frown her aunt's way, but Aunt Hilda ignored it. She seated the captain and Jonah on one side of the cloth-covered table and Jed and Mr. Blake on the other side. Aunt Hilda and Lily sat at either end.

"Let's bless our food, shall we?" Aunt Hilda looked at the captain. "Sir, will you do the honors?"

"I'd prefer you did, madam. I'm afraid I'm overcome by the delicious smells surrounding me."

Aunt Hilda looked pleased. "Of course."

Lily bowed her head, and Aunt Hilda gave thanks to the Almighty for their food. Once the prayer was said, the men dug into their meals with a flourish. Lily hid a smile, but Aunt Hilda's expression of satisfaction could not be concealed. If there was one thing Aunt Hilda respected it was a guest with a voracious appetite, unlike Mr. Everett, who picked at his food and never ate more than a snail's serving.

Mr. Blake sat back and belched loudly, causing the boys to giggle. "My compliments to the chef." He patted his belly. "Delicious stew and salt-rising bread—I ain't had better."

"I'm so glad you enjoyed it, Mr. Blake." Pride shone on Aunt Hilda's round face.

Jed and Jonah attempted to belch as loudly as their guest. Lily let the matter go. Far be it for her to embarrass their guest by pointing out her brothers' bad manners.

Captain Albright glanced her way with a spark in his eyes that could only be amusement. The corners of his lips twitched and Lily decided the boys could go on belching if it meant the man would actually smile.

Somewhere behind her a man cleared his throat. Lily froze. She didn't have to turn around to see who it was. *Mr. Everett.* She winced. Why hadn't she heard his horses and eerie, black box carriage approach? No doubt she'd been sufficiently distracted by her dinner guests, and now Mr. Everett had caught her being lenient with her brothers. The matter would no doubt spark a conversation about boarding school again.

Slowly she rose and met their frequent guest and benefactor. Despite the summer heat, he wore his usual black frockcoat, waistcoat, and breeches. A white flouncy cravat encircled his throat, and white stockings encased his legs from the knee down.

"Mr. Everett." Lily welcomed him with a small curtsy. "We didn't think you were coming tonight."

He stared down his long nose at her. "Why wouldn't I come? Have I not taken my evening supper with you for nearly a year?"

"Yes, you have." Humiliation simmered in Lily's cheeks, but she remembered her manners and indicated the people at the table. "I believe you're acquainted with our guests, Mr. Everett. They are lodging at the Stony Inn."

"Yes, we've met." A polite smile wormed its way across his face then vanished when his gaze landed on Lily. Well-manicured brows, graying slightly, met above his beak-like nose in a heavy frown. It was then Lily remembered that there was no place set at the table for him.

She sprang into action and collected Jonah and Jed's dishes. "Follow me, boys." She led them through the swinging wooden door and into the kitchen. Setting their plates on the table, she swung around and faced them. "Your chores are waiting. When you're finished with them, you may have your dessert."

"But, Lily—" Jonah's hands fisted at his side. "I've never known you to be so cruel. Here a sea captain sits at our supper table and you refuse me the chance to speak with him."

"He is our new neighbor, Jonah." Lily hoped her voice sounded both firm and kind. "You will have ample time to speak with him, as he will reside next door. Meanwhile, your chores are waiting because you chose to play in a cornfield all day."

The boys grumbled, but neither argued. They started toward the back door, dragging their booted feet with each step.

"Oh, but you must change your clothes first. Chores cannot be accomplished while one is wearing his Sunday best."

"Aw, Lily. . ." Jed kicked the corner of the wall. "I already changed once today."

"And now you must change again." Lily collected a plate, a water goblet, silverware, and a napkin for Mr. Everett. "Perhaps this inconvenience will teach you both to do your chores before playtime."

Leaving her brothers to their tasks, she reentered the dining room. She found Mr. Everett sitting in her chair at the head of the table. Papa used to sit there and, ever since his passing, Lily had filled his vacancy at the table. As she neared, she noticed Mr. Everett had pushed her plate off to the side, where Jed had been seated beside Mr. Blake. Aunt Hilda's frown was as heavy as her favorite iron skillet. Lily tried to ignore her aunt's displeasure as she arranged the place setting in front of Mr. Everett. Then she passed the bowl of stew his way. The captain was kind enough to hand her the bread board, and Lily sent him a grateful smile.

Lowering herself into Jed's vacated chair, Lily noticed the boy had spilled gravy on the white linen tablecloth. She discreetly covered it with her plate.

"As I was saying, gentlemen. . ." Mr. Everett helped himself to one piece of stew meat, a small slice of potato, one carrot, and two slivers of onion. If the man wasn't careful, he'd likely blow away on a gust from North Mountain. "We have expert craftsmen here in Middletown who will be more than happy to discuss your building endeavors."

"Good to know. Thank you." Captain Albright sat back in his chair. "The first thing I need is a barn and stable along with corrals and pens. My livestock will be arriving in spring."

"Pray, what sort of livestock?" Lily sipped water from her goblet.

"A flock of sheep, a herd of cattle, a pair of goats, a drift of pigs, a team of mules, and two fine geldings. I will, however, require mules as soon as I can make the sale."

"Surely going from sea captain to farmer will be quite a leap." Mr. Everett cut his portions into nibbles.

"A farmer and investor. I plan to sell commodities such as wool, various cheeses, barrels of apples, goat's milk soaps, produce, tobacco, and cotton to my family's company. They'll be sold and shipped overseas. Wool and goat's milk soap are quite popular in England."

"Are they now?" At the captain's nod, Lily continued. "Do you plan to make your own soap and cheese?"

"No, I'll hire craftsmen."

"Or purchase slaves." Mr. Everett ran his tongue over his lips. "I've grown so annoyed with employees quitting at my inn that I'm determined to own some slaves."

"But that's morally wrong." Lily couldn't hold her tongue. She'd been raised to regard all human beings as equal despite their differences in skin color or language. "Surely you wouldn't buy human beings like you'd purchase cattle."

"I would indeed." His gaze narrowed and one corner of his mouth twitched. "And it is not for you to tell me what I should or shouldn't do."

"Of course. My apologies, sir."

"When guests are present, ladies should be seen and not heard at the supper table."

Lily clenched her jaw to keep from arguing the point. Keep silent, indeed! Who made up that silly rule? No doubt Mr. Everett did, for she'd never encountered it before.

And she refused to keep quiet in her own home. "We kept sheep and other animals until my mother died."

"A very unfortunate time," Mr. Everett said. "I remember it well."

Lily did too. Thank goodness the boys were too young to remember how their mother had suffered with her illness.

She shook off the sad thoughts. "How will your animals be arriving, Captain?" Her heart skipped a beat when his dark eyes settled on her.

"They'll be coming down the pike from towns located in the upper Shenandoah Valley."

"Why, Captain Albright, you should have told me of your need for a barnyard of critters." Mr. Everett pressed his napkin against the corners of his lips. "I could have brokered a good price for you."

"Thank you, sir, and with all due respect, I brokered a fine deal for myself."

"Ain't that the truth." Mr. Blake chuckled. "No one dickers better than the cap'n."

Were the seller a female, Lily imagined she'd succumb to Captain Albright's charm and give him whatever price he wanted.

"And, like you, Miss Laughlin, I don't believe owning slaves is a decent practice." His eyes moved to Mr. Everett. "It's merely my opinion, of course, but there you have it."

The conversation continued with Aunt Hilda and Mr. Blake tossing their thoughts into the mix. All the while Lily watched the captain. His movements were smooth and confident, from the way he held his fork and set down his utensils, to the way he raised his goblet to his lips.

Mr. Everett cleared his throat loudly, causing Lily to realize she'd been staring. She dragged her gaze away from the captain. "Did you say something, sir?"

The older man's eyes narrowed and he appeared almost angry. "I asked if there's a swallow or two left of red berry wine. My palate requires it in order to digest this overly rich meal."

"Hmmph!" Aunt Hilda stood, as did the men, but only she marched off toward the kitchen.

As long as the men were on their feet, Lily took the opportunity to rise from her place at the table. "In answer to your question, Mr. Everett, there is more than a swallow of wine left." There was an entire root cellar filled with various wines and ciders made from fruit from trees which now belonged to Captain Albright. "If you'll excuse me, I will fetch it."

"Of course." Mr. Everett bowed slightly.

Their guests reclaimed their seats, but Mr. Everett remained standing and caught Lily's hand as she passed him, halting her steps. He brought her fingers to his lips and placed a sloppy, wet kiss on the backs of them. "My dear, you're as heavenly as an angel."

"Such flattery, sir." She tugged her hand from his grasp and stepped beyond his reach in case he had a mind to surprise her further. Mr. Everett had never expressed such devotion before. She was well aware of his intent and didn't want his public display of affection.

On the way to the kitchen, she rubbed the back of her hand against the skirt of her muslin gown. God forbid he pay her any special attention in private.

❤

After dinner, the men traversed from the dining room to the parlor where they engaged in small talk—or rather Silas Everett babbled on about his accomplishments. While pretending to listen, Mac took note of the teal walls and complementary sea-green woodwork. He admired several of the framed oil paintings hanging in an attractive cluster on one wall and depicting various landscapes. It was quite clear to him that the Laughlins were not typical farmers or tradesmen for Middletown, Virginia. Their home and furnishings spoke of their wealth.

Miss Laughlin entered the parlor balancing a silver coffee service and two plates containing thick slices of cake. Mac quickly took the large tray from her and set it on the sideboard, which stood against the far wall like a stately old soldier.

"Thank you, Captain."

"My pleasure."

Her blue eyes briefly met his gaze before sinking to the coffee service. She poured him a cup. "Sugar or sweet cream?"

"Neither. Thank you."

Miss Laughlin began serving the sweet treats, although Mr. Everett waved off both the coffee and cake. He seemed content with his wine.

But Mac had every intention of indulging.

"For you, Captain?"

"Absolutely." He smiled his thanks, which seemed to put Miss Laughlin in some sort of trance. It took her several seconds to recover.

"I believe that's the first time I've seen you smile, Captain Albright."

"Really?" He leaned his elbow on the sideboard. Hadn't he smiled at her numerous times since their meeting this afternoon? Apparently not. He leaned close to her. "Perhaps my frowns were due to my starving for delicious food and good company, both of which I have found in your home."

"Is that all it takes?" Her luscious lips curved upward, displaying a hint of a dimple in her cheek. "Then you're welcome to smile in this house often."

"I can hardly refuse such an invitation."

Mr. Everett cleared his throat. "Lily, be a dear and fetch my pipe and tobacco. I believe I left them in your father's study."

"Of course."

After dipping a quick curtsy, she stepped around Mac. Her delicate scent of honeysuckle and mint stirred something deep inside of him. He envisioned the lovely sea nymph of this afternoon, swimming in the creek and singing as if she hadn't a care in the world. Yet Lily Laughlin clearly shouldered the enormous weight of her family's welfare, and Everett seemed to only add to it. From what Mac had witnessed so far this evening, the man's arrogance alone deserved dressing down. If Miss Laughlin didn't do it, Mac might be tempted.

She returned with the requested items and then offered Mac a thick cigar. He couldn't resist and took one.

"We grow fine tobacco here in the Shenandoah Valley." Her proud expression slowly fell. "That is, you've got a fine crop of tobacco. Typical harvest is late September or early October if the weather holds."

"I'll remember that." Mac took a swallow of coffee.

"My brothers and I are willing to help if you need it."

"That's very generous of you. I may take you up on your offer."

"Captain"—Everett's voice shredded the easy conversation—"shall we step outside with our smokes?"

"Indeed." It would be terribly rude to light up in front of a lady.

He followed Mr. Everett's lead out the side door of the parlor. It opened to a brick lanai. The day's heat had cooled and a tepid breeze wafted over Mac. An enjoyable evening all around.

They lit their tobacco.

"Captain, I'm afraid I must forbid you from employing Lily's—er, Miss Laughlin's help with your harvest." Everett puffed on his pipe. "I would prefer that she dedicate herself to becoming the lady of the manor. Her brothers, those wayward brats, need to be in boarding school."

"I see." Mac drew on his cigar. Whatever plans were in place, they weren't any of his business, although, to be honest, he felt a measure of pity for Miss Laughlin.

"I've known Lily since she was a newborn babe." A cloud of bluish smoke issued from Everett's mouth when he spoke. "The apple of her papa's eye, she was, and he spoiled her rotten."

"So you've determined to undo the spoiling?"

"It's my duty, I'm afraid."

"You're the Laughlins' guardian then?"

"I'm more than that, Captain Albright." He leaned closer to Mac. "I have plans for Lily. . .when she proves she can be a lady of the manor, of course."

"Of course." The fop probably intended to marry her, but it wasn't any of Mac's concern. Old men married young ladies all the time, especially when they sensed their time to beget an heir was rapidly ticking by.

"I warned Reginald—Lily's father—that he would be sorry he didn't send her to finishing school abroad. But then war broke out and Reggie had every excuse not to send her. So now she will turn twenty soon and has no prospects whatsoever."

"Ah, so you'll deign to marry the poor girl." Mac meant it half in jest, but Everett didn't look a mite amused.

"I'm her last hope, I'm afraid."

"And she's your brightest future." At Everett's quizzical frown, Mac added, "What I mean is, Miss Laughlin possesses many charms, especially in the area of hospitality." He could think of a few more categories, but deemed it best to hold his tongue. "I will say this, however. My purchase of Laughlin property came as quite a shock to her."

"Lily will get over her surprise." Everett set down his pipe and patted the pocket of his waistcoat. "I just remembered. I brought Lily a book on etiquette. It was given to me by an upstanding Englishwoman who stopped at my inn to wait for the next stagecoach to Winchester. I must give it to Lily immediately so she can study it."

Mac took another draw on his cigar.

Everett emptied his pipe in the flower garden. "Do you play chess, Captain Albright?"

"I do, although I'm far from an expert at the game."

"What say you to a match?"

Mac pursed his lips and nodded. "Let's play."

Mac dropped his cigar and ground it out beneath his boot before following Everett into the house. Miss Laughlin sat in an upholstered chair, sipping amber liquid from a goblet. The boys had returned, wearing stained shirts and tattered trousers, and they along with Mrs. Gunther listened to Blake play a mournful tune on his squeeze-box.

"Look what I've procured for you, Lily." Everett thrust the book at her. "You must read it at once."

"Oh. . ." She gazed at the title.

Everett tapped its cover. "*Proper Etiquette for Young Ladies.*"

"Yes, I can read for myself."

"Then see that you do. It will help you become a true lady."

Two red spots appeared on her cheeks. "Thank you, Mr. Everett."

"And, pray, what are you drinking?"

"Why, apple cider, sir." Her voice sounded strained. "Would you care for a glass?"

"No, no, I still have my wine to drink."

Lifting her chin, Miss Laughlin returned her attention to Blake's music. Mac sensed her humiliation, and his heart ached for her. Perhaps there was a volume on gentlemanly manners somewhere that Everett could make use of.

The innkeeper sidled up to the gaming table in the corner of the room. "Run along now, Lily and Mrs. Gunther. I'm sure there are pots and pans to scrub." He lifted a chess piece and turned it in his palm. "Oh, and take your brothers. The captain and I are going to play a game of chess."

"We're not concerned with pan scrubbing tonight, Mr. Everett," the older woman said. "I'm enjoying the music and Mr. Blake's good company."

"So are we," piped up Jonah.

Jed nodded.

Everett frowned.

"What's more, I play a mean game of chess myself." Miss Laughlin set her goblet on the table beside the chair and stood. "So I hereby challenge the winner of the first game to a second match."

"I must object!" Everett's voice rose above the squeeze-box and Blake stopped playing. "A lady must not engage in such behavior as challenging a man to a chess game. . .or challenging a man. Period."

"But this is my home, not some public gaming room. My challenge is quite appropriate." Her gaze lit on Mac. "Am I correct, Captain?"

"I've known my mother and sisters to join in games of fellowship with guests in our home, so yes, I'd say you are correct, Miss Laughlin."

Her blue eyes glimmered triumphantly. "So you see, Mr. Everett. All is well. My challenge stands."

Everett's face reddened and a muscle worked in his jaw. Mac was sure that, as angry as he seemed, smoke would billow from his ears.

Even so, Mac couldn't subdue his grin. A greater incentive to win a game—or lose it—he couldn't recall. "I hereby accept your challenge, Miss Laughlin."

## Chapter Four

*L*ily sat at the game table behind her chess pieces. She eyed the captain and grinned at the confidence shining in his dark eyes. Papa had taught her how to play and she could put the best of opponents in checkmate in only four moves, if they moved their pawns the way she hoped the captain would.

"Watch out. She's as slippery as an eel when it comes to chess."

"Jonah!" Lily sat up a bit straighter, a smirk tugging at her lips. "How do you know whether an eel is slippery?"

"I read about it." He leaned on Captain Albright's shoulder as if they were the best of friends.

"You should be rooting for me." Lily pushed out a purposeful pout.

"Sorry, sissy, but us seafarers gotta stick together."

Jed put his arm around Lily's shoulders. He smelled like fresh air and dried grass. "I'm on your side, sissy."

"Thank you." She sent Jonah a look she hoped was as severe as any of their father's expressions.

At the other end of the sitting room, Mr. Blake played another tune on his squeeze-box, a treasure he claimed to take with him on sea and land.

"A wager, miss?" The captain arched a brow while a challenge shone in his dark gaze.

"Well—"

"Absolutely not!" Mr. Everett jumped up from his seat near the window. "I forbid it. Gambling is a grievous sin, and I'll not have Miss Laughlin be morally corrupted for your amusement."

"And yet, you offer a gaming room at the Stony Inn." The captain sent a wink to Lily.

"That's different. I only allow men to play."

"And become morally corrupted?"

"Bah!" Mr. Everett's face swelled, then reddened, indicating his fluster.

Lily sent a look toward the plaster ceiling. Why hadn't she noticed Mr. Everett's hypocritical philosophies before now? He'd embarrassed her in front of their new neighbor and his friend, and then expressed concern over her moral welfare. Such nonsense.

She regarded the captain through lowered lashes. What must he think of her, considering the circumstances of their meeting this afternoon and Mr. Everett's gift of a book on etiquette? Why Captain Albright must think she was a common shrew.

Mr. Everett clasped his hands behind his back. "She has no money with which to bet, Captain." He neared the game table and Lily shrank. "She's penniless, which is why I was forced to sell some of her deceased father's property. Besides which—" His arms made a swoop about the room. "I own the house and everything in it."

Lily gasped. *Haus am Bach*—gone?

A knot of shame tightened in Lily's chest and she fought to contain her emotions. So it was true. Aunt Hilda had been correct in her earlier assumptions. And if she wanted to remain in her beloved home, she would, no doubt, pay dearly.

Marriage to Mr. Everett.

Bile rose in her throat. Never! But then. . .how?

"Money isn't always the best prize." The rich timbre of Captain Albright's voice commanded Lily's attention. "For instance, if I win, Miss Laughlin, I shall dine at your table every night until my home is built and adequately staffed."

Lily's gaze sought Aunt Hilda's. Seated across the room, the older woman gave a slight nod before returning to her needlework. Lily couldn't see the harm in it. For now they had plenty of food.

"I accept the terms." Lily tipped her head as a gentle summer wind swirled in through an open window and cooled her nape. "And if I win?"

The captain stretched and locked his hands behind his head, but his onyx eyes never wavered from Lily's face. "If you win, I will give you three-fourths of this year's crops."

"Three-fourths?" A seed of hope sprang up in Lily. They could harvest as usual, and if Shona and his fellow tribesmen came this way, they would be willing to help. They had in the past. Lily and her family would not be penniless. They might even have. . .options!

"That's a generous wager."

The captain shrugged broad shoulders. "I'm not giving it away, Miss Laughlin. You must win it." He swept his hand over the chessboard. "Ladies first, so you'll be white." He turned around the chessboard. "Your move."

Lily quickly strategized. This game meant everything. *Lord, please. . . that this game would end in my favor. . .*

She slid the pawn above her king piece two spaces forward.

Captain Albright moved his knight diagonally, jumping his row of pawns.

Nibbling her bottom lip, Lily slid her bishop forward diagonally and positioned him a space away from her pawn.

The captain moved his far left-hand pawn forward two spaces.

Lily was motionless, hardly daring to breathe. It might happen!

"Have you fallen asleep, Miss Laughlin?"

"Hardly." She gave him a sharp look and moved her queen diagonally to the forefront.

"A bold move. Personally, I've found it's wise to protect royalty." He moved his pawn to lie in wait for her bishop.

Lily grinned. "Sir, you are a true patriot." She slid her queen all the way down the board. "Like any good American, you left royalty wide open for capture." A laugh erupted. "Checkmate!"

Captain Albright's smug expression vanished. He studied the board with a furrowed brow. Even Mr. Blake halted his music to cross the room and view the results.

"She's got you sure as I stand here, Cap'n." Mr. Blake laughed hard enough to shake his shoulders. "In only four moves!"

"Yes, I can see that," Captain Albright growled.

Lily silently praised God for her good fortune even though she knew the evils of gambling. However, she hadn't been the one to make the wager. Regardless, in just over a month, they would have their harvest—three-quarters of it anyway!

"I told you she's slippery." Jonah wagged his head.

Jed dissolved into laughter and did a victory cheer.

The captain narrowed his gaze. "Next time, I shall heed your warning, Master Jonah."

"Well, sir, never let it be said that I'm not generous." Lily straightened the board. "Captain Albright, you are welcome to dine with us any time."

A grunt was his only reply. He rubbed his jaw as if he couldn't believe he'd lost—and so quickly.

"You've inherited your father's love for gaming, Lily," Mr. Everett announced. "I see I will have to keep my eyes on you at all times."

"That's unnecessary, sir." She dreaded the thought and imagined answering to Mr. Everett would be like a jail sentence. "Unlike my father, I know when to quit. But I'm afraid I've grown ever so tired." She feigned a yawn. "Night is falling fast since autumn will soon be upon us."

The captain stood. "As much as I've enjoyed the food and company, and even the game-playing. . ." His dark eyes locked onto Lily's. "I'm afraid we must be off. We've planned for an early morning tomorrow." He turned to Mr. Everett. "I don't suppose I can talk you into giving us a ride back to town in your carriage."

"The invitation is open to you, sir. You are staying at my inn, after all."

"Thank you." The captain's gaze returned to Lily's. "We walked here this morning filled with a sense of exploration. However, I'm afraid my friend won't make the two-mile journey back without toppling to the side of the road."

Mr. Blake snorted. "Blame it on Mrs. Gunther's peach whiskey." He sent a wink Aunt Hilda's way. The older woman waved off the remark and—

Lily tilted her head. Was that a blush brightening Aunt Hilda's cheeks?

The men gathered their frockcoats and filed out of the parlor. Lily shooed her brothers upstairs. She breathed a sigh of relief to see Mr. Everett was the first man out of the house. She wouldn't have to endure one of his long and admonishing farewells. Lily particularly disliked it when he drooled over her hand. Thank God she'd been spared such a parting tonight.

Aunt Hilda and Mr. Blake exited the house next, leaving Captain Albright in the reception hall.

He turned to face her. "Thank you for inviting Blake and me tonight, Miss Laughlin. I enjoyed myself."

"You are most welcome, sir, and I meant what I said minutes ago. You and Mr. Blake may take a seat at our supper table any time."

"I will likely take you up on your offer."

As etiquette dictated—and, yes, she was familiar with etiquette, despite Mr. Everett's opinion—Lily offered her hand. The captain took it and brought it toward his lips, but then hesitated, peering up at her.

"You won't wipe off my regard on your skirt, will you?"

Lily's face warmed. So he'd seen her reaction to Mr. Everett's kiss tonight. She narrowed her gaze. "You won't slobber all over my hand, will you?"

"Definitely not."

His gaze looked aflame in the final glow of the setting sun. He brought her hand to his lips, but turned it at the last moment. His kiss landed on the inside of her wrist, sending a current up her arm.

"I suppose you wish to hear that I shall never wash this spot again." They were words Lily had spoken to Oliver Ashton before he joined the volunteers who defended Virginia's shoreline along the Potomac River. Little did she know Oliver had received similar reactions from all of Middletown's maidens—and he'd made the same promises to them as he had to her. *The cad!*

She tugged her hand from Captain Albright's grasp. He seemed an equally practiced charmer, if not more so than Oliver. But at least Lily recognized it now. She wouldn't be fooled again.

"Never wash your wrist?" The captain leaned toward Lily's ear. His warm breath sent a shiver down her neck. "On the contrary. I wish to hear you say that you'll bathe frequently, particularly if it means you'll be visiting your swimming hole of this afternoon."

An indignant cry left Lily's lips. She had a mind to slap his face. Instead she gave him a shove that barely budged him. How dare he mention the incident like it was some joke! Did he not realize the power it had to ruin her good name in Middletown?

*The rake. The scoundrel.* And just how much of her bath had he seen anyway?

He chuckled, a sound resembling the distant thunder of a blessed rainstorm. In seconds it drowned her anger until she succumbed to a smile.

"You, sir, are a rapscallion."

He bowed. "Guilty as charged."

Lily found it difficult to muster even a little displeasure when the captain's jesting reminded her of Jonah and Jed's silly pranks.

However, it wasn't the least bit amusing to imagine a sullied reputation. "You won't tell anyone of our accidental meeting this afternoon, will you?"

"I will not."

"And Mr. Blake?"

"I can assure you that he will also hold his tongue regarding the matter." The captain's expression lost all evidence of mirth. "Miss Laughlin, even rapscallions live by a code of honor, as it were. Thus, I shall never betray you. Tease you, perhaps. Betray you, never."

Lily believed him, although it made no logical sense to do so. But the lines around his eyes had softened and sincerity swam in his dark gaze.

Besides, she had no choice but to trust him.

"And on that promise, I shall bid you a good night."

"Good night, Captain." She gave him a slight curtsy.

He placed his top hat on his head. His broad shoulders blotted out the last of the daylight until he stepped outside. Leaning on the doorframe, she watched his long strides down the walkway. The heels of his boots clapped against the bricks with each step he took. All too soon, he was swallowed into Mr. Everett's box-like carriage.

Mr. Blake was the last one inside. As Aunt Hilda waved her white hankie, harnesses jangled and wooden wheels scraped against the earth, and the conveyance rolled toward town.

The awkward silence inside the coach thickened like pea soup as the carriage made its way toward the Stony Inn. Mac could think of only two reasons for it. Either Mr. Everett was miffed about the chess game and wager between Mac and Miss Laughlin or he was simply too tired for amiable chitchat.

The latter was what held Mac's tongue and likely Blake's too. It had been a long day, albeit a very good one. Mac was pleased with his investment—extremely pleased. Tomorrow he'd plot out where he'd build the barn and stable and, of course, his new home.

"Captain Albright"—Everett began, jerking Mac from his thoughts—"forgive my interference, but I hope you don't mean to have Lily—that is, Miss Laughlin—"

"Have her?" Mac shook his head. The man had nothing to fear from him. The news of Mary's death had caused something in his heart to die as well. He'd never love again.

"Yes, have Lily do fieldwork in order to obtain her winnings of the chess match."

A sudden inferno erupted in Mac's face and spread down his neck. Blake's grunted laugh only fanned the flames.

"Ah, yes, the harvest." Mac loosened his necktie. "The reason I offered it as a prize was because Blake and I will have no time to bring it in. It's a shame to let the fruit in the orchard and the grains in the field rot when they could be staples for Miss Laughlin's family."

"True, but I would prefer that Lily behave less like her devious brothers and more like the lady of the manor."

"So I heard you say earlier this evening." Shadows rose and fell across Everett's face as moonlight danced between lush treetops.

"After her behavior tonight, I'm sure you'd agree that it's time she corralled her energy and focused on more genteel duties inside her home."

"Pardon me if I speak out of turn, sir," Mac began, "but I saw nothing in Miss Laughlin today that hinted at a young boy's behavior. Rather, she was decidedly female."

"Decidedly." Blake rammed his elbow into Mac's ribcage. "And if she can cook as well as her aunt, she'll make some young swain a fine wife. Ain't that right, Cap'n?"

"Yes, we ate an excellent supper, and a lot of it." Mac glared at his friend then faced Everett again. He tried to gauge the man's reaction to the "young swain" remark, but couldn't decipher his tight-lipped expression in the murky darkness.

More silence filled the carriage as it rolled past homes and barns along the road. Finally they arrived in Middletown proper, which was no more than a fifty-acre settlement. Mac had done his research before selecting the area. According to the latest census, one hundred forty-four free folks and twelve slaves made their homes here. Quite a contrast to Alexandria and its more than eight thousand residents. But Middletown had its own claim to fame, as some of the best precision instruments were manufactured here along with fine clocks and watches.

The carriage halted in front of the Stony Inn, which doubled as a stage-coach relay station. At any time of day one could find citizens and visitors alike mingling in the dining hall or sitting at the recently built gaming table in the back room.

"Care to join me in a card game, gentlemen?" Everett peeled off his hat and handed it and his walking stick to a white-capped maid. She curtsied and scurried off.

"Not for me, thanks." Mac strode toward the wide stairway.

"Me neither. Early morning tomorrow." Blake's voice didn't hold much conviction.

Everett seemed to seize upon the fact. "One game, Mr. Blake. Surely you can sit through one game."

"Well. . .I suppose I can."

"I shall wish you both a good night." Mac paused and gave them a polite and parting bow. Then, accepting a lighted lamp from another maid, he climbed the steps to his rented room. He unlocked the door and a wave of heat crashed over him. Crossing the room, he opened the window, allowing the late summer breeze to ruffle the muslin curtains as it wafted into his quarters.

After shedding his overcoat, Mac unbuttoned his waistcoat then pulled off his boots. He pondered the events of his life that led him to Middletown. How different things were now compared to a year ago when he'd returned home with his British ally, Captain Taylor Osborn. Blake hadn't come along to Mac's family home that afternoon. He'd found acceptable quarters close to the wharves. At the time, the British army occupied Alexandria and Blake wasn't sure if he'd sign on with a merchant ship. He'd even pondered the idea of returning to England.

Meanwhile a squall gathered in Alexandria upon Mac's return. The

British and Loyalists welcomed him, so not all of his family's vessels were destroyed, as they would have been if he was a returning American hero. Nor was their home. However, the Patriots weren't so enamored of him.

Mac shook off the voices that still whispered "traitor" when he least expected it, although tonight they weren't quite as loud. Tonight he heard the sweet voice of a sea nymph singing in his head. He envisioned her plucky grin and vulnerable blue eyes.

*Lily Laughlin.*

Mac extinguished the lamp and crawled into bed. Hands behind his head, he watched the shadows play on the ceiling. His mind filled with certain moments of the day when her smile beguiled him, her laughter tickled him. Certainly, she had faced tough times, but a more joyful female he'd never met. What was it about her that set her apart from all the others? Why was she occupying his thoughts?

Part of Mac wanted to discover the answers to his questions, but caution rang loud and clear in his heart. The last thing he wanted to do was stir up trouble—and with Middletown's most prominent citizen, Silas Everett. Mac's plan was to carve out a small corner of the world for himself. By himself. And he had to succeed or succumb to a lifetime of failure. Father had agreed and granted Mac an early inheritance. Father had dubbed him the Prodigal Son, but, unlike the biblical character, Mac had no intentions of squandering his money.

No, he'd build a life for himself here in Middletown. A quiet life—alone. He'd subsist on what his land and animals provided and trade for what it didn't. Life would be infinitely easier that way. No more romantic entanglements. No more broken hearts.

Why, then, when he closed his eyes, did the vision of Lily Laughlin singing in Cedar Creek appear?

Mac was too exhausted to fight it so he allowed her to glide across his mind like a schooner across calm waters. Sleep came quickly.

# Chapter Five

*B*eneath her aunt's scrutiny, Lily made room for a jug of homemade
blackberry cider in the picnic basket.

"There. That should do it." Satisfaction glimmered in Aunt Hilda's blue
eyes as she stepped back and admired Lily's handiwork. She motioned to
Jonah and Jed. "Now, you boys work together and carry the basket over to
our favorite picnic spot near the creek."

They muttered unison "yes ma'ams" then each took hold of a basket
handle.

Lily couldn't imagine two men eating all the lunch Aunt Hilda packed—
the salt-rising bread, fried pork, sliced cheese, cold potato and sauce, various
raw vegetables from the garden, and last but hardly least, a sugary treat.
Although, if the captain should invite her and the boys and Aunt Hilda to
partake of the meal, there would be plenty for all.

"Do you think the captain will tell me more seafaring tales?" Jonah said,
reaching the opened doorway.

"If he doesn't," Lily replied, "I'm sure Mr. Blake shall oblige you."

Anticipation sparkled in his eyes. "C'mon, Jed, let's go."

The boys set down their burden long enough to push their caps onto
their heads. Then they resumed hauling the basket toward the meadow.

Lily tied her bonnet's yellow ribbon under her chin. Aunt Hilda pinned
her braided straw hat on her head. Together they left the house, closing the

side door so critters wouldn't make themselves at home while they were away.

"I hope our new neighbor doesn't decide that we're as irksome as raccoons."

"For bringing him food and drink in the middle of a hot summer day?" Aunt Hilda clucked her tongue. "Why would he?"

Lily didn't have a reply, but that didn't keep her insides from filling with odd flutters. Perhaps it was the captain's teasing the night before last or her fretting ever since that soon the entire town would hear of her bath in Cedar Creek.

Besides which, the captain had heard Mr. Everett say the Laughlins were penniless.

He'd promised to keep her secret. But, the question was, would he?

They tramped across the long grass, dented from where Jonah and Jed had recently trod. Lily sent up a prayer that God would shoo off any slithering snakes that might be hiding in the overgrowth. Knowing her heavenly Father heard her, she concentrated on the sweet scent of the meadow. A lively song came to her and she just had to sing it.

*"In Freedom we're born and in Freedom we'll live.*
*Our purses are ready.*
*Steady, friends, steady;*
*Not as slaves, but as Freemen our money we'll give. . . ."*

"Lily, look." Aunt Hilda pointed up ahead. "I think your singing summoned our new neighbor and Mr. Blake."

Squinting into the sunshine, she spotted Captain Albright greeting the boys. Within moments, he jogged over to them and relieved them of the heavy basket, carrying it in one hand as if it were feathery light.

"Nothing in the world like a big strong man." Aunt Hilda sighed dreamily.

"Why, Aunt!"

"I'm only statin' a fact."

Lily wanted to argue that it wasn't ladylike to remark on a man's stature, but the words evaporated on her tongue as the captain's broad shoulders tested the fabric limits of his ivory shirt. Finally shifting her focus, she realized her aunt wasn't staring ahead at the captain but somewhere else. Lily followed her line of vision to Mr. Blake, who strutted toward the captain.

"Aunt Hilda!" Lily nudged her. "Don't tell me you're sweet on Mr. Blake."

"Oh, pish! I'm too old to be sweet on anyone or about anything." She punctuated her statement with her usual defiant nod.

"If you say so." Lily smiled, suspecting her aunt was as human as any female. Despite her gruff, Aunt Hilda had blushed two nights ago as if she were sixteen again.

"Well, this is a pleasant surprise." Captain Albright set the basket down just as Lily and Aunt Hilda arrived at the picnic spot. He swept off his hat. "To what do we owe this unexpected visit?"

"My aunt packed a lunch for you and Mr. Blake." The flutters in Lily's midsection multiplied. "She hated the thought of you two men starving to death out here."

"Starve? With all this fruit hanging from tree limbs? Why, I feel like the first Adam in the Garden of Eden."

Lily felt mesmerized by the captain's attention.

"Three-quarters of it is your crop, Miss Laughlin."

Aunt Hilda nudged her and Lily realized she'd missed what he just said. "I beg your pardon, sir?"

"The fruit? You won three-quarters of the harvest a couple of nights ago."

"Oh. . .yes. Of course." She composed herself.

"But I must admit your gift has arrived just in time. Blake was ready to eat one of his boots, and I confess to being famished myself."

Lily smiled at his jesting.

"And you will join us, won't you?"

Lily looked beyond the captain to where Mr. Blake unpacked the picnic basket. He'd already found the jug of blackberry cider. Jed and Jonah practically hung over his shoulders, and Jonah was already peppering the old sailor with questions.

"We don't want to impose," Aunt Hilda said. "We understand you're a busy man."

Lily held the blanket out to him.

"No, no, you must stay." Captain Albright took a position between Lily and her aunt. His cotton shirt smelled like sunshine and manly musk. He set his arms across their shoulders and moved them toward Mr. Blake and the boys. "To leave now would be to rob Blake and me of your excellent company."

Lily peeked up at him. He smiled and it looked most genuine. Her heart started to race like it did before she sang a solo in the church choir.

"We're happy to stay if you insist, sir." Aunt Hilda made it sound like it was some grand acquiescence.

His expression of pleasure remained. "I do, indeed, insist, Mrs. Gunther." He turned his dark gaze on Lily and it warmed her face more than the summer heat. "And Miss Laughlin."

"Thank you. It's the perfect day for a picnic."

"That it is," the captain agreed.

Lily took the large blanket from him and spread it out near the base of a willow and close to where Mr. Blake continued to unpack the basket. Already her brothers were plucking up food and stuffing their mouths.

"Where are your manners, boys?" Lily sent them her best scowl. "We haven't thanked the Lord for His provisions. And you might let our guests select their lunch first."

"Ah, but you are my guests, Miss Laughlin."

The captain's mild admonishment fell over Lily like a shroud. The meadow, the access to Cedar Creek, this acreage—it no longer belonged to them.

She swallowed the sorrow threatening to strangle her. "You are correct, sir. Please accept my apology for overstepping as I did."

"None required." His gaze seared her. "I only meant that you, Mrs. Gunther, and your brothers should make a lunch plate for yourselves before Blake gets his hands on the rest of it."

"Aye, I plan to eat my fill, that's for sure." Mr. Blake chuckled.

"But you're right, Miss Laughlin, we should ask a blessing." The captain's suggestion put a frown on Mr. Blake's face, causing Lily to wonder over the men's faith—or lack thereof. "Perhaps one of you, young masters, would care to pray over our meal."

Jed volunteered for the task, making Lily proud.

"Good bread, good meat, good God, let's eat!" He cheered like a raucous sailor and Jonah laughed.

Lily's mouth fell open. Such sacrilege! And the guffaws that sprang from Mr. Blake and the grin on the captain's face would only make it more difficult for her to reprimand Jed later.

Perhaps Mr. Everett was right about boarding school.

Lily eyed her aunt, who didn't seem troubled by Jed's impertinence. Instead Aunt Hilda plopped down beside Mr. Blake and began eating.

"Miss Laughlin?" Captain Albright waved her toward the picnic lunch.

Lily's insides twisted. "Suddenly I'm not very hungry." Between the captain's reminder that this was his property and her obvious failing when it came to training up her younger brothers, Lily felt defeated. She took a step back. "I think I'll go home. I've got plenty of chores waiting for me."

"And wait they will." A shadowy frown moved across his face. "You need refreshment." He neared and took her elbow, guiding her toward the food. "Besides, it is, as you said, a perfect day for a picnic."

"Yes, of course." The words came rather mechanically, for there was no heart in them. But at the same time, Lily didn't want to appear rude.

"And as long as I've got your ear, would you mind terribly if I bend it?"

"Lily's good at bending ears," Jonah spouted, rubbing his.

"That's not what the captain meant," Lily scoffed.

"She's also good at pinching," Jed put in.

"My, my, Miss Laughlin, such glowing attributes from your brothers." Amusement shone in Captain Albright's inky gaze. "Did I tell you that I have four younger sisters?"

"You did not, sir."

"Yes, well, I do and, as a boy, when my older brother and I weren't teasing them, we enjoyed frightening them with grass snakes, bugs, and worms."

"Your poor sisters." Lily cast him a look of reprimand while a feeling of genuine pity crept over her. Nothing gave her the frights more than snakes, although she'd never admit it to Jed and Jonah lest a serpent appear in her bedcovers one night.

Grinning, the captain took a wide stance and locked his hands behind his back. "Both amusements sent the girls crying to our mother who, of course, told our father when he came home from a long day at his shipping business. The end result never boded well for my brother and me."

Lily froze. It was the most the captain had revealed about himself. The information shed light on his softer side, although not with regard to his poor terrorized sisters.

The gloom hovering over Lily lifted somewhat, and she wrestled with a smile before helping herself to a slice of buttered bread, a slab of fried salted pork, and two pickled beet eggs—all her favorites.

The captain began adding food to his plate.

"No one can scare Lily," Jed announced with his cheek bulging. "Me and Jonah tried, but she's not scared of nothin'."

The captain turned, and Lily didn't miss the gleam in his eyes. "Ah, the ultimate compliment, Miss Laughlin." He finished filling his plate and found a grassy spot near the tree trunk beside her. "I suspect you're quite proud of your brothers."

"Indeed," she fibbed. In truth, she felt no accolades. The boys' bad manners and Jed's misuse of the English language caused her a measure of shame. She shouldn't have allowed them to fall behind with their studies, but with Papa's death. . .

"Cap'n, have you sampled the potatoes?" Blake asked. "They're a marvel."

Aunt Hilda looked pleased, but waved the compliment away.

Lily tried to gauge the captain's reaction as he bit into a slice. "Mmm, they are indeed tasty. I've never eaten cold potatoes in such a tangy sauce."

"So glad you like them." Aunt Hilda aimed her reply at Mr. Blake. "An old German recipe."

Lily peeked at their new neighbor. Glimpsing his raised eyebrows, a giggle passed through her lips. It appeared the captain was as intrigued by the older couple's odd behavior as Lily.

"I could be mistaken, but"—he leaned toward Lily—"for Blake I think it was love at first *bite*."

His play on words tickled her. "I've heard Aunt Hilda say she missed feeding a man with a healthy appetite."

"Thus the way to some men's hearts is truly through their stomachs."

"Quite right, sir."

Captain Albright's lips formed a grin seconds before he took another bite of food. "She is a grand cook," he managed with his mouth full. "I'll swear to that."

Lily glanced across the picnic blanket in time to see Aunt Hilda put a handful of olives on Mr. Blake's plate.

"Miss Laughlin, about my bending your ear. . ."

She steered her attention back to the captain. "You may proceed, sir."

"Thank you. It's regarding the placement of my home."

"Oh?"

"Yes. It would seem that in keeping with the rest of my neighbors, my home should be built nearer to the road."

"But then you would be forced to cut down a large portion of our fruit trees." She caught herself. "*Your* fruit trees."

The captain merely nodded his head.

Lily looked off to her left. "Wouldn't you rather build your home on the hill?" She perceived questions pooling in his eyes. She stood. "Allow me to show you?"

He pushed to his feet in one fluid move. "Lead the way."

Lily began a trek toward the top of the hill, although she didn't really lead the captain. She had a difficult time keeping up with his long strides, and she couldn't mask her attempts to catch her breath. At last he slowed.

"Forgive my hurry, Miss Laughlin."

Breathless, she could only bob her head.

He offered his arm. She slipped her hand around his elbow. The warmth from his flesh beneath his sleeve found its way into her palm. Although she didn't need assistance walking up the incline, it might keep him to a slower pace.

"Quite the informal picnic today." It was a sorry excuse for any improprieties, but all Lily could offer.

"I think that's the way picnics should be. Informal and enjoyable."

Charmed, she dropped her gaze to the clover as a meadow breeze threatened to unseat her straw bonnet.

They reached the property's apex, and Lily drew in a breath of sweet-smelling air. "'Tis a fair view, wouldn't you say?"

"I would, indeed."

"When I was a girl I used to dream of being a princess and building my castle on this very spot." She laughed. "It's my father's fault. He always called me his princess."

With the smile lingering on her lips, she pointed straight ahead. "In my childish mind, the back of my house would face the east and the shadow of the Alleghenies." She twirled around. "The front of my house would face the orchard, but of course, a wide swath would be cut in between the trees to make a circular drive so all my guests would be greeted by the sight of elegant fruit trees as they rode up to the house and left it later." Lily indicated directly westward where the Blue Ridge Mountains spread out along the horizon, looking like a long line of smoke.

"Hmm. . ." The captain rubbed the backs of his knuckles beneath his chin. Was he actually thinking about her girlish ideas? He certainly didn't appear to be on the brink of a good laugh as many men would be, men like Mr. Everett.

"You could even build your house into the hill and have a natural root cellar in which you could store your preserves and your late harvest of fall vegetables, such as squash and potatoes." Another idea struck. "Why, Captain, you could build a poop deck on your roof and entertain guests there. Just think of the views!"

His chuckle sounded like it came from deep inside. "A poop deck on my castle, eh?"

Lily smiled and shrugged.

"As creative and tempting as it is, Miss Laughlin, I don't believe your idea will work. I need ample space for my barn and stable and a yard for the animals. If I build up here, there won't be room. My property ends at the eastern foot of this hill."

"Well, you won't want to live downstream from your barnyard, sir."

The captain's brow furrowed. "Good point."

"Besides, there is already a barn and stable standing, although they have been neglected for more than a decade. After Mama died, Papa lost interest in farming and set his sights on various other opportunities. Little by little he sold off the remainder of his animals, saying it was easier to purchase milk, beef, and pork from the neighbors."

With his hands on his hips, the captain's gaze took in the surrounding field and woods. "So where is this barn?"

Lily pointed southward. "On the other side of the creek." She stared up at him and noticed she stood eyelevel with his broad shoulders. "Have you not seen the stone bridge?"

"I have not, and I thought I walked the perimeter a couple of days ago." He arched a brow. "However, I did get somewhat distracted."

Lily didn't know whether to slap him or laugh. Her face flamed, and not even a gust of wind cooled it.

"Forgive my teasing, Miss Laughlin. If you haven't already guessed, I possess a wicked sense of humor."

"Wicked indeed, sir, for your remark pains me. The incident of our first meeting has kept me awake for the better part of the past two nights. I fear that my reputation will soon be ruined."

"I told you that I will never betray you. My word is good."

"Is it? Your humor, as you call it, tells me I cannot trust you."

Lily took three strides toward home, intent on leaving the man to discover the barn on his own, but the captain's hand clamped around her wrist. His hold on her seemed both gentle and determined.

"Forgive me, Miss Laughlin. I had no idea my teasing caused you pain. Please believe that I wouldn't have dared such a remark if anyone else was present." The soft lines around his eyes and the intensity of his swarthy gaze beseeched her. "I promise I will not tease you in that manner or mention our initial meeting again. Will that put your mind at ease?"

Lily worked the inside of her bottom lip between her teeth as she wondered whether to believe him. She prayed the Holy Spirit would guide her, as He alone had heard her sobbing when Oliver was killed.

And then to discover that he'd played her for a fool. . . It was all too much.

But this man was not Oliver, and Lily supposed he deserved his own chance at earning her trust.

But could she afford to give it to him?

Did she really have a choice? He could at any time tell the tale of catching her in the most immodest display, and she'd be ruined.

The captain brought her hand to his lips and placed a kiss on her gloved fingers. "Truly, I am sorry for embarrassing and wounding you. It won't happen again."

His words seemed most sincere, and she believed him. "I accept your apology." It would be unchristian to do otherwise.

"Then we are friends again?"

"Friends?" Every taut muscle in Lily's body unwound and relaxed. So he just wanted his neighbor to be his friend. Certainly, she could grant him that much. "Yes, we are friends."

"Good." He smiled, revealing a strong set of teeth and brightening his entire countenance.

Lily tipped her head. "You should smile more often, Captain. It does you credit."

"Then I would say your friendship brings out the better man in me."

She rolled her eyes at his flattery. "Shall I show you the stone bridge? My father had the same mason who built the foundation of our home construct it."

"Yes, please, Miss Laughlin. Lead on."

# Chapter Six

*M*ac crossed the bridge behind Miss Laughlin, trying to recall the last time he felt as bad for injuring someone else's feelings as he did about hurting hers. Perhaps it was the brutally honest way in which she addressed him. A man knew just where he stood with Lily Laughlin. No coyness. No games or trickery such as were found in the parlors of unattached females. Only blatant honesty.

*Like Mary...*

She stopped in the middle of the bridge. "Isn't this lovely? I know for sure it holds a pony, a cart, and a little girl." Her eyes twinkled.

"The princess?" His remark earned him one of Miss Laughlin's bright smiles. Dapples of sunlight filtered through overhanging tree branches and danced on the top of her bonnet. The latter's yellow ribbon matched the color of the curls framing her lovely face. "Lead on, Your Royal Highness."

The dimple in her cheek winked at him before she turned and led him across the stone overpass.

"Take heed, Captain, this bridge is quite slippery in the winter."

"Noted." He could see how the uneven footbridge could easily ice over. Its sides came only as high as Mac's boots. They would hardly prevent a man from toppling over into the creek if he slipped and stumbled backward.

Leaning over the side, Mac saw straight down to the creek's bottom. Fish swam by, trout by the looks of them. Yes, he could subsist off his newly acquired property, especially with such amiable neighbors.

He followed Miss Laughlin to the other side of the creek. After push-ing aside low-hanging tree branches and tall shrubbery, they stepped into a vast clearing, albeit a very overgrown one. As she said, the barn was badly weathered, but erect from this vantage point. Corrals that had seen better days divided up the rest of the property.

"I did not see this before." Mac wondered how he could have missed it, although he had glimpsed the copse of fruit trees nearer to the road on this side of Cedar Creek.

He strode to one of the wooden fence posts and found it so rotted that a kick from the bottom of his booted foot toppled it and broke it into pieces, scattering hundreds of small bugs.

"As I said, it needs much work." Miss Laughlin's voice trailed off while an unmistakable apology creased her forehead.

"I'm grateful to have something to work with."

"But perhaps not." She directed his attention to the barn. "It appears the roof has collapsed."

Mac fought his way through the tall grass and weeds and even saplings before reaching the barn. He stopped and Miss Laughlin smacked into his backside.

"I beg your pardon." He faced her. "I didn't realize you'd followed—and so closely behind me."

"Again, my apologies." She stared up at him with wide, azure eyes. "But you see, my brothers were wrong. I am afraid of something."

"Oh?" Mac put his hands on his hips.

"Snakes." She glanced all around them before bringing her gaze back to his. "When you said you teased your sisters. . ." She heaved a sigh. "I could only feel immensely sorry for them."

Mac laughed. "Your little brothers haven't tormented you with a snake yet?"

"Oh, yes, they have. But I pretended to be unaffected." Another glance at the thigh-high grasses. "So now you know a second secret."

"I'll carry it to my grave." His right hand over his heart, Mac succumbed to a grin. "But fear not, Your Royal Highness, I suspect the snakes heard us coming and slithered away."

She moaned and her frown deepened. If she didn't appear so genuinely stricken, Mac would have continued with his trek. Then, again, she didn't wear tall boots. Her leather shoes with their ribbons that crisscrossed at her ankles wouldn't be much protection against a copperhead or timber rattlesnake.

He scooped her up into his arms and she gave a startled cry. "Whatever are you doing?"

"Protecting you from snakes." He caught her scent, one that reminded him of fragrant wildflowers. "They can't sprout wings or grow legs, so you are safe in my arms." Her lack of protest made Mac chuckle, and he couldn't deny the enjoyment of feeling her arm around his neck and her lithe body pressed against his chest.

He strode toward the barn. The door stood ajar. Mac kicked it open wider, and sounds of scurrying critters reached his ears. Hay particles drifted downward from the sloping loft, shimmering in the many shafts of sunlight. Above, he could see the sky where the roof had caved on the far side of the structure.

Miss Laughlin sighed in his arms. "It's worse than I imagined." She turned her head to look at him, obviously forgetting their faces were but mere inches apart.

Mac suddenly ached to kiss her. All that prevented him from doing so was the glimmer of innocence in her blue eyes. But then she confused him by touching his whiskered jaw.

"You're a very handsome man, Captain Albright." They weren't exactly words of an innocent. He frowned. Or were they?

"You're quite lovely yourself, Miss Laughlin. However, if you keep up this discussion, you're liable to get yourself kissed."

She gasped. "Oh! No, I didn't mean..." Roses bloomed in her cheeks, and Mac couldn't recall feeling more amused. Perhaps *naive* better described Lily Laughlin. "Forgive me for my unladylike behavior." She tipped her head. "As for your good looks, surely, you must hear compliments all the time."

"On the contrary. I receive innuendos galore, but I find that I much prefer your directness to gestures behind fluttering fans at stuffy galas." The urge to kiss her was steadily increasing and becoming more difficult to ignore. "Besides, we men are beasts who require our fiery egos to be frequently stoked."

"I shall remember that, sir." The tips of her full lips lifted and tempted him further.

Had she no idea of her effect on him, or was she a practiced flirt?

An odd sensation at his feet caused Mac to turn and glance at the dirt floor. A fat snake slithered across the toe of his boot. Miss Laughlin spotted the reptile and inhaled sharply. Her grip around his neck tightened until Mac could barely take in air.

"It's a harmless black racer," he managed to eke out.

She loosened her hold on him.

"Look. He's already disappeared into the shadows."

"Harmless, perhaps, but quite bold."

"A bit like you, perhaps."

Her blue eyes turned to ice. "You compare me to a reptile, sir?"

He winced. "Poor attempt at humor."

"Ah, well, the likes of failed humor have happened to me too, although I am quite harmless."

He wondered. Miss Laughlin's pretty pout and arresting blue eyes might convince a man to head toward the altar.

But not him!

Another of Miss Laughlin's gasps claimed his attention. "Don't move a muscle." Her warm breath tickled his neck. "There is a skunk over there."

Without a muscle twitching, Mac slid his gaze to his left. Sure enough. The black-and-white furry creature watched them through beady dark eyes.

Mac stepped backward slowly. If he could just reach the entryway without the skunk turning on them. . .

Two more measured paces and Mac's shoulders touched the door. He formulated a plan then held Miss Laughlin closer so he could whisper it to her. "On three, I will set you down and you will run like the wind toward the stone bridge. Understand?"

She replied with a slight nod.

"One," Mac whispered, "two. . .three."

In a single, fluid move, he set Miss Laughlin's feet on the ground and jumped back. Then he kicked the barn door closed before dashing behind her across the long grass and through the brush. They stopped only when they reached the center of the stone bridge.

She sounded breathless, and her bonnet had fallen backward, revealing her glorious golden hair. "Captain, I believe we came away from that encounter unscathed, from both snakes and skunks."

"I believe you are correct." Mac bent forward and placed his hands above his knees. The short sprint had winded him, but within moments his breathing returned to normal.

Miss Laughlin lowered herself onto the side of the bridge and placed her delicate right hand above her heart. "I haven't run like that since springtime when I chased Jonah through the yard after he refused to come in for the night."

Mac grinned. "It's been a while for me also." He sat down beside her. "So let me get this straight. Princesses sprint?"

His jest earned him a playful jab in the ribs.

They quieted, and nature's cacophony settled around them. Noisy tree frogs croaked while insects hummed and buzzed and birds chirped. Subtle splashes in the creek hinted at the presence of fish, and in the far distance, musical notes from Blake's squeeze-box drifted to them on the warm breeze.

"This is a beautiful place." Mac watched the dappled sunshine twirl on top of Miss Laughlin's silken head.

"Yes, and truth to tell, I shall miss it."

Mac stopped himself before asking why. Of course she referred to his purchase of her property. "You, Miss Laughlin, are welcome here any time."

"Thank you." She took to studying the toes of her soft suede shoes.

Mac cupped her chin. Her misty gaze met his.

"I fear I'm being foolishly sentimental." She blinked as if repelling tears. "Who can really possess land? God is supreme owner of all the earth."

"Miss Laughlin, you are a friend and—"

"Then you must call me Lily."

"Lily. . ." He liked the way her name rolled off his tongue. "And you must call me Mac."

"Captain Mac?"

"Just Mac." He lowered his hand. "I'm no longer a sea captain, except in formal circumstances."

"Will you miss being a sailor?"

"Not a bit. I'm a landlubber through and through." Leaning forward, his forearms on his knees, he rubbed his palms together. "Should a wave of nostalgia wash over you or any member of your family, you're more than welcome to come and sit on the stone bridge, fish in the creek, or take an afternoon b—"

"Don't you dare say it!" Her eyes became narrowed slits.

"An afternoon swim." He grinned.

"Hmph!" She jerked her chin. "I know what you were going to say."

"But I refrained." He chuckled and her displeasure at him vanished.

"I can't stay miffed at you when your smile is so...transforming."

"Ah, so the princess reveals her weakness to the rapscallion." He arched one brow. "How very unwise of you. I might be tempted to take advantage of it."

"But you won't."

The confidence gleaming in her eyes was surprising. Did she believe in him more than he believed in himself?

She shouldn't.

"Lily, I confess that I'm not the gentleman you might think I am."

"I know." She folded her hands in her lap. "The war changed everyone in some way."

He sent her a side glance. "I gather from what Jonah blurted last night that you lost your true love in the war."

"Yes, but as it happens, Oliver Ashton wasn't mine alone, even though he led me to believe otherwise." She clenched her hands. "Oliver was paying court to most of the young ladies here in Middletown. His dalliances were uncovered after his death, so I had plenty of young ladies with whom to commiserate."

"He tricked you?" Mac grimaced. "You deserve better."

"Thank you." She unclenched her hands and rubbed her palms along the printed fabric of her skirt. "But it's over and done with and of no importance now."

Mac's gut clenched.

"Why are you not a gentleman, sir?"

Mac took in her expression, her interested gaze and slightly parted lips, and settled on revealing half the truth. "I had a true love too." The words seemed to come from another entity and not from his own mouth.

"Her name was Mary and, although we never spoke of love and marriage, I planned to ask her father for her hand after the war. But when I returned to Virginia last year, I learned she had died while I was at sea." What he refused to say was that Mary's brother Henry was one of the crewmen who was forced to walk the plank after the British frigate took command of his vessel. The Hanovers said they would never forgive Mac for returning home while their son did not.

"How terribly sad."

"She died without knowing I planned to come back for her. No understanding between us was ever discussed." He sank his gaze into Lily's blue eyes. "That is one of my deepest regrets."

She placed her hand over his.

Mac pulled away. "I don't want your pity."

"And I'm not giving it." She sat straighter with hands folded in her lap once again. "I only meant to show you some kindness and understanding."

"Thank you." He regretted his harshness. "Kindness and understanding have become foreign to me, but, ironically, they are exactly what I need."

"It's my hope that you find a renewed sense of happiness here in the Shenandoah Valley. Did you know the native Indians call the valley 'the Daughter of the Stars'?"

"No, I did not." It didn't escape Mac's notice that she'd changed the subject. His shoulders sagged forward. Seemed Lily Laughlin wasn't a stone-throwing Christian. Could it really be possible that she understood—and cared?

A putrid cloud of raw stink wafted to them from the south side of the creek. Lily produced her hankie, covered her nose, and stood.

"The skunk has found us."

"At least part of him has." Mac didn't see the creature anywhere, but its presence could not be ignored.

He coughed and followed Lily off the stone bridge and up the creek bank. To the distant right, Blake shoved his squeeze-box into its sack while Mrs. Gunther and Lily's brothers deposited leftovers into the picnic basket while holding their noses. By the time Mac and Lily reached the picnic spot, Jonah and Jed were carrying the picnic basket away as fast as their feet could take them.

"We'll see you at supper then." Mrs. Gunther waved a hand in the air. "Dreadful creature, the skunk. Why God breathed them into existence, I know not."

"The cap'n and I've smelled worse." Blake tossed a glance Mac's way. "Ain't that right, Cap'n?"

"I can't rightly say." Mac's eyes were beginning to water. While the skunk didn't directly spray them, the wind seemed to carry its stench over hill and dale.

Lily turned to Mac. "See you later, friend."

He replied with a gracious bow and then watched her cross the meadow with her golden curls bouncing freely.

## Chapter Seven

"I smell something utterly dreadful." From his place at the table betwixt Jed and Jonah, Mr. Everett gave his vegetable chowder a whiff.

"It is not my soup, sir." Aunt Hilda glared at the man. "If you must know, a skunk made an appearance near our picnic this afternoon, hence the lingering odor blowing in the wind from the creek."

"Picnic?" Mr. Everett sat ramrod straight, but his frown seemed reserved for Lily alone.

"It was such a fine day—"

"Not even Sunday afternoon." He punctuated each word while glaring at Aunt Hilda, and then at Lily. "Did you not have work to do?"

"Yes, but we'd finished by noon." After she'd replied, Lily wondered why she felt the need to explain herself. She and Aunt Hilda were not in Mr. Everett's employ, nor were they his slaves.

How had Lily ever thought the man had their best interests at heart, or even honorable intentions? Clearly, Mr. Everett looked out for his holdings, not her family. Were Papa still alive, he'd despise his longtime comrade's behavior.

Mr. Blake finished his soup with a slurp that caused Jonah and Jed to snicker. "Tastiest vegetable chowder I've ever eaten."

"Glad you enjoyed it." Aunt Hilda looked pleased.

"I admire a woman who knows her way around a galley. . .er, I mean kitchen." Despite the harmless misspeak, Mr. Blake's compliment pinked Lily's aunt's cheeks.

"Again, I find a picnic on Friday quite extraordinary." Mr. Everett's frown seemed permanently etched into his aging face.

"I'm afraid you're correct, sir." Captain Albright—Mac— lifted his napkin to his lips. Any lingering food vanished, but his lips quivered with obvious amusement. "Some of us purposely neglected our work and enjoyed the summer day." His gaze touched on Lily from where he sat beside Mr. Blake. "However, I did decide where I shall build my house, and I plan to call it Fairview Manor."

A thrill passed through Lily. She'd never known a man to take her suggestions to heart. "I drew a sketch for you." The words vaulted into the air before she could think twice about sharing them. Surely Mr. Everett would scold her for doodling her time away.

"A sketch?" Mac arched a brow.

"Of your house. Rather, of the one I fancied as a girl."

"I look forward to seeing it."

"It's time to put away childish things, my dear Lily." Mr. Everett spooned the tiniest bit of soup into his mouth.

"Of course you're correct, sir." She'd expected the harsh remark, but it deflated her nonetheless, mostly because he spoke the reprimand in front of guests.

"It's thought to be quite prestigious for young ladies to spend considerable time sketching, drawing, painting, and the like," Mac said. "Appreciating the arts is a subject taught in finishing schools all over Western Europe. I know because I have younger sisters."

"Ah, then you're something of an expert with young ladies, hmm?"

"I wouldn't go so far as to claim that, Mr. Everett. I am, after all, still a man."

*And a fine-looking one too. Kind and compassionate. . .*

As if she'd spoken the words aloud, Mac sent her a smile that caused her heart to skip.

Oh, what was the matter with her? She'd thought of him and little else since they parted earlier in the afternoon. Mac succeeded in charming her more so than Oliver Ashton ever had.

Jed slurped his chowder, causing Lily to wince. How often had she reminded the boys to sip and never slurp? She sighed and forced her shoulders to relax. It seemed Mr. Everett's chiding nature had rubbed off on her. *God forbid*! However, she would not do as he did and reprimand the boys in front of guests. Never again would she wound their spirits that way.

Mr. Blake lifted his bowl and drank the remaining liquid. Mr. Everett appeared horrified by his actions. But then Jed and Jonah emulated their guest and he groaned aloud.

"Lily, honestly, these boys must be taught better table manners."

"Why, sir, they cannot help it." Her cheeks warmed. "They enjoy my aunt's tasty chowder."

"And tasty it is too!" Mr. Blake dragged his napkin across his mouth.

"You're too kind." Aunt Hilda stood and surveyed the table. "Since most of you are finished, I'll bring out our main dish."

"The soup is adequate fare, Mrs. Gunther." Mr. Everett's frown deepened, if such a thing were possible.

"Speak for yourself, sir." Mr. Blake moved his stout frame back against the chair and belched. "I'm just getting started."

Chuckling happily, Aunt Hilda made her way to the kitchen.

Lily blinked, amazed the man could hold so much food. Perhaps he'd come back from the war half-starved.

She decided on some polite conversation. "Do you have family, Mr. Blake?"

"No family to speak of, miss. I've been on m' own since the age of fourteen."

"Not much older than me." Jonah perked up and, once again, Lily had to force herself not to correct his grammatical error in front of others. She would work extra hard with him on his book learning.

"That's right, Master Jonah, and I hired onto a ship docked in London and never looked back."

Unease spiraled through Lily. She wished Mr. Blake would not encourage Jonah's grandiose notions.

The old seadog cocked his head to one side. "But, you see, I didn't have any family who loved me and missed me like you do."

The tension pinching Lily's shoulders eased. She looked at Jonah. "I would miss you most of all, I think."

"Aw, sissy. . ."

Lily smiled at his brightening cheeks.

"So are we to assume, Mr. Blake, that you are British?" Mr. Everett narrowed his gaze. "You certainly sound British."

"Born a Brit, but I'm as American as Independence Day." His wide chest puffed out with obvious pride. "During the last conflict with England, I was prepared to die for my new country. Of course, I'm glad it didn't come to that."

Aunt Hilda returned, carrying a pan of cornmeal and mutton cakes. "I'll bet you've never tasted this fine dish, Mr. Blake. Our family enjoys it." The older woman's gaze found Lily. "Isn't that right?"

"Quite right, Aunt."

The guests helped themselves, and Mac held the tray while Lily forked a cake onto her plate. His manners were impeccable and, combined with his charm and good looks, Lily figured his days as a bachelor were numbered. The unmarried ladies of Middletown would see to that, and he'd best look out for Cynthia Clydesdale.

She lowered her chin, but watched him surreptitiously. With Aunt Hilda's blessing, their guests had removed their frockcoats, as the house had grown uncomfortably warm in today's late summer sun. And, in addition to dining in his waistcoat, Mac had rolled up his shirt sleeves to his elbows, allowing Lily full view of his muscled forearms.

Mac glanced her way, and Lily quickly removed her gaze from his powerful-looking arms. She thought over what they'd discussed before the skunk so rudely interrupted them. Certainly, Mac would love again, no matter how deep his wound from losing Mary. Wouldn't he reconsider the idea of marriage, especially once his home was built? Papa always said a woman made a house a home and a man presided over both.

Of course, Papa never ruled with fists of iron, and she suspected Mac was not a man to do so either. Mr. Everett, on the other hand. . .

Lily vanquished the unwelcome thoughts of the man. Ever since she'd learned Mr. Everett sold off Laughlin land, she'd lost a goodly amount of respect for him. However, she couldn't blame Mac for purchasing it. After all, he'd had no idea of the land and owner's history.

Her thoughts still heavy, Lily cut into her mutton cake. She smiled when Mr. Blake praised Aunt Hilda for another scrumptious dish. Both he and Mac helped themselves to another cake while Mr. Everett ate his soup ever so slowly—and without a single slurp.

The meal ended and Jonah coerced Mr. Blake into regaling him with more sea adventures. Aunt Hilda requested a few lively tunes on the squeeze-box. Mr. Blake claimed he could oblige them both, although he preferred to sit outdoors. Aunt Hilda led the way. Mr. Everett, too, left the house to smoke his pipe. As she walked to the parlor beside Mac, Lily decided to take advantage of her time alone with him. It seemed the perfect opportunity to show him the sketches she'd drawn.

"Please, sit and rest yourself." She fidgeted with the ribbon in her hair. "May I show you my sketches?"

"You may, of course." Mac dropped down onto one side of the settee.

Lily slid her drawings from the folder which she'd hid in a drawer of the corner writing desk—one of Papa's favorite pieces of furniture. She could still see him in her mind's eye, sitting there, writing letters or figuring his accounts.

She focused on her guest once more. "You'll find these quite amateurish, I'm afraid. But at least it'll give you a better idea of what I attempted to describe earlier today."

Mac's expression reflected his obvious interest, but Lily had a feeling he was merely being polite. Handing him the sketches, she took the seat beside him.

One by one Mac inspected them and Lily wished he'd say something.

"See how I included a rooftop poop deck for entertaining?"

"Yes, I noticed it immediately." He tapped the paper with his forefinger. "I even noticed the captain's wheel at one end."

Lily smiled, praying she hadn't been too presumptuous. "Of course these are pictures from my imagination. I wouldn't dare expect you to emulate them. It is, after all, your land and your home."

"Finally warming to the idea, are you?" Wearing a hint of a smirk, he sent her a wink.

Lily looked away, reminded, again, of his wicked sense of humor.

Mac set the first drawing aside and perused the second one. "The square, saltbox design is quite popular. I see it everywhere I venture. However, instead of a sloping roof, you've drawn a flat one to accommodate my. . .*poop deck*."

"That's correct, sir." She watched his expression. "But you may have other ideas. As I said, it will be your home, not mine."

"So you have." Mac's dark gaze seemed to slice right to her soul. "And what of the indoor layout of *this* house? I've seen the dining room and parlor. . ."

"Would you care to see my father's study and the sewing room?"

"I would, indeed."

"Then I shall give you a tour."

Lily stood and led the way out of the parlor. They walked through the central hallway from which each room could be accessed. Decades ago, they'd welcomed various important guests and politicians, but after Mama died, hosting parties here at *Haus am Bach* came to a halt.

Reaching the back of the house, Lily stood in the center of a long hall-way. "Down this way is the sewing room, which also serves as the ladies' drawing room, although it hasn't been that in many years." She explained why and appreciated the way Mac paid attention. Why, he even appeared interested in what she had to say.

She led him to her father's study. The walls had been painted a masculine shade of blue. At one end, two wide bookshelves stood on either side of the limestone hearth. Two well-worn leather armchairs faced it, and an elegant Hepplewhite round table and two chairs filled the space on the right side of the room.

Mac paused to stare out the curtain-framed windows, his hands clasped behind him. With his feet spread apart in a wide stance, he looked very much like the sketches of sea captains that Jonah looked at for hours.

If only her brother would attack his studies of reading, writing, and arithmetic with such gusto.

"I like this room," Mac said, glancing at Lily from over his shoulder. "It's comfortable and has character, unlike so many men's studies these days which seem. . .sterile."

"Papa would be pleased to hear you say so. I can still see him sitting in the chair over there, warming himself by a blazing hearth. Even though the anniversary of his death will be soon, I still expect to see him in this room, at his writing desk, in the parlor, or at the dining room table." Sadness washed over her.

Mac's softened expression seemed to say he understood.

Eager to change the subject, lest she dissolve into tears, Lily pointed upward. "On the second floor are four bedchambers. I won't show them to you because they are...lived in." A kind way to say the rooms were in slight disarray, especially the boys' bedchamber. "There is one larger master bedroom, and three smaller, yet spacious rooms." Lily and Mac ambled back to the parlor. "Presently, my parents' bedchamber is unoccupied and used as a guest room, although our visitors have been few and far between now that Papa's gone and Mr. Everett has taken over."

Mac gave a polite smile in reply and, after reseating himself on the settee, resumed his study of her drawings.

Lily watched. Anticipation gathered inside of her like puffy white clouds in an azure sky. At last she could stand the suspense no longer. "Do you like them?"

"I think—"

"Or are my sketches so terrible they don't warrant a response?"

Mac's mouth opened.

"Give me your honest opinion."

"If you allow me a chance to speak, I will." He chuckled, and Lily's face blazed with embarrassment. "I think you have managed to capture a unique style that's very much suited to my personality."

"Truly?"

"Yes." Could that be appreciation in his gaze? "The style of the house is different enough that I shall, no doubt, impress my family and the scant few guests I plan to entertain. And, without the sloping roof, I'll gain more space inside for the rooms on the second floor."

"Exactly!" Lily almost giggled. "And, if you build the back of the first floor into the hill, you can build a root cellar off the kitchen in which to store your late harvests of potatoes, squash, and the like."

"You mentioned that before. A marvelous idea. Thank you."

"You're very welcome." Lily felt like she might burst from jubilation. No other man except Papa had ever appreciated her artwork, and Papa most likely only made a fuss over it because she was his flesh and blood. "I'm so very glad you like the drawings."

"So I gather." Amusement flared in his eyes. "May I keep these?"

"Of course. Take them."

"A most excellent gift, Miss Laughlin."

"Lily, remember?"

"Lily." His dark eyes shone like thick, polished obsidian for the briefest of moments before his expression turned more businesslike. "I'll send these sketches off to my architect in Alexandria. These will give him an idea of the house I want and he can take it from there." Mac began rolling up the drawings.

"An architect?" Lily hadn't gotten beyond that statement. "My sketches in the hands of a true architect?"

"Is anything wrong with that?"

"No. Only that I have an untrained hand."

"Then you possess a divine gift." He held up the drawings. "These are better than some I've seen from artists in Paris."

"You flatter me, sir." Indeed, his words sent a heated rush into her cheeks.

"But not falsely. I mean it." He looked quite sincere. "You're quite talented with a piece of charcoal."

"Thank you." She smoothed her yellow printed gown over her knees.

"May I ask a personal question?"

"Of course. We are friends." Lily leaned closer to tease him. "And you do harbor two of my secrets already."

The edges of Mac's lips moved upward but didn't quite form a smile. "It's about the innkeeper." He glanced over his shoulder toward the open window. Mr. Everett's chiding tone blew in on the evening breeze. No doubt he was speaking to one of Lily's brothers.

She sighed. "What about him?"

"May I inquire as to your relationship with him?"

Lily found the question somewhat odd, but couldn't see any harm in answering it. "Why, he was one of my father's best friends. I've known him all my life, and since Papa had no will, the magistrate appointed him our guardian now that Papa is gone."

"Only your guardian?"

"Yes." She tilted her head. "Pray, why do you ask?"

His brows furrowed. "I ask as a friend because you seem ignorant of Mr. Everett's intentions."

Unease tickled the back of her neck. "I know of them, and the very thought makes me ill."

Mac leaned forward, resting his forearms on his thighs. A lock of his thick, ebony hair fell onto his forehead, giving him a rakish look. "If it's the age difference that troubles you, it shouldn't. I can testify to older men marrying younger women. It frequently happens that way."

"It is not his age, but the fact that I do not love him and I never will that makes me unwell in spirit." Lily stood and began pacing in front of the hearth. Again, Mr. Everett's voice swept in from outside, but this time Mr. Blake's craggy reply followed.

"Do not trust your feelings," Mac said. "The heart is, indeed, deceitful and desperately wicked."

Lily recognized a piece of biblical truth in his remark.

"I realize that some unions are born from love," he continued, "but not all. Many marriages are business arrangements or pairings of practicality."

"How utterly romantic of you, sir."

"How utterly honest." His dark eyes seemed to pierce Lily, and she couldn't ignore his cynical tone. "Surely, you can see why it might benefit you to consider Mr. Everett, once he declares himself, of course."

"I will not!" A knot formed in her chest and she closed her eyes. "Lord, may that day never come when he does approach me."

"Have you any other prospects?" Mac's voice was soft and devoid of its previous cynicism.

"Well, no. . ." From the corner of her eye, Lily spotted the gaming table, on top of which the chessboard was laid out. During their chess match, Mac had heard Mr. Everett say she was penniless. "Ah, so that's it." This conversation suddenly made perfect sense.

"That's what?"

"You think I should marry Mr. Everett because I'm a penniless waif." Lily grabbed hold of the mantel. A hurt as deep as the sea washed over her. Here she thought she had a trusted friend in the good captain, but he obviously considered her far less of an equal socially and far more of an unattached female in need of a husband. "Well, I'm sorry to disappoint you, but I'm not that desperate."

"As you say."

She curled her right hand into a fist. Heat rushed into her cheeks. "My father left us in good financial standing. He told me so long before his death." Lily knew things could have changed since her conversation with Papa. And, as Aunt Hilda said, Papa loved the gaming table, although he didn't possess the knack for placing bets. But Lily refused to believe all their money was gone, especially after the sale of their land. "There should be no reason for me to be forced into a loveless marriage with a man twice my age." She nibbled her lower lip. "I've got to find Papa's last will and testament. I feel certain the document exists. . .somewhere."

Mac stood and stepped toward her. "I cannot say what you should or shouldn't do. I merely wanted you to be aware of the situation, as it seemed quite obvious to me that you were not."

"Thank you. But I am aware of it." *Unfortunately.* Lily shuddered, imagining herself married to Mr. Everett. She stared at the tips of her black slippers peeking out from beneath her gown. In a word, the idea disgusted her.

Mac cupped her chin and she lifted her gaze. "I really only meant to repay your kindnesses of the meals and the drawings with the gift of knowledge." His smile looked rather sad. "I could not have my new friend ignorant of Everett's plots."

"God forbid." Lily hated to think what else Mr. Everett might have in mind for her family. "And we cannot be friends. I understand that now."

A frown furrowed his brow. "Why on earth not?"

"Because you are socially superior to me."

Mac dropped his hand to his side before tossing his head back and laughing. The sound echoed around her while delighting her at the same time. "I care very little about what is socially acceptable and what is not."

She grinned at his declaration, because he could not be serious. "You speak like a true pirate, sir."

A lasting smile still toyed with the edges of his lips, but as he opened his mouth to speak, Mr. Everett strode into the room.

"It appears that a storm is on the horizon. I think it's time to go."

## Chapter Eight

*Y*ou're besotted. Admit it."

"I will not." Mac pushed off the tree trunk on which he'd been leaning. He had rented a team of mules, a wagon, and sundry equipment from James Hawkins, the blacksmith and liveryman. In the last week, he and Blake had proceeded to pull down what they could of the old barn. The rest would be burned over time. But now Mac felt soreness in muscles he didn't realize he possessed. Worse, Blake's goading irritated him to no end. "You would do well to button your lip, my friend."

"Why? I freely admit that I'm besotted."

"With what?" Mac cocked a brow. "Mutton cakes or pork chops?"

Blake snorted a laugh that had a good-natured sound. "I always hoped for finding a sturdy woman who could cook, and Brunhilda Gunther is certainly that."

"You'll get no argument from me."

"At last!" Blake flung his stocky arms toward the sky. "We agree on something."

Mac groaned. He was tired of their verbal sparring.

"You haven't seen Miss Lily in days. Methinks ya miss her." Another amused snort. "Why, just look at yourself, staring aimlessly between the two properties, longing for a glimpse of her golden head."

"I am hoping Mrs. Gunther comes soon with your lunch so you'll quit your incessant blather!" Truth to tell, Blake's words hit the mark.

Mac inhaled the sweet smell of drying grass but winced as the muscles surrounding his ribcage protested. Nonetheless, the question lingered. Why hadn't he seen Lily? Was she unwell, or had he offended her last week? It was the latter that haunted him. Yes, Everett's intentions were none of his business, but Mac had only been looking out for Lily—as one friend looked out for another.

Or so he told himself.

But now here he stood, gazing across a meadow of wildflowers, hoping she'd walk out of the house, accompanying her aunt with her picnic basket of good eats.

"Come to think on it, I haven't seen them two rascals either." Blake scratched his stubbly chin. "Maybe they're ill, although Hilda didn't mention it."

And Mac had been too full of pride to ask. The last thing he wanted was for Lily to get the wrong impression about their...friendship.

"And we haven't been asked to evening supper in a long while." Blake placed his hands on his hips. "What say you to us walking over there and inquiring?"

Before Mac had a chance to reply, Mrs. Gunther appeared at the kitchen doorway. In one hand she carried the picnic basket, and in the crook of her other arm, she held the familiar blanket. Blake needed no prompting and crossed the meadow to relieve her of her burdens. Within minutes, the couple selected a shady spot upon which to spread the picnic blanket. Similar to noontime the past several days, Mac had no plans to infringe on their meal together.

Except, he could scarcely believe that Blake had, at long last, fallen in love. *Besotted* was an apt word to describe his friend's peculiar behavior.

"Captain Albright." Mrs. Gunther's voice stopped him as he strode toward the stone bridge. She stood and fluttered the paper in her hand. "Lily asked me to give this note to you."

A wave of encouragement splashed over Mac. He backtracked and accepted it. "Thank you."

As soon as the conversation resumed between Blake and Mrs. Gunther, he stepped a ways off and opened the missive. His first thought was that

Lily displayed neat penmanship. His second was that it filled nearly the entire page.

Reading on, Mac was sorry to learn that Blake had guessed correctly. The boys had come down with a fever and peculiar rash, but they were on the mend now. Lily wondered if Mac would attend church with them tomorrow. She was scheduled to sing.

"What answer would you have me give my niece, Captain?"

He turned to find Mrs. Gunther standing only a few feet away. "I'll give the matter some thought." He hadn't attended church in years. Did he really want to restart a habit that had been forced upon him in the first place?

"I'm afraid I need your answer now. There'll be no picnicking for me today. I need to be getting back home. With the boys sick all week, the housework piled up."

"Then you needn't have troubled yourself to pack us a lunch."

"Lily insisted." With a light laugh, Mrs. Gunther tucked strands of her hair into her white mobcap. "She saw you and Mr. Blake through the window. She said you were standing on the edge of the meadow, looking hungrier than bears in springtime."

Mac grinned. *So she'd been watching them, eh?*

"Please ask Miss Laughlin to accept my apology for not inquiring over her and the boys. It wasn't neighborly of me."

"Don't fret yourself, Captain." Her lips curved into a rather sly-looking grin. "I think Lily had a hunch you were thinking of her—them."

*Only continually!*

"So what about church tomorrow? Will you attend with us?"

"I'll be a good sport and go if you will, Cap'n," Blake said from his lounged position on the picnic blanket.

Mac felt slightly coerced, but how could he refuse? He'd already blundered by not checking on his neighbors. He should have known things were far too quiet next door. Besides, he longed to hear Lily sing again. "Please tell Miss Laughlin that I am most happy to accompany her—your family— to church tomorrow."

"Good news then." Smiling, Mrs. Gunther whirled around. "We leave promptly at seven thirty."

"In the morning?" Deep creases lined Blake's forehead. "But, Hilda, that's after Saturday night."

"It is. So you'd best leave the gaming table early, you old scamp." With a laugh, Mrs. Gunther bent over, removed Blake's hat, and kissed the top of his graying head. "Leave the picnic basket on the kitchen doorstep when you're through with it."

Blake's grin grew wide enough to reveal a few dark gaps where teeth had once been. "You see that, Cap'n? She kissed me."

"She's a very courageous woman." Mac watched Mrs. Gunther retreat across the meadow. "Lord knows I wouldn't kiss you for a pouch of Capped Head Half Eagles." He dropped down on the picnic blanket and drew the basket closer to himself. "Now, let's see what's for lunch."

The following day, Mac rented a buggy and a team of horses from Mr. Hawkins, at the livery. He recalled that the church wasn't a far walk from his property, but if Jonah and Jed had been ill, it was better they ride the short distance. Besides, Mac didn't want to chance soiling Sunday clothes by walking. It had rained last night and, though the sun promised to shine this morning, everything from rooftops to gravel roads had gotten soaked.

Passing the dining hall at Stony Inn, Mac didn't see Silas Everett, which suited him just fine. Mac didn't want to get drawn into the middle of a prickly situation. He'd done his best by revealing the truth to Lily. Now he would stay out of the way.

The clock chimed seven as Mac and Blake left the inn. They didn't wait long before the rented vehicle pulled up in front.

Mr. Hawkins waved away the payment. "See you at church soon."

Mac's expression of obvious surprise caused the liveryman to grin.

"My wife is good friends with Miss Lily Laughlin. We visited last night and Lily told us you'd be there." He jumped down from the buggy and waved. "See you soon."

News certainly traveled fast in Middletown. Mac would remember that. He climbed up onto the buggy. Blake hopped up beside him.

As they bounced along the rutted road toward the Laughlins' home, Mac listened to his friend voice his conundrum for at least the third time since last evening.

"I want to marry Hilda, but I'm not a landlubber. I don't even like farm animals, unless they're roasted to perfection. I only came out here to help you settle."

Mac heaved a bored sigh and cut a glance at Blake. He hardly resembled the seaman he claimed to be. In fact, he appeared every inch the perfect gentleman. Wearing dark boots and tan breeches, a fawn-colored waistcoat and a dashing blue frockcoat, he seemed to belong in Mac's new life here in Middletown.

"There's no other occupation I know," Blake lamented. "How will I support the both of us?"

"You might discuss the matter with Mrs. Gunther before despairing. She may not wish to remarry, and then your fretting has been for naught."

"Oh, she wishes to marry, all right. I feel it in m' bones, and m' bones don't lie. But I'm a sailing man. I have been all my life. It's the only work I know how to do."

"Tell your bones to keep quiet. Perhaps if you don't listen to them you'll hear the right answer."

"If you say so, Cap'n."

"I do." It was advice that Mac wished himself to take. He hadn't moved to Middletown to get ensnared by a lovely member of the fairer sex. Quite the opposite. He'd relocated from Alexandria in order to live alone off his prized land and occasionally entertain family members. . .yes, on his rooftop portico, once he got it built.

He noted the farms he passed. Had someone told him before the war that he'd end up building in a remote village in the Shenandoah Valley, Mac would have enjoyed a good laugh at the prediction. Yet, here he was.

He pulled the team to a halt in front of the Laughlins' manor. Jumping down, he avoided several puddles and walked toward the house to greet the two ladies. They met him in the walk and, immediately, he noticed Lily's pale complexion. He didn't care for the dark half moons beneath her eyes, either. However, he very much enjoyed the way the peach-colored gown hugged her slender frame. She'd draped a light swag of the same hue across her shoulders, and an ivory bonnet hid her lovely golden hair.

Blake had transferred to the back seat, and he patted the space beside him. Mac assisted Mrs. Gunther into the buggy then turned to Lily. "Are you certain you're well enough to attend church this morning?"

"Oh, yes, I'm feeling much better." She smiled in a way that caused Mac to wonder. "I'm a bit tired after coming down with the same fever the boys had, but definitely on the mend now."

Once again Mac felt guilty for not inquiring, but promised to be more neighborly in the future. He offered his hand and Lily placed her gloved fingers in his palm. He helped her up into the buggy. "Where are the boys?"

"They ran off ahead with a group of their friends," Mrs. Gunther answered. "Obviously, they have regained their health. And if they're late for the service, I won't stop the reverend from boxing their ears."

Chuckling, Mac climbed up beside Lily and grabbed the reins. A delightful fragrance of blooming honeysuckle wafted to his nose. "Dare I admit to having a reverend box my ears on more than one occasion?" With a flick of his wrists, the horses jerked forward.

"None of us would be shocked to hear your confession, Captain." Lily leaned playfully against his arm while Blake's chuckle filled the coach. He glanced back in time to see Mrs. Gunther's wide grin as she adjusted her puffy light-blue cap whose lacy trim outlined her round face.

"Thank you for bringing a carriage for us," Lily said softly.

"Entirely my pleasure, Miss Laughlin."

She smiled and the entire carriage seemed to brighten. Indeed, she looked healthier than she had only minutes ago.

The ride to the church was a short one—too short as far as Mac was concerned. He had enjoyed Lily's proximity. As they strode to the white, wooden structure, Mrs. Gunther paused to make introductions to a small group of ladies congregating near the doorway. Lily murmured something about rehearsal and set off into the church with only a brief smile and wave for the cluster of females.

Mac doffed his black top hat.

"I've never met a naval officer before," a bonneted brunette by the name of Miss Cynthia Clydesdale said. She followed up with a bat of her dark lashes. "Did your wife accompany you today?"

How Mac longed to fib and say he had a wife, for he knew what was about to follow. But his new life here dictated honesty. The truth of his past might appear soon enough, but he'd hate for his new community to consider him a liar from the start.

"I am unmarried, miss."

The young lady squealed. "Oh, Mama, did you hear that?"

Mac cringed inwardly. Everyone in the churchyard heard her reaction. He lowered his head and toyed with a piece of gravel beneath the toe of his boot.

"The captain is not married. We simply have to invite him to dinner."

Mrs. Clydesdale stepped closer to Mac and inspected him through one round eyeglass. He would have laughed out loud at the woman's conduct if he wasn't convinced that he'd offend the well-intentioned matron and, perhaps insult Mrs. Gunther too.

"Yes, you're a fine specimen of a man." Mrs. Clydesdale turned to her daughter. "Dinner on Tuesday night it is."

Miss Clydesdale giggled and clapped her gloved hands together.

"Then you must dine with us on Monday," a freckle-faced female declared. She turned and pleaded with her mother who, of course, agreed. Monday night it was.

Mac decided to put a stop to the dinner invitations, kind as they were. "Ladies, I beg your pardons, but I cannot dine with you this week. I'm in the process of clearing my land. I must work from dawn to dusk."

A collective moan rose from the group.

"How about the following week on a Wednesday then?" A young lady in a straw bonnet with a large pink ribbon came forward. Since she was small in stature and her hat swallowed up so much of her head, Mac couldn't get a glimpse of her face. "I'm one of Miss Lilyanna Laughlin's closest acquaintances."

"Mrs. Hawkins, I presume." Mac just had that "feelin' in his bones," as Blake liked to say.

Her bonnet bobbed. "I'm Isabella Hawkins."

"I'm acquainted with your husband, madam, and any friends of Miss Laughlin's are friends of mine."

"How very excellent, sir." Holding the top of her hat, she lifted her gaze to his face. Arresting hazel eyes met Mac's stare. "Then you're aware that my husband is Mr. James Hawkins, the blacksmith and liveryman in town." She pointed toward the right where a group of men stood conversing near a wagon, Silas Everett being one of them. Mac spotted Mr.

Hawkins with a baby on his hip.

"You have a very healthy baby by the look of him."

"Her. You would have known that if she kept her bonnet on her sweet bald head."

Mac chuckled.

"So a week from Wednesday then?"

"Yes, madam. Thank you."

The other females started clucking and twittering in unison until Mac wasn't sure which conversation to follow. He hurriedly retrieved his pocket watch and glanced at the time. "Ladies, please. . ."

They quieted.

"We had best be seated soon. I believe the service is about to begin." Mac bowed out and headed for the open church doors.

Inside the building, he discovered the smallest of cloakrooms before he entered the sanctuary. Sunshine filtered through brightly colored stained-glass windows that presided over two columns of neatly aligned benches. Mac sensed a cheery atmosphere about the place, quite the opposite of the impersonal, echoing monstrosity that was his family's church in Alexandria.

He slid between two polished wooden pews, pushed back his coattails, and took a seat beside Blake. He set his top hat beside him. "I gather you weren't interested in meeting the throng of young ladies in the churchyard."

"I thought I'd leave all the charming to you, Cap'n."

"Thanks for that."

Blake chuckled until Mrs. Gunther shushed him, and Mac wondered if the old seadog had ever darkened a church doorway before in his life. Surely he must care deeply for Mrs. Gunther if he offered to attend today. After all, it had meant that he bathe last night, roll out of bed early this morning, shave, tie his shaggy mop of hair into a gentlemanly queue, and don the best clothes he owned.

Yes, it was love, all right!

Silas Everett appeared to Mac's right. He removed his stylish black top hat and nodded a silent greeting. Mac returned it in kind, and then Everett sat in the pew in front of him. Jonah and Jed showed up in the side aisle, breathless and with apple-red cheeks, but clean and neat, except for Jed's shirt, which had come untucked in the back. The boys slid in beside their aunt, who had the wisdom to place Jonah between herself and Blake, separating the rascals.

A white-robed minister came through a side entrance and walked to the center pulpit. He greeted the congregation then led them in a hymn. The singing was accompanied by a woman playing the pianoforte and a man on the violin. They played loudly enough to cover any singer's off-key notes, Mac's included.

At last it came time for Lily's solo, the moment Mac had been anticipating. She gracefully walked to the minister's vacated pulpit, pushed back her shoulders, and lifted her gaze to somewhere above the rafters, as if she could see through the roof and into heaven itself. After a brief musical introduction, she opened her mouth and sang,

*"Jesus, Lover of my soul,*
*Let me to Thy bosom fly.*
*While the nearer waters roll,*
*While the tempest still is high."*

The words Mac recognized, but the melody was unfamiliar and hauntingly beautiful, made more so, perhaps, by Lily's emotive soprano.

*"Hide me, oh my Savior, hide,*
*Till the storm of life is past.*
*Safe into the haven guide,*
*Oh, receive my soul at last."*

She sang like an angel and Mac was captivated. Again. What's more, he didn't know a single, seasoned sailor who hadn't breathed similar words while navigating over stormy seas. The song's spiritual meaning wasn't lost on him either, but surprisingly, the song touched a place deep within his being—a place that Mac wasn't aware existed until today—right now. It was a place in his soul where pleasure and pain converged in the most inexplicable way. He nearly sighed with relief when Lily's solo ended, and yet he wished to hear the song again. How strange his reaction to a piece of music and mere words on a page.

As Lily made her way down the aisle, Mac glimpsed Everett slide over as if to make room for her beside him. But she walked on by and slipped into a place that Mac quickly created for her, causing something of a chain reaction all the way to the end of the pew.

"Did you like my song?" Lily whispered.

"Very much," Mac whispered back.

The answering smile on her face made Mac want to belt out his own chorus of hallelujahs. If only his family could see him on this fine morning, sitting in church beside a lovely young lady who possessed a talent for song that could only be divinely given.

Perhaps Lily Laughlin would make a believer of out him yet.

# Chapter Nine

*L*ily bounced baby Amanda in her arms. "Oh, Issie, she's getting so big."

Issie's features exuded sheer delight. "Isn't she though?"

"And pretty." A longing inside of Lily bloomed like the daisies in her flower garden. She ached for a loving husband and children of her own, just like her lifelong friend, Isabella Hawkins, had been blessed with.

As if sensing her thoughts, Issie leaned closer. "Someday, Lily, I'll be holding your baby."

"I doubt it." The thought of marrying Mr. Everett made her shudder despite the rising temperatures in the churchyard. "I fear I'll die a poor old maid."

"Nonsense." Issie giggled. "Why, Captain Albright can't seem to take his eyes off you."

"He's our new neighbor."

"So?" Issie held the top of her wide-brimmed bonnet as a gust blew around them and bowed treetops. "Neighbor or not, the man is smitten. It's obvious."

"Oh, stop, Issie." Lily slid her glance to where Mac and several men conversed beneath the shade of a tall, black walnut tree. He looked her way and Lily smiled politely and quickly returned her gaze safely back to Issie.

"And you're sweet on him too."

"Well, how can I help it? He's a charmer—like Oliver Ashton ten times over."

"Forget Oliver." A pucker furrowed Issie's brow. "The poor man is dead. Let him rest in peace." Baby Amanda fussed, and Issie plucked her daughter from Lily's arms. "There's a man who is very much alive over yonder, and he is obviously interested in you."

"I'm his only friend so far in Middletown." For as much as Lily yearned for romantic love, the idea frightened her. She knew so little of Mac. . . What if he'd made promises to another young lady in Alexandria? She couldn't stand the thought of being humiliated again.

"Captain Albright accepted our dinner invitation a week from this Wednesday. You'll come too, won't you?"

"Well. . ." Lily knew of no other obligations.

"I'll put Amanda to bed and we'll have a casual late supper."

Lily smiled. "I would enjoy nothing better than to visit your home and dine with you and James."

"Good. Then it's settled." Issie's happy smile peeped out from beneath her ridiculously large hat. "I'll go tell James immediately."

Lily watched her best friend's haste to tell her husband the news. Perhaps Mac would feel more comfortable knowing his neighbor would be in attendance too. However, the cluster of young ladies standing nearby was a clear sign that Mac would not be lacking in invitations.

One young lady in particular stood out among the throng, Cynthia Clydesdale. Her pretty face, nut-brown hair, and figure-flattering light-blue dress with its cerulean sash caused several male heads to turn. Surely Mac noticed her, and Cynthia made no effort to hide the fact that she wanted a husband. She'd planned to be married by now, but Oliver Ashton had fooled her too.

Mac backed away from the conversing men and Cynthia stopped him by touching his arm. He politely tugged on the brim of his black top hat and seemed interested in Cynthia's prattle. Why, the lilt in her voice carried across the yard. Mac gave a nod, and Lily heard him thank Cynthia for whatever it was she'd said. Then he made his way toward Lily.

"Are you ready to leave?"

"Are you?" Lily leaned forward. "Seems Miss Clydesdale would prefer that you stay."

"The attractive young woman in the blue gown who spoke to me just now?"

So he had noticed Cynthia's comeliness. The fact caused Lily pangs of jealousy—pangs she quickly tamped down. "Captain, surely you're accustomed to young ladies throwing themselves at you."

"You would think so, wouldn't you?" A guffaw escaped him. "The truth is, I find meeting members of the fairer sex more difficult the older I become."

He offered his arm and Lily threaded her hand around his elbow. They strolled toward the carriage.

"I fear I am to be a bachelor forever."

"Don't feel badly. You're in good company. I'm destined to be a penniless old maid as I would rather die than marry a certain gentleman whose name we shall not mention."

At the utterance of her last word, Mr. Everett hailed them. Lily moaned and Mac chuckled softly.

"Hark, that certain gent summons you."

"Forgive me for not sharing your amusement." Lily watched Mr. Everett's rapid approach. His features were shadowed by a dark scowl. She clung a bit tighter to Mac's arm.

"Lily, I insist you ride home in my carriage." Mr. Everett sounded a bit breathless from his canter across the churchyard. "This is the way we've done things since your father died, and I believe he would be quite vexed by your behavior this morning." He glared at Mac. "I hope you aren't the sort of man who would risk a young lady's reputation by publicly commanding her attention."

"Sir?" Mac frowned. "I'm merely escorting Miss Laughlin to the buggy. She's recovering from a fever. I wouldn't have her walk home."

"And the display in church?" With pinched features, Mr. Everett moved toward Lily. "What do you have to say about that?"

Lily took a half step back. Mac moved forward, causing her to feel quite protected. It occurred to her that she hadn't felt such a measure of security since Papa died. And to think of the gratitude she'd felt when Mr. Everett told the magistrate he'd step in as executor. He'd taken advantage of her grieving family. Now that she knew of his intentions, Lily wanted to stay as far away from him as possible.

"Have you no answer?" He gave a grunt. "I was thoroughly humiliated."

"I have no idea what you're referring to." Lily searched her memory and came up with nothing.

"You sat next to me," Mac muttered, tilting his head closer to hers. "It appears Mr. Everett took offense to that."

"Then I'm sorry for you, sir. There was nothing shameful about selecting my family's pew. Besides, Mr. Blake and Captain Albright attended today at our invitation."

"You obviously did not read that book on ladies' etiquette that I gave you." Mr. Everett lifted his chin, sniffed, then brushed away flakes of dried leaves from his black lapel. "What a pity."

"You are wrong, sir. I read every word." She spoke the truth, although she hadn't studied the volume for Mr. Everett's sake. She hoped to glean an impeccable comportment for...

She stared up into Mac's face. Yes, she'd read the book for him. She would freely admit it, at least to herself. But she hated the idea of embarrassing her new friend, especially since it sounded as though he hailed from a sophisticated family in Alexandria.

"I'm certain proper etiquette," Mr. Everett scoffed, "does not dictate the obvious pursuit of a man while in the house of the Lord."

Lily opened her mouth to answer, but found herself speechless. Her face flamed beneath the accusation. She glanced around, wondering if others heard him, and tears pricked.

"You are mistaken in your assumptions, sir," Mac said. His tone left little room for argument. "I've known Miss Laughlin barely a month, but in that short time I have learned she is not a young lady who behaves unseemly."

The memory of being in Mac's arms while they surveyed the barn rushed to the forefront of Lily's mind. She'd told him straight out that he was handsome and he said she was liable to get herself kissed. How disappointed she'd been when a skunk interrupted their intimacy.

Lily suddenly wished for the Second Coming. Perhaps she deserved this dressing down in front of all her church family. She attempted to slip her hand from Mac's arm, but he flexed his muscles and held it in place.

Amazingly, and in spite of Mr. Everett's flare of temper and wild assertions, Mac's expression registered complete calm. No furrowed brow. No creased forehead. No frown pulling his mouth downward.

Reverend Kasper joined their threesome and Lily's knees weakened with relief. The reverend was not quick to accuse or judge. She introduced Mac and carefully kept her eyes averted from Mr. Everett. The two men shook hands.

"You are new to Middletown, I hear."

"Yes, Reverend, I am." Mac sounded pleasant enough.

"Welcome." The reverend's bright gaze shifted to Lily before returning to Mac. "I think you will find happiness here in our quaint corner of the world."

A half grin played across his lips. "How can you tell?"

Reverend Kasper grinned also. "Call it divine intuition."

"Then I'm glad for it, as Middletown is feeling more like my home every day."

"Good." The minister clasped his hands together. "Oh, and I should mention that my wife and I have been invited to the Hawkinses' home next week as well, so I look forward to our getting better acquainted, Captain."

"Likewise, sir."

The reverend gave a bow, smiled at Lily, and moved on.

"What is occurring next week?" Mr. Everett asked. "I am not aware of any invitations."

Mac cleared his throat. "Miss Laughlin shouldn't stand in this breeze much longer. As I said, she is recovering from her illness. We had better make for the buggy."

"Had you communicated your need of a vehicle, Captain, I would have shared mine, as I have done since your arrival." Mr. Everett emphatically punctuated his last several words.

"You have been most gracious, Mr. Everett."

Lily heard the tightness in Mac's voice before he turned with her still on his arm. They strode to the gravel opening where the horses and various styles of vehicles had been parked. She exchanged waves with Carolina Givens, who sat in the back seat of her father's wagon. However, Lily didn't miss Mac's signal to Mr. Blake. With the man's hand at the small of Aunt

Hilda's back, Mr. Blake steered her away from her gabbing friends, although Aunt Hilda got in a few parting words.

At that moment, Jed and Jonah came tearing around the church building, chasing the three McGuire boys. Mac whistled through his teeth, causing Lily's ear to ring. However, it brought her brothers to a standstill. Miraculously, they followed Mac's lead to the buggy.

As her brothers barreled onto the seats, one in front and one in back, Lily noticed the knees of Jed's trousers were caked with dirt. His Sunday clothes would have to be washed. . .again.

"Pardon my whistling for your brothers." Mac spoke close to Lily's ear while he assisted her into the carriage. "I fear I acted on impulse."

"It did the job. Besides, my hearing shall return shortly." Lily laughed at Mac's look of concern.

His frown ebbed. "You're sporting with me."

Her smile lingered. "That I am, sir."

He rolled his dark eyes before helping Aunt Hilda into the coach. But Lily had glimpsed the amusement that stole over Mac's face. Knowing she was the culprit of his good humor pleased her.

Could Issie have been correct about a mutual romantic attraction between Mac and her? Was that why Mr. Everett was so livid in the churchyard and the reason he'd been behaving oddly all week? Such a thing would certainly foil his plans—

Plans which crimped Lily's insides at the mere idea of them. He'd already sold off a fair portion of their land. What else did he have in mind?

Mac cinched the last of two valises and glanced around his rented room. After returning the buggy to the livery and thanking Mr. Hawkins for its use, he procured a wagon and a team of mules from the man who promised to ready the animals and drive the wagon to the inn. Hawkins's manner encouraged Mac. Perhaps he'd find a friend in the good-natured blacksmith.

Upon returning to the inn, Mac asked Blake to change clothes and pack up his things. They were leaving. Mac refused to tolerate any more of Everett's rude behavior and insinuations. Paying the innkeeper daily seemed, in a way, like he condoned it.

And he didn't.

He opened and closed his right hand as the temptation to slam his fist into Everett's jaw came over him once more. The urge this morning had been powerful enough to make Mac want to forget the reverend's teaching on loving thy neighbor and extending him grace.

He breathed in deeply, then exhaled slowly. He wouldn't resort to violence. He couldn't, even for Lily. His future here in Middletown had only just begun, and Everett seemed to have influence on a good number of citizens. Mac had guessed that days ago, and talk among a few men in the churchyard this morning confirmed it. Seemed several of them had secured loans from Everett and he'd hiked up their payments, imposing severe constraints on the debtors' budgets.

More reason to move out of the Stony Inn. The less Mac knew about other men's financial affairs, the better.

A knock sounded at the door.

"Enter," Mac called.

Blake shuffled in. "I'm all set if you are. The wagon's out front."

Mac grabbed his valises and followed Blake downstairs. He paid their bill to a maid who furnished him with a receipt. Mac had offered to pick up all expenses if Blake would help him get started with his new life as a landlubber.

Yet one more good reason to leave; he'd save money. And he'd need every coin to achieve his goals.

The desire to prove himself to his family swelled inside of him. He longed to show them he wasn't the reprobate and traitor—even murderer —that the Hanovers and others in Alexandria had made him out to be. The accusations from former friends and neighbors wounded Mac deeply. While it was true that the only way he could stay alive was to fight his own countrymen, Mac's actions put questions into his brother's and father's minds and tears into his mother's and sisters' eyes.

Well, he'd show them—all of them—that he wasn't a ne'er-do-well...or worse. As he prospered, he'd prove it. He'd regain their respect.

But first he had to build his barn and stables and then his home. When Father gave him his inheritance, he promised to send a crew to help Mac with construction. The men would arrive shortly.

From the far end of the block, James Hawkins caught Mac's eye and waved. Mac lifted his hand in thanks and the man faced forward and walked on. Blake occupied himself with loading their belongings into the wagon. Mac's tumultuous thoughts preoccupied him. Perhaps as he made the acquaintances of more men in Middletown, although never allowing himself to be sucked into their woe, he would no longer so easily succumb to Lily's companionship.

And then, like daylight turned to dusk, thoughts of Lily turned to memories of Mary. She'd grown into spinsterhood waiting for his return and died before he reached American soil. Mac had mourned her death, certainly, but now he felt more guilt than sadness. Mary had a bold and solid faith—like Lily's. But unlike Lily, Mary never affected him the way his pretty new neighbor did. The truth of it was, Lily distracted him beyond all reason.

And Mac couldn't afford any diversions. They would surely be his downfall, and he must not fail. Not this time.

"So where to, Cap'n?" Blake climbed onto the front seat of the long, wooden wagon.

"Home, Blake." Mac held the reins in his hands and snapped them over the mules' backsides. Determination filled his entire being. "We're going home."

# Chapter Ten

*D*id you never construct a hideout when you were a boy?"

"No, never did." Blake halted his squeeze-box serenade. "But what you're building resembles a house my mother rented when I was a boy."

"Surely, you're joking." Mac tossed another piece of plank from the barn onto the makeshift roof of his new home and guest quarters. A good thing he and Blake hadn't gotten more time to burn the entirety of barn wood and, equally as fortunate that the seven-foot-high stone foundation only needed minor repairs. "This hovel will protect us from the elements, but only temporarily. I hope to have my new barn and stable built by the time the winter comes."

"I've spent many winters in a hut like you've thrown together." A sorrowful glimmer entered Blake's eyes, one Mac never noticed before. "Now you know why I thought the sea was the queen herself and the ships on which I sailed were palaces."

"Hm. . .well, I suppose that explains why you never complained of cramped quarters and a hammock for a bed."

"Not I, Cap'n, although I admit that on most nights I was too full of rum to care where I slept."

His friend spoke the truth there.

Mac threw more remnants of the barn onto their makeshift living quarters. Afterward he rubbed his palms together to rid himself of the wood dust and grime. "Well, my friend, this shall be a camp you'll not soon forget."

"I'll take your word for it." Blake snorted and began playing a mournful tune.

"Play something more lively, will you?"

"If it's lively you want, then that's what you'll get." Blake pumped out the melody of "Yankee Privateer." Soon the two of them sang,

*"We sailed and we sailed,*
*And we kept good cheer.*
*We're not a British frigate,*
*But a Yankee privateer."*

Blake chortled. "Remember how we sang that tune and made Cap'n Osborn's face redder than stewed tomatoes?"

"I remember." Smiling, Mac gathered twigs and small pieces of wood for a fire. "We're lucky he didn't hang us."

"Aw, he knew it was all in good fun."

"That he did—and he had a long fuse, which certainly helped matters."

"I'll say." Blake clamored to his feet and tucked away his instrument.

"Done playing?"

"Aye. I'm mighty hungry now. I think I'll head over to Hilda's and see what she's made for supper."

Something deep inside Mac warred within him. He had sought Lily out in the churchyard, even protected her from Everett. His actions hadn't gone unnoticed. He'd seen how the congregating church members looked on. Then he and Blake left with the Laughlins and Mrs. Gunther. Mac could only guess what the talk of the town was at supper tables all across Middletown.

It was for the best that his friendship with Lily ended here and now.

"You comin', Cap'n?"

"No."

"No?" Blake tipped his head. "Why not?"

After dumping an armful of dried wood onto his growing pile, Mac faced his friend. "I didn't move to the Shenandoah Valley to get mixed up with a young lady."

"The Laughlins and Hilda are your neighbors."

"True, but I've not been careful where Lily is concerned. This morning Everett pointed out the fact that I could jeopardize her reputation by my overly friendly actions."

"Bah!" Blake waved off the notion. "What do you care what that strutting peacock says?"

"I have to care, Blake. My future depends on it."

"You're makin' a mistake, Cap'n. Falling in love only betters a man."

"Or breaks his heart."

"Miss Lily won't do that."

Mac clenched his jaw then took in a long breath. "I've got my future to secure before I entertain notions of taking a woman to wife." And, God forbid, Lily would choose to wait for him until she became an old woman—like Mary. Despite the fact he despised Everett, Lily might do well to marry the man. She'd have everything a woman could want—well, almost everything. However, it was as he'd told her: marriages weren't always made out of love but out of need and practicality.

"Suit yourself, Cap'n, but my belly is leading me to Hilda's supper table." Blake headed in the direction of the stone bridge.

Mac longed to follow for no other reason than the rumblings in his belly. The porridge at the inn this morning had tasted like paste. He could use a hearty meal.

With hands on his hips, Mac contemplated the hovel he created. The sheer discomfort of it would spur him on to building his barn and, perhaps, even digging the foundation of his house before winter arrived. Nearly every coin he owned had been invested in the land on which he stood. Every dollar had gone toward beginning his new life.

And, in spite of his feelings, there was no place for Lily in this new world he now called home.

Lily found it hard to believe that a week and a half had passed since Issie's invitation. Seemed like months, but finally Wednesday evening arrived, cold and gloomy, and bearing the reminder that autumn would soon be at hand. Harvest time was rapidly approaching. As she walked toward the Hawkinses' home, Lily's ideas of bringing in the harvest teetered. If only

Shona and his native friends would come around in the fall and offer their help it would ease her troubled mind. Papa had employed them the past few years when the men showed up, asking for work. Payment for their labor came in the form of shares in the harvested crops so they could feed their families. However, it was always a gamble for the men, as opportunity dictated their schedules. A bigger farm promised larger shares in wheat, corn, fruit, and vegetables, while the Laughlins' smaller one produced far less.

Lily wrapped her hooded cape more tightly around her shoulders as cold rain pelted her from all sides. If she arrived at the Hawkinses' home soaked to the bone, it would be her fault for not accepting Mr. Everett's offer of his carriage. But she'd come to realize how Mr. Everett's kindnesses carried with them subtle indebtednesses, and she wished to owe the man nothing.

Except she and her family owed him everything. They wrote out a list, and Mr. Everett had the foodstuffs delivered. If they needed material and thread, Mr. Everett saw to it they got it. For months now she and Aunt Hilda had been spared the walk into town. It had been hot and humid, so they figured it was just as well. And, of course, they were still reeling from the void Papa's death left in their hearts. Now Lily wished she hadn't begun to rely on Mr. Everett, and yet she was forced to, as he was the executor of whatever funds and assets existed in Papa's estate.

Mr. Everett still claimed they were penniless.

Lily clenched her fists. They couldn't be! It didn't make sense.

Lily passed Mac's orchard, wondering if she would see him tonight. They very idea made her heart drop like a stone. Mac had made himself scarce these past several days, and when Lily waved to him across the meadow, he'd turned away as if he hadn't seen her. Mr. Blake said Mac battled some inner tempest, but he refused to elaborate, as any loyal friend would. Did that tempest have anything to do with the broken-down old barn and the rotten fences which once made up a prime barnyard? Perhaps if Mac had known just how much work lay ahead of him, he wouldn't have purchased the acreage.

Well, Lily had nothing to do with the sale, and it seemed to her that if she'd accepted the idea, Mac ought to accept it also. Even so, she couldn't blame him for being miffed. A lot of extra time and work had to go into tearing down the old in order to build the new.

The rain let up and Lily hurried on her way up the pike. At last she reached Issie and James's small farm. Although a blacksmith and liveryman by trade, James liked to putter around in his garden, and he possessed quite the green thumb. Issie, too, had developed impressive agricultural skills over the years. She'd grown up on a farm not too far away. Her parents still resided there.

The lacy curtain on the front window fluttered and, moments later, the door opened wide.

"Don't tell me you walked all the way here." Issie clucked her tongue.

"All right, I won't tell you." Lily shrugged out of her soaked cloak. "However, I believe the evidence speaks for itself."

"Indeed." Taking the wet wrap, Issie excused herself and proceeded toward the kitchen. Lily guessed she would hang the cloak on a peg near the open hearth.

Brushing the moisture from her dark-blue printed gown, Lily wished once more that she had accepted the offer of Mr. Everett's carriage. He seemed not to mind that he wasn't invited. Then again, Mr. Everett preferred rubbing elbows with the upper class who passed through Middletown and stayed at his inn.

Issie returned, with raindrops staining her blue-green gown. Lily felt instantly guilty. However, Issie didn't seem to care. She looped her arm around Lily's and together they entered the parlor where a fire in the stone hearth blazed and warmed the room. Lily greeted Reverend and Mrs. Kasper with a smile and a wave. They stood at the far end of the room, conversing with James.

"Amanda is asleep and dinner is ready." Issie's hazel eyes glimmered with accomplishment. "We are just waiting on Captain Albright."

"Is he coming?" Lily held her hands out to the brightly burning flames.

"I thought so." Frown lines peeped out from beneath the auburn curls on Issie's forehead. "But you should know. He's your neighbor and—"

"I haven't spoken to the man for over a week, and Mr. Blake, the captain's companion, is careful not to say too much. Therefore, I haven't a clue as to what's going on with my new neighbor."

"I see."

"But it would seem," Lily whispered, "that I have offended him somehow." Issie gasped. "What sassy thing did you say?"

"I don't know." While Lily had only just recently met the man, she missed their friendship. "Perhaps I spouted some nonsense and he didn't know I was joking." It's all Lily had come up with after rehashing their Sunday morning and ride back home together.

"Well, perhaps you both can settle things tonight." Issie turned to face James. "Captain Albright is coming, is he not?"

"As far as I know." His gaze fell on Lily. "I had assumed the two of you would arrive together."

Lily pulled her shoulders back. "Now why would you assume that, James Hawkins?"

"No reason." He graced her with a lopsided grin. "No reason at all."

"Except that when you left the churchyard on the captain's arm" —Reverend Kasper put in—"everyone, including me, thought you two looked like a match made in heaven."

"What am I to say?" Lily shrugged. "You men are fickle beings."

"Ah, yes, well, I have heard the same from my lovely wife."

Mrs. Kasper admonished him with a gape and a playful slap on his arm.

As if on cue, a succession of firm knocks on the front door wafted into the parlor. It seemed Mac had arrived after all. James hurried to let him in.

Lily stared at the fire and tamped down a sudden case of fluttery nerves. Silence fell over the room as the men's voices drifted in. Then, finally, Mac darkened the doorway. He looked rough, from his crumpled clothing to his whiskery jaw.

"Another guest who chose to walk on this rainy night," James said, reintroducing everyone for Mac's benefit. "And, of course, you know our good friend, Lily Laughlin."

"Miss Laughlin." Mac gave a hasty bow and barely set eyes on her before following James across the room.

"You know what I think?" Issie leaned close to Lily.

"What?" Lily bent her head to hear.

"I think you've terrified the poor fellow."

Lily's giggle caused several heads to turn, although not Mac's. She quickly sucked the smile off her lips. "He's a weathered seaman who fought in the war," she whispered to Issie. "A woman would not terrify him."

"So one would think." Issie's hazel eyes reflected the firelight. "But I'm sure there's room for an exception."

"It's just as well anyway. We were only friends." Lily wondered why she felt like she'd just fibbed. "Besides, after Oliver broke my heart, there's nothing romantically left for another."

"Oh, Jehoram! Why must you consistently raise poor Oliver from his grave?"

"I understand his family is suffering from great need. Mr. Ashton can barely tend to his chores because he's so distraught. Their money is gone. The younger girls have no shoes and they'll need them in the coming months." Sorrow settled over Lily. "I wish I could help, but I have nothing to offer."

"Where did you hear that news?"

"Mr. Everett." Lily almost hated to cite her source, but the man did overhear much talk, being the town's innkeeper.

Mrs. Kasper stepped in close. "I heard you make mention of Oliver Ashton."

"Yes, ma'am." Lily turned her way.

"Mr. Ashton is not there—in the grave."

"Of course." Lily inclined her head. "He is with the Lord."

"No. . .well, yes." A moment's confusion settled on the good woman's features. "What I meant was Mr. Ashton's body was never recovered. It's only a marker in the cemetery."

Stunned, Lily wondered why she'd never known about it before now.

"His kin wanted it that way," Mrs. Kasper added. "But if I was not the strong believer I am, I might believe the tale that Oliver Ashton haunts Middletown, as some have suggested."

"Oh, I believe he does haunt Middletown," Issie said with a tiny smirk curving her mouth. "Why, not a day goes by that he doesn't pervade Lily's thoughts."

Lily hurled a glance upward. "Oh, hush."

"Seriously, now. . ." Mrs. Kasper stepped in so closely that Lily caught a scent of the lavender sprigs in her brunette hair. "Mr. Will Weston, who claims to be the last one to have seen Oliver alive, ran to our home several months back, insisting that he heard Oliver's continual moaning breeze over the top of North Mountain."

"And that, of course, would be fiction," Issie said, looking unimpressed. "Mr. Weston is known to be something of a drunkard."

Lily nodded in agreement.

"That's true, although my husband will tell you that there is a deep spiritual side to Mr. Weston. He. . ." Mrs. Kasper glanced over her shoulder as if to make sure they weren't overheard. "He sees things."

"I'm sure he does." Issie laughed lightly. "After enough libations, any man—or woman—is a visionary."

Another giggle bubbled up inside Lily. "In all due respect, Mrs. Kasper, our hostess is correct, especially as it pertains to the matter of Mr. Weston's bad habit."

"I agree, and yet I find the tale inexpiably mysterious."

Lily resisted the urge to shudder. "Oliver Ashton is not alive. If he were, someone in Middletown would have surely seen him—someone who didn't frequent the many taverns up and down the pike."

Issie glanced over her shoulder before batting her lashes at Lily. "It would appear, dear friend, that you have recaptured Captain Albright's attention."

# Chapter Eleven

*M*ac despised these sorts of social outings, although he knew they were necessary if one wanted to blend into a new community. Truth to tell, he only agreed to the Hawkinses' dinner invitation because he knew Lily planned to attend.

And that was the problem. Lily was here. Mac needed to stop putting her before his own plans and his very future. Because of her, everything had changed, most predominantly his accommodations. It had not been an easy task, dressing in dingy lighting while rain poured through rotted logs and the sorriest excuse for a roof. Perhaps he'd been hasty, checking out of the Stony Inn, but at least he could boast of a clear conscience. He in no way funded Mr. Everett's endeavors, which may or may not include his plans for his pretty neighbor.

As for Lily, her effervescent laughter never failed to reach his ears, whether from across a meadow or the Hawkinses' parlor. How had this happened, and in so short a time?

Blake's voice clamored for space in his head. *Besotted.* But Mac refused to succumb to peculiar feelings of the heart now—if ever.

He dragged his fingertips across the stubbly growth quickly overtaking his jaw. He hadn't attempted to shave for tonight's dinner event, but plenty of men in Middletown sported beards. Mac just didn't appreciate the look—or feel—on himself. What a fool he'd been not to pack a razor, but while at the Stony Inn, he'd made daily trips to Mr. Corbin's shop. Corbin specialized in wig-making, shaving, beard-trimming, dentistry, and blood-letting. Mac rubbed his whiskered jaw once more. Despite Corbin's quacksalver ways, the man did a close shave, and his shop was only two doors down from the inn. Yes, there had definitely been an advantage to staying in town.

Mrs. Hawkins seated everyone around the dinner table. A knot formed in Mac's chest when Lily sat beside him. Mrs. Kasper and the reverend's places were directly across the table. The ladies, close to their hostess, and the men, near their host, most likely for the sake of conversation.

After politely holding Lily's chair, Mac lowered himself into his. At least with her next to him at the table, he would escape her captivating blue eyes. But if he'd overheard correctly, only minutes ago, she exclaimed something about the cur who broke her heart being. . .alive? Surely Mac hadn't heard correctly. After all, it was a fact that he was lousy at eavesdropping. Years of standing too close to firing cannons had dulled that sense, and yet, he always heard Lily's voice—even in his dreams.

The reverend stood and called for everyone's attention. "At Mr. and Mrs. Hawkinses' request, I agreed to ask the blessing on our meal."

He prayed, and Mrs. Hawkins began passing dishes. Mac's stomach gurgled with anticipation. While Blake ate three hearty meals a day, courtesy of Mrs. Gunther, Mac hadn't eaten much at all these past few days, and he was famished.

"Captain, I hope you won't find us too presumptuous," James Hawkins began, "but several of us townsmen, including myself, would like to offer our skill and muscle to help build you a barn."

Mac wondered if Lily had anything to do with the offer. "Well, I—"

"It's a way we like to welcome newcomers," the reverend added.

"Yes, and those of us participating figure we can give you a couple of hours at the end of the day beginning next week." James took a quick bite of his dinner. "We'll likely complete the project in a fortnight."

"That's very thoughtful of you." Mac would be crazy not to accept. Father's crew still had not arrived. "Thank you."

"All we ask," Mrs. Kasper put in, "is that you host a party afterward—to christen your new barn. We women will bring all the food you men can eat."

"But of course the gathering must end early enough"—the reverend waved a finger—"so that no one is late for church the next morning."

Chuckles flitted around the table, but it was the lilt in Lily's soft laugh that captivated him.

Except captive implied many things—things like commitment to a woman, marriage, children. Mac battled to rid his mind of such notions daily. First things first. He needed to succeed at this endeavor!

The conversation shifted to James's admitted favorite topics: farming and profitable crops. Mac listened carefully, as he wanted to be proficient with crops next year. He marveled at the way James's young wife, Isabella, added to the conversation. Clearly, she was James's helpmeet, that biblical reference that Mac had heard bandied about during his school days.

Mrs. Hawkins laughed softly at something James just said. Her face glowed beneath the light of the tapers. The love the young couple had for each other was as obvious as the rain splattering against the windows.

Two bites of food later, Mac started fearing his hovel would be completely flooded when he returned. Puddles had been accumulating when he'd left for the Hawkins' place with Blake's mutters following him to the pike.

"Wait till you taste Issie's strawberry and rhubarb cake." James wagged his head, and several strands of his brown hair slipped from their queue. "Rhubarb is a wonder, all right. Grows like a vegetable, but tastes like a fruit—a bitter fruit until sugar is added."

"It cooks up nicely," Mrs. Hawkins said, "and when I added my sweet, ripe strawberries, I preserved much more than last year."

"I purchased the root stock from a Massachusetts salesman." James held his fork just above his plate. "He claimed rhubarb is gaining in popularity in New England."

"I've heard of rhubarb from my trips to the Orient," Mac said between mouthfuls of the tasty chicken and dumplings. "It's noted for its medicinal qualities, although I couldn't tell you which ones."

"How very interesting, Captain." Mrs. Kasper smiled. "Won't you miss your seafaring days by becoming a lowly farmer in Middletown?"

"Not at all, madam. I'm glad to be away from the seashore, and I'm eager to test my book knowledge of caring for animals, planting, growing, and harvesting fruits and vegetables."

"And you won't find Middletown dull?" The woman tipped her head in a way that reminded Mac of his mother.

"Not at all." He noticed Lily kept her gaze averted.

*Good!*

True, she and her family had made his first week in Middletown quite exciting, but now Mac was determined to be serious about his work on his new property. He and Blake had been pulling down rotted fence posts, and Mac would see to getting the floor of the barn leveled. The scattered plashes of rainwater today told him that the floor was anything but even.

Pounding at the front door halted the table talk. Mac stifled a grin when James grudgingly pushed to his feet. The lag in conversation allowed him several more bites of his dinner. He selected a flaky biscuit from the bread basket parked in front of James's placemat and took a bite of buttery goodness.

"My compliments on the meal, Mrs. Hawkins." Mac dabbed the corners of his mouth. "Everything is delicious."

"Why, thank you, sir." His hostess's eyes glided to Lily, who sipped her fruity wine but said nothing.

Part of Mac longed to engage her in conversation, but the other part—the practical part—wanted to encourage her to ignore him all the more.

Even so, he supposed he owed Lily an explanation for his sudden turnabout. He avoided discussing the matter—and her—because he hated to hurt her feelings.

But there was always a chance she'd understand.

James returned and stood behind his wife. He placed his hand on her shoulder. "Lily, that was Mr. Temmes at the door, speaking on behalf of Mr. Everett. Evidently your guardian has sent his carriage for you due to the inclement weather."

"He is not my guardian, though he's given himself the title."

James lifted his shoulders. "The wind has picked up and it's raining harder. Mr. Everett is concerned that the pike will flood and he won't get that ostentatious carriage of his back to the inn. Therefore, he's requesting that you leave here at once."

"I've been rained on before." Lily lifted her chin.

*Stubborn woman.* She ought to gratefully accept the ride so she didn't catch her death. Mac glanced around the table. The Kaspers and Mrs. Hawkins stared at their dinner plates.

"Actually, Mr. Everett is not requesting." James's tone turned iron hard. "He is insisting, and he's waiting in the carriage for you."

"It's probably best you go, Lily," the reverend said with a glance at Mac.

*It's none of my business.* Mac decided to focus on his wine glass. He brought it to his lips and drained the liquid, enjoying the way the grape mixture warmed his insides. It rivaled imported Madeira. Did the Hawkinses have grapevines on their farm and make the wine, or had they purchased it? If the former, perhaps he could cultivate such a vineyard. His father could ship it all over the globe.

Lily set her linen napkin on the table and stood. Mac and Reverend Kasper politely did so as well.

"I'll fetch your cloak." Mrs. Hawkins left the dinner table and disappeared into the kitchen.

"Thank you for inviting me tonight." Lily kept her gaze trained on James. "I've enjoyed myself immensely."

"A pity we were only getting started with our fellowship."

Lily set her hand on James's arm. Then, after throwing out a parting smile that landed on no one in particular, she left the room.

Guilt the size of a schooner's mainsail billowed inside Mac. He knew full well that the last thing Lily wanted was to be alone with Silas Everett. Blast it all! How could Mac deny a friend in her time of need?

Except she wasn't a friend.

Although she didn't know that yet.

"Perhaps I shall request a ride home and save myself another soaking." At Mac's announcement, the mood in the room suddenly lightened.

"A fine idea." James wore a wide smile before dashing to the front door and halting Lily.

Mac came up behind him.

"Our friend wishes to beg a ride home." James clapped Mac behind the shoulder blades. "I'm sure Mr. Everett won't mind sharing his coach."

For the first time all evening, Lily met Mac's gaze. A tenuous little smile danced across her lips. "No, I'm sure Mr. Everett won't mind at all."

♥

Lily took Mac's proffered arm. The rain pelted them as they hurried to the awaiting carriage. Mr. Temmes, the driver, opened the door. Mac assisted Lily inside before propelling his brawn into the coach. He sat beside Lily, and Mr. Temmes closed the door.

Sitting across from them, Mr. Everett rapped on the ceiling, signaling his driver onward. An awkward sort of silence settled over them.

"Did you enjoy your little dinner party, Lily?" Mr. Everett's voice sounded tight and, in the darkness, it seemed devoid of a physical body. "A cozy gathering, I assume."

"A pity our dinner was interrupted," Mac grumbled.

Lily shivered and tugged on her cloak. Disappointment, like the damp chill in the air, seeped into her bones. Mac had changed. He was no longer an agreeable fellow, a friend, and she mourned the loss.

"Well, you needn't have left the party, Captain." Mr. Everett gave a pompous sniff, one Lily heard frequently. "I've been meaning to ask, does one still address you as 'Captain'? You're no longer in military service."

"If you wish, you may refer to me as Mr. Albright. I answer to both."

Lily couldn't keep silent. "But addressing you as your former military rank is a show of respect, is it not?"

She felt Mac stiffen beside her. Obviously, she'd said the wrong thing.

"Ah, Miss Laughlin, I'm proud of you." Mr. Everett copped his usual condescending tone that seemed reserved for Lily. "Obviously you have read the book I gave you on ladies' etiquette."

"I did, indeed, sir."

"Then I shall refer to Middletown's newest citizen as *Captain* Albright."

Mac faced the rattling glass window. Water trickled down the pane. "Thank you for sharing your carriage, Mr. Everett. I hope you don't mind my intrusion."

"Of course not."

"Well, the two of you share the same destination," Lily said. "It only seems logical that you would travel back to the inn together."

"Oh, no, my dear, the captain and his friend checked out of my inn over a week ago." A note of mockery tainted Mr. Everett's otherwise smooth tenor. "Apparently they prefer a shanty that the captain hastily threw together to the comfort of my rented rooms."

"A shanty?" The carriage rolled over a bumpy stretch, sending Lily bouncing into Mac's arm. "Where have you constructed such a place. . . and why?"

"On my property, of course, and I have my reasons."

Lily felt thoroughly rebuked. "Of course."

The carriage hit a rut, throwing Lily forward. Mac caught her before she slammed against Mr. Everett's knobby knees, then he tucked her hand beneath his elbow. The conveyance lurched again, and Lily clung to his arm a little tighter. He slid his warm hand over her fingers. An act of contrition for his harsh tone? Whatever the reason, a tiny thrill passed through her. In the darkness Mr. Everett couldn't see their shared intimacy, which made it oddly thrilling.

A frown began weighing heavy on her brow. But if Mac despised her, why was he holding her hand? She had been sure that he was miffed at her for some silly reason, one she could not fathom. Yet, he left a warm home and Issie's delicious chicken and dumplings for a damp, bone-jarring carriage ride. And the way he held her hand so secretly and with the utmost tenderness. . . What did it all mean?

Mac cleared his throat. "I felt it would be more of an incentive to build my barn and home if I wasn't in a soft bed each night."

"Indeed." Mr. Everett snorted as the carriage swayed to and fro. "Mr. Blake said your hut is regrettably flooded, so you may well be uncomfortable tonight."

"I've been wetter."

The temptation rose up in Lily to offer Papa's room as temporary shelter, but she held her tongue. He would most likely refuse anyway.

"Of course, you and Mr. Blake are welcome to take refuge at the Stony Inn tonight." Mr. Everett's voice returned to its familiar haughtiness.

"Thank you, sir, but no."

Foolish, perplexing man. Why would he not accept Mr. Everett's offer?

After a few more jolts and jostles, the carriage pulled to a halt on the pike.

"I dare not ask Mr. Temmes to attempt your drive, Lily." Mr. Everett's tone was quite matter of fact. "The carriage wheels will sink for sure."

"It's not a problem. I appreciate the ride." Even though it was only a mile's jaunt from James and Issie's farm.

Mac released her. "I, too, am grateful, sir." He climbed out and extended his hand to Lily.

She clasped it and pulled the hood of her cape around her head before jogging to the front door. Surprisingly, Mac followed her.

"Please come in and I'll make you some hot tea or coffee."

"That's not necessary. I merely want to speak with Blake." He paused. "I presume he's warming himself inside your home."

"Of course." The razor-sharp edge in his voice wounded her. "But first perhaps you'd like to tell me what I've done to offend you. We were friends the Sunday before last, but recently you've behaved like you hate me. Then in the carriage just now—"

"I owe you an explanation, yes."

"Please enlighten me." Lily stood just inside the house, allowing Mac only a few feet of shelter.

"You have not offended me."

"Then what has caused your briny mood?"

"Can we discuss this another time?"

Lily tamped down the desire to say that now was as convenient a time as any, except Aunt Hilda's call of welcome made her swallow the retort.

"Captain Albright!" Aunt Hilda peeled Lily's cloak off her shoulders. "Give me your outerwear and I'll hang it up to dry."

"Actually, Mrs. Gunther, I can't stay," Mac said.

"In other words, he *won't* stay." Lily tasted her bitterness on her tongue. A more capricious man she'd never met! "I'll find Mr. Blake at once."

"He's in the parlor near the fire." Aunt Hilda's tone was ripe with the same befuddlement that had rotted Lily's mood.

She headed that way, but overheard her aunt add something about Mr. Blake getting soaked to the bone. Lily found the aged seaman in an upholstered armchair near the hearth. His shirt and trousers looked oddly familiar. Had they belonged to Papa?

He stood when she entered. "Greetings, Miss Lily. Did you enjoy the dinner party?"

"It was far too short to be much fun, I'm afraid."

"I figured as much when Mr. Gilly Gaupus stormed out of here with intentions of fetching you with his carriage."

She smiled at his somewhat tawdry term for Mr. Everett. "Yes, well, the captain rode along"—thank goodness!—"and now he's in the entryway, wishing to speak with you."

"Right-o." Mr. Blake sauntered from the room, in no hurry it seemed.

Lily removed her gloves, crossed the Persian carpet, and stood with her hands outstretched toward the hearth. She shivered when the warmth of the fire met her chilled body. Although summer's final days were upon them, today's gloom and steady rain made it feel like the end of autumn.

Aunt Hilda's exuberant pitch drew Lily's attention. Footfalls thundered up the stairs. Then a long shadow fell across the room. Lily turned to find Mac standing in the doorway.

He leaned one shoulder against the archway. "It appears I'm staying for the night."

## Chapter Twelve

*L*ily turned back to the crackling hearth. The floorboards creaked in a familiar way and signaled Mac's footsteps as he came up behind her.

"Your aunt has gone upstairs to ready your father's room. I hope you don't mind that Blake and I stay there for the night."

"Why would I mind?" She swung around to face him. "It's the neighborly thing to do, seeing as your shack is washed out. Of course, I didn't know you were living in such conditions as Mr. Blake didn't say anything about it." Her arms went stiff at her side and she leaned toward him. "And you haven't spoken to me in over a week! Not even a friendly wave across the meadow. All I received were scowls."

"About that, Lily."

"The Kaspers and the Hawkinses think you hate me now because of your surliness toward me."

He cringed. "Lily. . ."

"And then you dare such intimacy as holding my hand in the carriage. Your actions went far beyond mere protection, and I can't for the life of me figure out why."

"My actions in the carriage are evidence of my true feelings, Lily. But I cannot—I won't—give in to them."

The fight drained out of her. "I don't understand."

With stealth-like movements, he stepped beside her and put his elbow on the mantel.

"Allow me to be candid."

"As you wish." She glanced toward the doorway. Presumably Mr. Blake had followed Aunt Hilda upstairs, and the boys were in their bedroom. "I think we're guaranteed a few minutes' privacy, so speak your mind."

Mac's chest expanded with the depth of his next breath. "I don't want to be your friend, Lily."

His words stung, though she pretended otherwise. "Yes, so I gathered." She looked away. "But I hope that doesn't mean we're enemies."

"It's not what you think."

"Oh? And what do you presume that I think?" Despite her efforts, snips of cynicism made their way out of her mouth.

"I'm not angry with you."

"Really? You act it."

"I'm a horrible actor, so please accept my deepest and most sincere apologies."

"You're apologizing for your poor acting abilities?"

"I'm apologizing for my boorish behavior. I attempted to act as though I didn't care about you. The truth is I do care." Sincerity swam in his dark eyes. "At the same time, I cannot allow myself the luxury of your pleasant company." He began studying the chimney's stonework. "It's why I've determined to discourage you."

"So you made your decision to dissolve our acquaintanceship after church last Sunday?" She shivered as the dampness of her dress seeped into her skin.

Mac shrugged out of his frockcoat and set it about her shoulders, wrapping her in his woodsy scent. Quite an unlikely gesture from a non-friend.

"Admit it, Lily." He tugged on the lapels, drawing her closer. "Everyone who saw us leave together two Sundays ago now believes we have an understanding."

"I have heard nothing to that effect."

"And, tonight, did the Hawkinses and the Kaspers not assume that we would arrive together?"

"Well, yes. . .but only because we're neighbors and the weather is inclement."

He grunted. "It was not because we're neighbors nor is it due to the foul weather." He released his coat and Lily stumbled back. "To be honest, I'm surprised at your naivety."

"You are filled with compliments tonight, Captain." Her chin trembled slightly and Mac's features softened.

"I meant no insult." He clasped her fingers, but pulled away as if he thought better of taking her hand. "The fact of the matter is, I have invested every coin I own into my property and a chance to start my life anew. I've made mistakes, Lily, misdeeds for which I must atone. I cannot afford to get distracted by a golden-haired beauty with beguiling blue eyes, enchanting smiles, and a captivating singing voice."

"Are you referring to me?"

"I know of no other neighbor who poses such a threat." Mac's eyebrow quirked.

"Such puffery, sir." Surely he mocked her. No one ever regarded her as a beauty.

"I don't engage in feigned flattery. To be blunt, I am a man, Lily, and you are probably the loveliest young lady I have ever set eyes on." He spoke in a tone scarcely above a whisper that sent delight swirling through her. "If you think the two of us can enter into a platonic relationship, you are misguided." He rolled his left shoulder. "I speak for myself, anyway."

She gaped at him, a frown pinching her brow, but then the reality of his words struck her. "Oh!" He had just confessed his attraction to her. In truth, she was equally as fascinated by him.

Her face warmed at the admission.

"When I said I'll never marry, I meant it."

"And I took your word for it."

"Yet, I would hate to give you the wrong impression by continuing our friendship."

"I see."

"Do you?" He lifted one ebony eyebrow. "I never want to imitate that cad who broke your heart."

"Oliver?"

"Yes, him. I don't think I could bear it if I hurt you."

"But you did wound me by not being forthright sooner."

"And for that, I am sorry." He stroked her cheek with the backs of his fingers, sending a surge of delight through her, but further confusing her too. He didn't sound like a man eager to be rid of their association. Rather, he sounded like a caring friend.

However, there was one thing Mac overlooked.

"Despite your feelings, it does not change the fact that we are neighbors. Here in Middletown we all help each other and count it all joy to do so."

"Yes, I've gotten that impression."

"So I hope you won't forbid me to attend your barn raising party."

"I wouldn't dream of it." A hint of a smile tugged on the corners of his mouth. "I may even ask you for a dance, which might be to my peril."

A laugh bubbled out, but it was a heady feeling to imagine that she had some strange power over Mac's emotions. "I will refuse you, of course—for your own good."

The tiny lines around his eyes vanished and an expression of what could only be disappointment shadowed his features.

"You see, Captain? I have your best interests at heart."

The corners of his mouth quirked as if he fought off a grin. "On that note, Miss Laughlin, I shall retire for the night." He bowed slightly.

She replied with a polite dip and watched his retreating back. "Oh, but aren't you forgetting something?"

He halted. "A final kiss, perhaps, sealing the dissolution of our friendship?" He spun around, resembling a snorting bull. "How dare you tease me in such a manner when I have been—"

"Your coat?" Lily slipped from beneath the garment, instantly missing its warmth, and held it out to him. She exercised every ounce of will to keep from laughing at his chagrined expression.

He snatched it from her with a glower that warned her not to even smirk.

She didn't. . .until he left the parlor. It was only then that she allowed herself a giggle.

A final kiss. . . Did he really believe she'd suggest such a thing? He thought quite a lot of himself.

Lily inched closer to the hearth and replayed their conversation over in her mind. Once more he had vowed to remain unwed. Lily wished she were a man so she could assert such a bold claim. But the fact was, she would need to marry sometime in the future. How else was a penniless girl to support herself—that's if she were, indeed, penniless? She still believed Papa hid his will somewhere.

But where?

Fear and frustration weighed down on Lily. After harvesting three-quarters of this year's crops, she and her family could no longer rely on monies earned at the fair from jams, jellies, and pies fresh from the orchards or the bread and cornmeal from the grain fields. Their yield had never been enough earnings to live on anyway. Mad money, Papa used to call it, for it usually was divided up and used for gifts at Christmastime.

Was Lily really down to the only option available to her? Marrying Mr. Everett—presuming he would declare himself. Could she abide such a union if only for the sake of her family?

Lily closed her eyes and beseeched the God of the universe. *Lord, please provide me with a way to support my family. A means to survive.*

After several more moments in silent prayer, a sense of calm fell over Lily. Her heavenly Father owned the cattle on a thousand hills. If she trusted Him, she'd want for nothing—

Not even for a darkly handsome husband who resembled her guest upstairs.

♥

The tapestry-papered walls and oil paintings did not reflect a poor man's bedchamber. Chunky mahogany furniture made Mac feel right at home. Clearly, this was a man's dwelling place. Nary a hint of female touches graced the room.

"As I told John"—Mrs. Gunther cast a quick but adoring smile at Blake—"help yourself to any of my brother's garments." She opened the doors to the wardrobe. "Lily and I keep meaning to go through his belongings and give to charity what Jonah and Jed don't wish to keep, but some other task always claims our attention."

"I appreciate the offer. You're too kind."

"Just being neighborly." Mrs. Gunther circled the room, straightening a chair, adjusting the privacy screen, and then pausing at one side of the bed to plump pillows. "Hang your damp clothes by the hearth to dry." She indicated the lively flames dancing behind the ornate three-paneled iron grillwork.

"Thank you, I will." Mac was humbled by the woman's graciousness, especially given his rather flinty conversation with Lily. To Lily's credit, she hadn't collapsed into a fit of tears, a fact that encouraged him to be completely honest with her.

Why, then, did it pain Mac to imagine that Lily might be crying her eyes out right now?

"Mrs. Gunther." His words halted the woman as she reached the doorway. "Would you check on Lily before retiring?"

"Certainly, but why?"

"I may have unwittingly hurt her feelings."

"Be honest, Cap'n. Nothin' unwitting about it. You don't appreciate the girl's company." Blake made him sound so crass. "You got work to do."

"Ah, so you told Lily what was on your mind, did you?" Mrs. Gunther dipped her chin. "She's been wondering what bee got into your breeches." Neither humor nor concern showed on the older woman's lined face. "I'm sure she was glad you spoke up. My niece manages best when one is straightforward with her."

"Yes, ma'am."

"I'll bid you a good night, gentlemen." With a parting nod, Mrs. Gunther left the room.

"Breakfast is at seven sharp." Blake removed the coverlet atop the wide bed.

"And hopefully this rain will stop by morning." Mac moved the heavy drapes aside and peered out the window. Rain splashed against the glass pane and preceded a dark, moonless sky. "We should start felling trees and think about constructing a cabin in which to live while my house is being built." He turned and faced Blake, now tucked beneath the bedcovers. "In the future I can use it as a shelter for farmhands if I'm successful enough to afford them."

Blake raised himself up on his elbows. "Cap'n, I been doin' some thinkin' of my own, and I decided I'm goin' back to Alexandria."

Mac barely contained his disappointment. "Why?"

"The sea is beckonin'. I can hear her callin' me, even with those mountains standin' in the way."

"I thought you loved Mrs. Gunther."

"I do, and I plan ta marry her. But I can't be a landlubber, and I told her so."

Mac set his hands on his hips. "You proposed marriage?"

"I did." Blake's wide grin nearly reached his earlobes.

"And what did the lady say?"

"Well, after she got done chucklin'—"

Mac smiled, imagining the scene.

"—she said I had to dedicate myself to pleasing God and prove to her I can financially support the both of us."

"Not an unreasonable request." Except for the pleasing God part. But it explained Blake's renewed desire to work aboard a ship. Sailing was the only occupation he knew, and he knew it well. "I wish you the best, my friend."

"Oh, I ain't leavin' for a few weeks yet. Hilda said Middletown is lucky if the stage comes through once a month. Sometimes more. But it brung us a couple of weeks ago, so I figure I got some time yet to help you out." He yawned loudly. "We'll start choppin' down trees tomorrow."

Mac carefully picked through Lily's father's belongings in search of appropriate bedtime wear and extracted a linen nightshirt, made of quality material. His body suddenly ached for dry, clean clothes and a soft bed, even if it meant sharing it with Blake.

"It appears Mr. Laughlin was a man of some means." Mac unbuttoned his waistcoat, shed it, then untied his cravat.

"I'd say so." Another loud yawn.

"Makes a man wonder why Everett claims the family is destitute and were it not for his good nature the Laughlins and Mrs. Gunther wouldn't have bread on their table."

"Hilda is used to high livin', but she knows things changed with Everett in charge now."

"Undoubtedly." Mac pulled off one soaked boot, glad for a pair of dry socks tonight. "This home has a subtle elegance about it that I admire."

"Hilda said they used ta have a hired man that tended the horses and buggy. Everett let him go and then sold the team and conveyance."

"So that the Laughlins are dependent upon him, no doubt." Mac yanked off his other boot. "It's obvious what that man's doing. He's using the Laughlins' inheritance for his own benefit."

"Now, Cap'n, don't get yerself all riled before bed. You'll toss n' turn all night and neither of us'll sleep a wink."

Hanging his wet socks over the wrought iron screen in front of the hearth, Mac grumbled that Blake could sleep anywhere and on anything. A vision of Lily's golden hair formed in the flames, and Mac shoved aside the thought of her marrying Silas Everett in order to keep her home. He balled his fists. The very idea of the man touching her tensed Mac's every muscle.

But it was none of his business. What Lily Laughlin did or said and where she went—and with whom—was of no concern to him. As of tonight, they weren't even friends.

The finality of it caused a dull ache to lodge in Mac's chest. Not since Mary had he gotten along so well with a member of the fairer sex.

But that's exactly what he wanted, wasn't it? No diversions. He'd moved to Middletown for solitude on a rambling farm. The life of a recluse sounded so good in theory.

Why, then, was he now having doubts?

Chapter Thirteen

*M*ac opened his eyes to bright sunshine spilling into the bedroom. The sight cheered him. The rain had dissipated and now he could work on felling the trees for his cabin and leveling the barn's floor before building commenced.

Rolling onto his back, he stretched, noticing Blake had already risen. Soft mutters and constant shuffling on the far side of the room indicated his friend was dressing for the day. Mac decided to do the same and tossed aside the bedcovers. As his feet met the carpeted floor, a series of thuds filled the room followed by a terrific crash and then Blake's moans.

"What in heaven's name is going on over there?"

"Sorry to wake you up, Cap'n." Blake appeared around the dressing screen, still wearing his nightshirt and rubbing his forehead. "Guess I got what I deserved for snoopin'."

"Snooping?" Mac strode toward him and noticed the tiny line of blood trickling down the side of Blake's face. He stepped over to his frockcoat and plucked the handkerchief from his inside pocket. Handing it to Blake, he sized up the small puncture wound above the man's left eye. "You're bleeding, but I think you'll live."

Blake grunted a laugh. "I been hit with worse than the corner of a metal box."

"What were you looking for?" Mac stepped toward the mess on the floor. Men's fashionable top hats and other accessories, along with piles of folded documents, littered the floor.

"Hilda said to help myself to anything, so that's what I was doing." He stepped lightly over the mess on the floor. "Look here, Cap'n." He indicated a tiny room with shelves on three walls. "It's a closet, chock-full of every kind of accessory a man could want."

Mac wagged his head. "This isn't booty. These are Lily's father's belongings, Mrs. Gunther's brother. Have you no respect for a dead man's property?"

"Well, sure I have, and I only meant to peek in the boxes. I never intended 'em to fall on my head."

Mac hunkered down and began accumulating the various items. He lifted a white powdered wig that curled at the temples. The style had fallen out of fashion some time ago, although there were men who couldn't let go of the practice.

Several small velvety pouches caught his eye, and Mac captured one by the drawstring. After peering inside, he poured its contents into his palm. Gold coins glimmered in his hand, aided by the sunlight streaming through the adjacent window.

"Will you look at that! They're guineas, Cap'n."

"So I see."

"How many?"

Mac counted them. "Five and twenty."

"Twenty-five pounds and then some. And there's twelve such pouches." Blake collected them and tossed them to Mac. A quick inventory told him each pouch contained the same amount.

"How much all together, Cap'n?" The excitement in Blake's voice made Mac smile. What's more, it sent relief spiraling through him. Lily and her family were not penniless.

"It's three hundred pounds, more or less."

"A English gent could live quite comfor'bly on that amount in London. Maybe more so here in Virginia."

"Yes, I'm sure the cost of living is quite a bit lower here in Middletown than in London." Mac stood. "You know that this means?"

"The Laughlins aren't dependent on that overbearin' fop, that's what it means. And look here. . ." Blake collected a fistful of paper bits in all different shapes and sizes. "It seems a whole gaggle of men were indebted to Mr. Laughlin." Blake did his best to sober. "May he rest in peace."

"Wherever he is, I'm sure he'll be resting much easier now that his family won't have to rely on Everett—at least for a while. In fact, if they are mindful of their expenditures, these funds should sustain them until Lily is twenty-one and can legally replace Everett as guardian."

"I can't wait to see Hilda's face when she sees this money. Why, my findin' it might just make up for me snoopin'."

Mac grinned. "You'd best hope so, old man. You'd best hope so."

"We shouldn't tell the boys." Lily stared at the coins piled on Papa's bed. She had assumed Mr. Everett had taken possession of Papa's money and that it was gone. And perhaps Mr. Everett believed the sum was gone, hence his selling a parcel of their land to Mac. But they were not penniless. "Jonah and Jed would likely let it slip, and without the protection of a man, we'd be at the mercy of thieves." Why did the image of Mr. Everett flash across her mind?

"That's probably wise, given your brothers' ages." Mac's soothing deep voice penetrated her anxious thoughts, and the tenderness in his raven gaze lent her a measure of confidence. "Besides, I feel quite sorry for the thief who enters this house, given your ability with a pistol, Miss Laughlin."

"How do you know I have any ability? I didn't fire Papa's weapon. I merely pointed it at you."

Aunt Hilda gave a startled cry. "Lily, you didn't!"

"It was their first day here, Aunt, and I thought these two were trespassers." She waved her hand in the air, hoping to quell further discussion on this subject.

A warm breeze blew in, fluttering the heavy drapes.

"Anyway, it's over with. Captain Albright and Mr. Blake have forgiven me."

"Right you are about that, lass." Mr. Blake stood by, grinning.

"Indeed we have." Mac quirked a grin then returned his focus to the coins.

"I don't want Mr. Everett to get his hands on this money." Lily looked to Mac for additional advice. "Do you think he knows about it?"

"I doubt it. Everett strikes me as a man who wouldn't leave it here if he did."

"Cap'n is right." Mr. Blake copped a wide stance, his fists on his hips. "Besides, the box was wedged in tight on the shelf and topped with a fine layer of dust."

"And a blessing you found it, my little apple dumpling." Aunt Hilda pulled on Mr. Blake's cheek, sending a shadow of crimson across the weathered seaman's face.

Lily giggled, wondering how Mac could continue his brooding.

"If I were you, Miss Laughlin"—he said, ignoring the mutual affection going on between the older couple—"I'd pop up a corner floorboard and stash the money beneath it."

"What a good idea. I wouldn't have thought of that hiding place."

"And it appears the loans your father made were small. Were I in your place, I would return the slips of paper to their signers and forgive their debts. This will rally those men to your side, should you find yourself opposite Mr. Everett in court. He is, after all, your legal guardian."

"That's true. . ." Lily supposed the right thing to do was to inform Mr. Everett of the money. But then he would take it, and she might be forced into marrying the man. On the other hand, this newly found small fortune would buy her time. She could now afford to remain single.

Still, it wouldn't last forever. Lily needed to figure out what to do with her life. Becoming a governess was a respectable position, but then what did she do with her brothers? And the thought of giving up her home was almost as bad as the notion of marrying Mr. Everett.

"The boys should be done gathering eggs," Aunt Hilda said. "How about a nice hot breakfast before we begin our daily routines?"

Mr. Blake was on Aunt Hilda's heels as she left the room.

Lily began scooping coins into pouches, not caring how many were in each. She'd only make use of a coin or two now and again. Otherwise she was liable to raise suspicion.

"This money will buy you some time, Lily." Mac's voice fell over her like a cloak of deep velvet. "You needn't fear Everett's marriage proposal, supposing it comes. You have choices."

"I know. Thank you." She met Mac's gaze. "And you needn't fear me. I'm not husband-hunting. Truly, I never was."

His features hardened and Lily looked away. So he was determined to be more of an adversary than a friend. Fine. So be it.

He said nothing, but his booted gait clapped a steady rhythm against the floor all across the room and into the hallway. His footfalls grew faint as he descended the stairs, and then Lily couldn't hear them anymore.

"I noticed that neither Captain Albright nor his friend Mr. Blake have graced our dinner table for two weeks."

Mr. Everett's smile wriggled like an angleworm across his thin lips, and Lily didn't miss the possessiveness in his statement. *Our* dinner table? Could the man get any more presumptuous?

"Rather refreshing, I think. Silence is, indeed, golden."

Lily stared at her plate to hide her hurt.

"The captain and Mr. Blake are working from morning to night." Jed spooned a bite of venison stew into his mouth.

Lily stabbed a potato. "Jed's right. There's quite a lot of activity going on next door." But, alas, the barn's christening had been put off for another week. According to Issie, the old foundation was in need of more repairs than first assumed, and Mr. Talbot, the mason, was busy with another job.

Lily ate the potato, musing as she chewed. From what she'd glimpsed between the trees and what the boys reported to her, the construction was humming right along.

"Have you been across the creek to visit the captain and see the beginnings of his new barn, Lily?"

It sounded like an accusation, and she clenched her jaw. "No, sir. The captain and I are not friends." At her brother's curious frowns, she added, "As it should be between an unattached female and a bachelor."

"Absolutely correct, dear Lily."

She heard the approval in the man's voice and cringed. She despised Mr. Everett's compliments as much as his admonishments. As far as Mac was concerned, Lily had caught him watching her while she weeded the flower garden last Tuesday morning. And then, he walked through the orchard on Friday while she and the boys picked the last of the ripening pears. He joked with her brothers but didn't say a word to her. Lily pretended she didn't care.

But she did.

Honking geese flew past the open window, signaling autumn's arrival.

"The man has let himself go." Mr. Everett cut an already bite-sized piece of carrot and nibbled on it. "The captain now resembles a trapper who stayed in the mountains too long."

"What's wrong with mountain men?" Jonah glanced up from his meal. "The ones I see at the trading post don't cause trouble. They leave town about as fast as they come in."

Lily swung her gaze to Mr. Everett, anticipating a snide reply.

Jed spoke up first. "Captain Albright said his whiskers keep ladies from fawning all over him."

Lily rolled her eyes and Aunt Hilda chuckled.

"I have never had a single woman complain." Mr. Everett kneaded his smooth jaw and Lily lost her appetite. "Then again, I keep a neat appearance."

"Unlike you, sir, the captain is too busy for ladies." Jonah forked food into his mouth.

"For your information, I am an extremely busy man myself. I have newly purchased slaves who need taming, and customers who depend on me."

A glance around the table told Lily no one seemed impressed, least of all herself. Worse, the last of the respect she had for him blew away on the wind when he announced some days back that he'd bought slaves to work at his inn. Imagine, buying human beings like one purchases farm animals! The practice was morally wrong. She had made her feelings known—and suffered Mr. Everett's many admonishments. The man's arrogance annoyed her more than ever. His subtle reminders that she and her family were in his debt had worn out their welcome.

Besides, they weren't true.

"Master Jonah, you and I have never gotten a chance to get to know each other." Mr. Everett set down his fork. "I have business in Alexandria and, as you know, Mr. Blake will be setting off for the same location soon." He leaned forward as if to tempt Jonah, who sat across the table from him. "Would you like to join me? I'll make sure you see clippers and schooners to your heart's content."

"Would I ever!" Jonah's face lit up like a thousand stars on a clear summer's night.

"Now, wait a moment." Lily wanted to pound her fist on the table. Mr. Everett hadn't consulted her, and school would begin after harvesttime. It had taken some pleading and one of Aunt Hilda's fruit pies to convince Mrs. Kasper to allow Jonah and Jed back into her classroom.

"And, Master Jed, would you also like to embark on this adventure?"

"Sure I would!" He turned toward Lily with puppy dog eyes. "Please, sissy, let me go too."

"I haven't even given my permission for Jonah to go."

"We don't need your permission." With an arched brow, Mr. Everett sipped from his wineglass. "I am these boys' legal guardian."

"That means we can go!" Jonah pumped a fist into the air as if he were cheering on a cockfight.

Lily's patience came to an abrupt halt. She stood so fast she knocked over her chair.

Aunt Hilda gasped.

"Mr. Everett, if you take my brothers on this trip when they ought to be in school, I will never forgive you!"

"Oh, bah!" Mr. Everett chuckled lightly. "You will forgive me because it's your nature, so stop your theatrics."

Lily's knees turned to pudding beneath swarming rage. Thoughts of the hidden coinage gave her courage to react. "Get out! Get out of my house this minute." She rounded the table and removed Mr. Everett's bowl and goblet. "I am tired of your highhandedness, sir. I'm sick to death of your insults, reprimands, and idle prattle, so leave at once and find yourself another supper table."

Mr. Everett didn't budge. "I think you're forgetting something, Lily."

"No, I am not forgetting anything."

"This is my house now."

"I'm afraid I will have to see proof of that, sir."

"Very well. I can provide you with the documents, although you won't understand them. All you need to know is the deed is in my name." Mr. Everett's tone sounded deadly calm. "If anyone should leave the manor, it should be. . .you."

Lily refused to back down. "Papa wouldn't leave it to you. He knew I loved my home, so that means you somehow found the funds to purchase this house, and everyone in Middletown knows you've never been a man of great wealth. Besides, I do not recall *Haus am Bach* ever being up for sale."

Mr. Everett expelled a bored-sounding sigh. "If you must know, I won this house in a card game."

Lily gasped and Aunt Hilda's hand flew to her throat.

He stood and stepped forward, towering over Lily. "I hoped to spare you the humiliation, my dear, but it seems you cannot leave well enough alone. It's one of your many weaknesses."

"Of course." She rolled her eyes. "And you are ever so perfect."

"Do not sass me." Mr. Everett grasped her arm and gave it a hard yank. Unprepared, Lily dropped the bowl. It clattered against the floor, sending stew in every direction.

"Now see what you've done, you foolish girl?" He gave her a shake.

"Let go of me!" Lily twisted but Mr. Everett only held on tighter.

"Leave her be!" Aunt Hilda shouted, rising from her place at the table.

"You're hurting me!" Lily winced as Mr. Everett's fingers bit into the soft flesh of her arm.

"Let her go!" Jonah threw his bowl of stew at Mr. Everett, clocking him in the head with the wooden bowl and sending food dripping down his black frockcoat.

Jed rounded the table and kicked Mr. Everett in the shin. The man howled.

Lily pulled from his grip and ran to Aunt Hilda, who enveloped her in the protection of her sturdy arms.

The muscle in Everett's jaw convulsed while he bent to rub the lower half of his leg. A piece of carrot had lodged in his graying hair and on another day, Lily might have laughed.

But not today. Not now.

"You will regret your actions, you impudent boys." Mr. Everett's bellow echoed into the farthest corners of the dining room. His eyes moved to Lily. "And you. . ."

He straightened and Lily shrank into Aunt Hilda's embrace.

"You will suffer the most for this act of insolence and betrayal." He shook a long, slender finger at her. "I have tolerated much from you, but no more, Lily. No more!"

"I have tolerated much from you also. My entire family has. You've insulted, chided, and humiliated us. Worse, you seem to enjoy doing it in front of guests." Lily pulled away from Aunt Hilda. She couldn't stop the words. They were out of her mouth as fast as they formed on her tongue. "I can't imagine what my father saw in you that would make him call you his friend."

Without a word, Mr. Everett left the room.

"I guess this means I won't see any ships." The disappointment in Jonah's voice, his crestfallen expression, caused tears to spring into Lily's eyes. Why couldn't she have kept her mouth shut, if only for Jonah's sake? Then, again, she didn't trust her brothers in Everett's care.

Having found his top hat, Mr. Everett stomped out of the house and shouted to his driver. Next, the sound of his carriage wheels crunching against the gravel pike replaced the weighted silence inside the dining room.

Lily's stomach clenched. Silas Everett might be gone now, but he would be back.

## Chapter Fourteen

ac knew the song. Who didn't? Popular during the Revolutionary War and then years later during the Second American War of Independence. But why was it roaming around in his head, its words stirring his dreams?

Reluctantly, he opened his eyes to the pinks of dawn on the horizon—and Lily Laughlin's musical adaptation of "Johnny Has Gone for a Soldier."

*"Here I sit on Buttermilk Hill,*
*Who could blame me cryin' my fill,*
*And all my tears could turn a mill,*
*Johnny has gone for a soldier."*

With a curse on his lips, Mac got to his feet. What in the world was that confounded woman doing, singing so early in the morning? As if to mock him, Blake's hard snores reached Mac's ears.

Jonah and Jed's voices wafted from the other side of the creek and coaxed their sister on.

"The fish like your sad song, Lily." It sounded like Jed. "Keep singing."

*No!* Mac balled his fists. Every time Lily sang it touched his soul and put a chink in the protective barrier around his heart.

He strode for the stone bridge and stopped short when he spotted his neighbors. He'd gone many days without seeing her, but she still succeeded at pervading his thoughts—and now, evidently, his dreams too.

Lily sat on a boulder in a sunny yellow-printed dress, a large shawl draped around her bare arms. Mac longed to caress her skin and discover if it was as soft as it looked.

"Sing, Lily." Jonah cast his line from his place in the creek. He'd rolled his trousers to his knees.

Jed hadn't the need to hike up his breeches. He stood beside his older brother, wielding a net.

*"I'll dye my dress, I'll dye it red.*
*In the streets I'll go begging for bread.*
*The one I love might soon be dead,*
*Johnny has gone for a soldier."*

Mac's jaw slackened when Jonah caught a trout and Jed scooped it up. Even the fish leapt from the depths when Lily sang.

He put his hands on his hips, angry that she should possess so much power by merely singing a song.

"Ahoy, Captain." Jonah had obviously found Mac's secluded lookout.

Mac lifted one hand in greeting while Lily's blue eyes bored more holes in his self-made fortification.

*"Me o' my I love him so,*
*Broke my heart to see him go,"*

Mac's insides warmed beneath her scrutiny.

*"And only time will heal my woe,*
*Johnny has gone for a soldier."*

Mac couldn't look away and an all-too-familiar sense of longing swept over him. How he wanted to cross the bridge, scoop Lily into his arms, and kiss her ripe, pink lips.

He tore his gaze from hers and bit down hard on his back teeth. He would not be caught like a fish!

"I wasn't ready that time, Lily," Jonah groused. "Sing another verse."

"No, I've sung enough songs for this morning." Without another glance Mac's way, she stood and picked her way to the worn path. A slight breeze blew strands of her golden hair onto her cheek. "Let's bring your catch to Aunt Hilda. We'll eat well at breakfast this morning."

"You can come and eat with us, Captain." Jed held up a passel of fish on a string. "We caught plenty."

"Quite impressive, and thanks, but no." Mac watched Lily's retreating form. Ruefulness pinched. She hadn't greeted him, even out of politeness. Sang to him, perhaps—and how he wished she meant those words for him.

But, wait, no, he didn't want that!

Mac's mind fought and flopped like one of Jonah's recent catches. Who could blame Lily for neglecting a formal greeting? Part of barricading his heart was ignoring her, although he'd explained his decision. She seemed to understand. So why did that parting frown, creasing her otherwise smooth forehead, reflect sorrow?

But perhaps she was thinking of Oliver Ashton when she sang her mournful love song. He'd heard rumors of the young heartbreaker alive and hiding in the mountains. Seemed ridiculous to Mac. Why would he hide? He'd volunteered to fight. It wasn't as if he'd deserted. His family would give anything to have him back home.

Did Lily believe the nonsense? Was she pining away for a ghost? Mac didn't think she was the type, but maybe he'd been mistaken.

*Bah!* What did he care?

He stomped back to camp, setting his sights on his new barn. The mason had filled in the gaps between the planks. The structure was almost finished now, and a finer barn in Middletown could not be found—at least that's what James Hawkins continually said. In another week, the remaining wooden shingles would be nailed onto the sloping roof and, of course, the women in town were looking forward to the party a week from tomorrow.

Would Lily come?

Of course she would.

Mac churned out a guttural moan. He looked at the heavens and shook his fist. "I don't care! Do you hear me, God? Lily can dance her heart out with any man she chooses. I will feel nothing. Nothing!"

He stared upward at the rapidly bluing sky. It promised to be another perfect day. Lowering his hand, he marveled at himself. Why did he assume his frustration over Lily was God's fault?

But of course, it was. The Almighty had blessed Lily with an incredible gift of song. Each note touched the heart of every listener, and Mac believed in giving credit where credit was due.

He neared the ten-foot circle of stones. Their campfire had long since died out, so Mac collected an armful of twigs and lit another. He made coffee, which aroused Blake from his sleep.

"G'mornin', Cap'n."

"Morning," he grumbled.

Blake scratched his head and next his jaw. "I wonder what Hilda is makin' for breakfast."

"Fried fish would be my guess. The Laughlins were out fishing this morning."

"Was Miss Lily with the boys?"

"Yes, but who cares? Surely not I."

"Oh, no. Not you." Blake snorted and hurried to dress. "I'll bring you a meal if anythin's left." After tugging on his boots, he jogged toward the stone bridge and disappeared into the overgrown shrubbery. More work to do. Good.

Mac felt like a heartless blackguard. He lifted a rock outside the campfire site. He worked it in his palm before hurling it toward one of the new fence posts.

*Blast it all!* His behavior was despicable. He shunned Lily but gratefully accepted the meals Mrs. Gunther sent over with Blake. He put Jonah and Jed to work whenever they traipsed across the meadow and asked to help. No wonder Lily felt grieved. Were she one of his sisters, he would deal severely with the rogue who hurt her.

And he was that man.

Mac clenched his jaw and hunkered down. He lifted a long stick and poked the campfire. The sound of coffee rolling in the metal pot joined with the cacophony of birdsong overhead. But Lily's voice played louder in his mind. As he toiled today he would no doubt hear her sweet laughter and her call for her brothers. He might take a break and walk through his orchards just to get a glimpse of her hanging clothes on the line or weeding one of her gardens.

Another piece of Mac's inner fortress crumbled while he watched the smoky flames inch higher, higher, as if daring him to be honest with the Creator of fire, the heavens, and earth, the sea and every living thing in it. He recalled such a Bible verse, one of many he'd been forced to recite from memory during his boyhood.

Mac tossed the stick into the fire and stood. He was no fool. He knew he'd never take on the Almighty and win. Once more, he lifted his gaze to the vastness above. The flaming orb rising in the east made him squint. "All right, maybe I do care, just a little."

♥

Lily heard Mr. Everett's approaching carriage and glanced up from where she sat beneath the shade of the house. There was no other sound like it— fat, wooden wheels grinding slowly into the rock, sand, and dirt that made up the pike. No other families' buggies or wagons made similar sounds, other than, perhaps, the horses' hooves that pounded the earth and an occasional whinny.

Rising from the wooden bench, Lily hugged the bowl full of fresh peas she'd shelled and hurried into the kitchen. As she set her burden on the kitchen table, the smell of baking bread assailed her senses. Her stomach protested its emptiness. Since eating a substantial and leisurely breakfast this morning, they'd skipped lunch, making the promise of suppertime all the sweeter.

"I believe Mr. Everett is here," Lily called to her aunt.

Aunt Hilda grunted, but didn't look up from her work table where she prepared venison chops, courtesy of James Hawkins. He'd shot a buck and shared the meat with them. Soon a portion of the chops would be sizzling in an iron skillet over open flames.

Lily strode through the house and met Mr. Everett outside the front door.

"Good afternoon, my dear." He sounded friendly enough, even after the incident four days ago. He'd stayed away all that time, leaving Lily to fret about what he might be up to next.

"I suppose you have come to evict us from our home." She folded her arms.

Mr. Everett smiled. "Now, Lily. We had a bit of a tiff, but I rose above it." He arched a brow and leaned toward her. "Certainly you have also."

"That depends on what you've got in mind for my family and me."

"Ah, then we must talk." He handed his walking stick and top hat to her.

Lily almost accepted them when she glimpsed Mac standing at the edge of the orchard. He carried an axe on one broad shoulder, and he seemed rooted in place, watching them with a dark expression. His gauzy shirt was unbuttoned and fell open halfway down his chest, revealing a sheath of ebony hair that matched his thick beard. Lily smiled. He resembled a black bear. Here's hoping a neighbor didn't mistake him for one.

"Lily."

The exasperation in Mr. Everett's voice carried her back to the present. A good thing Mr. Everett's back was to Mac. If he'd seen her response to her neighbor, he'd surely reprimand her for gawking, and another argument would ensue.

Why, oh why, did Mr. Everett press her on trivial matters? Hadn't her family suffered enough this past year? Lily felt like she walked on thin ice and was about to break through and drown. She couldn't manage any more than that which stood before her now.

"Mr. Everett"—Lily lifted her chin, hoping she appeared braver than she felt—"I am not your servant or the housekeeper. If you will recall, you dismissed Mrs. Cruthers this past spring and hired her at your inn."

Mr. Everett expelled an impatient sigh. "I see you plan to be stubborn."

"Not stubborn, sir. I'm merely behaving the way my father raised me."

"I see." His lips wiggled as though he held back a smile or, worse, a laugh—at her. "Let's go inside, shall we? There is much to discuss."

He politely indicated the doorway and Lily entered the house ahead of him. A warm breeze ushered her in, circling her ankles and cooling her temper. Reaching the central passageway, she spun around to face her guest who had a habit of making himself at home. As was his custom, he placed his walking stick in the umbrella stand and hung up his hat on the ornately carved mahogany hall tree. Peering at himself in the mirror, he licked his palms before smoothing down his severely parted hair. Then he shrugged out of his frockcoat.

"It's unusually hot for the fifth of September, is it not?"

"I don't think so." Lily loved the summer weather. Often it lasted until well into October.

"Let's sit in the parlor, shall we?" Mr. Everett made his way there before Lily could reply.

She reluctantly followed him into the room. Of late she'd become bored with the bold teal color on the walls and the deeper green of the painted woodwork. She dreamed of a brighter rose-printed paper, a chair rail, and a berry color paint beneath it. Of course it would appear quite feminine, and if Mr. Everett really owned the house. . .

Lily closed her eyes as the same question coiled around in her mind like the vipers she feared so terribly. How could Papa gamble away their home? It simply didn't make sense. If he'd wanted to bet, why hadn't he used the coinage that Mr. Blake found?

"I've done some thinking the last few days," Mr. Everett began in a nasally tone.

"Oh?" Lily dropped into a nearby chair and folded her hands. "I presume you've arrived at some decision."

"Indeed." Smiling, he sat on the settee and crossed his legs. "It's more important than ever that I make my business trip. Therefore, I have decided to take your brothers along."

"No." Lily pressed her lips together for a moment, deciding her reply had come out much too harshly. "You see, I convinced Mrs. Kasper to let them back into her classroom, and school will begin soon."

"This experience will teach them far better than any classroom."

"That might be true, but I. . .I need them." Truth to tell, she didn't trust Everett.

"Why?"

Lily swallowed hard. "To help with chores. Why, my shoulders will ache from carrying the laundry basket up and down the steps. Aunt Hilda washes our clothes, but I hang them. When they're dry, it's up to Jed to take the garments off the line and carry the basket upstairs again." A deep sigh escaped her. "Unfortunately for me, he ran off with Jonah today to help

Captain Albright, forcing me to lug that wicker monstrosity up the steps and my shoulders really do hurt."

"Bah!" Brittleness flattened his tone. "You must accept the fact that laundry is women's work, and you have proved my point. Your brothers need a father figure."

"You, I suppose." The sarcasm tasted sour on her tongue and she struggled for self-control. Closing her eyes, she pretended that Papa was in the room. What would he say to Mr. Everett's offer?

Dismay weighed heavy on her heart. She knew the answer. Papa would allow the boys to go.

Lily flicked a surrendered gaze at Mr. Everett. "Perhaps you make a good point, sir."

"Ah, I knew you'd come around and see reason."

"I know the boys will be excited to go with you, especially if your offer of showing them tall ships in Alexandria's harbor still stands."

"Of course." Mr. Everett leaned forward. "I hope to persuade a captain to allow the boys a firsthand look at a ship."

"My brothers will be very happy." This defeat weighed heavily on Lily's shoulders. However, if she didn't allow this trip, Jonah's fascination with the seafaring trade would escalate all the more and she'd never get him to settle down and do schoolwork. "When will you leave?"

"On Monday morning, providing the stage is on time."

Lily dipped her chin and studied the block design on the Persian carpet beneath her feet.

"I believe Mr. Blake is leaving the same day."

Again, Lily only nodded. How sad to see the man go. He had brightened their sad, ordinary existence with his exciting tales of ships, pirates, and battles at sea. With each story, Lily imagined Mac in command, his face to the wind.

"Lily, did you hear what I said?"

She blinked. "Pardon me, I did not." She touched her forehead. "I have so much on my mind of late." Too much of Mac on her mind to be sure!

"We'll be gone for a month, unless the stage will make an additional stop in Middletown. That's my goal, you see, to convince more investors like Captain Albright to settle here. We'll get more frequent stops in town—"

*And more customers at the Stony Inn.*

"—which, in turn, will bring mail regularly and more business to our sleepy little town."

"I wish you much success," she said, not truly understanding how more people, more businesses, and more traffic would benefit Middletown.

"In any case, I accept your apology for your appalling behavior last week."

Lily couldn't recall apologizing, but she supposed she'd been quarrelsome and unappreciative. As arrogant as he could be, Mr. Everett had seen to her and her family's needs since Papa died. Lily knew things could be so much worse.

"I'm glad you see things my way." Mr. Everett lazed back on the settee. "I shall make the announcement at supper tonight."

## Chapter Fifteen

When Lily spotted five sun-bronzed Indian men walking down the pike in their buckskin trousers and linen shirts of various styles, she stood and excused herself from the dining room table.

"Where are you going?" Mr. Everett's question resembled an accusation. "Sit down at once."

"Forgive me, sir, but I must tend to an urgent matter."

She hurried from the room despite Mr. Everett's calls for her to return. This was the escape she'd prayed for.

The insidious oaf! With her family around the supper table, Mr. Everett had informed the boys of their trip and, as Lily anticipated, they cheered. But then Mr. Everett began a long, rambling account of why the Bible stated that it was not good for man to be alone. Lily's mouth had gone dry and tiny prickles of fear shimmied up her spine. She guessed a marriage proposal was forthcoming—a very public marriage proposal!

Dread weighed her movements as she fled the house. Mr. Everett knew that out of politeness she wouldn't refuse him with her family present. As his discourse droned on, Lily predicted she would not get the chance to refuse him at all if he took his leave after their meal. He'd surely tell everyone in Middletown of their impending wedding and then Lily would be forced into a union she didn't want. In fact, just a few minutes ago, the very idea tempted her stomach to empty its contents of Aunt Hilda's shepherd's pie.

But then she'd spotted Shona and his tribesmen.

Jogging toward them, her feet lightly touching the walkway, Lily waved to get the men's attention.

They came to a halt when they saw her, and Shona gave her a wide, toothy grin.

"Miss Lily." He placed his hands on her shoulders. "It is good to see you." His features fell. "But I was sorry to hear about your father's untimely passing."

Lily could only nod. Papa's absence still didn't seem real.

"How is your family faring?" His hands fell to his sides.

"We're managing. Mr. Silas Everett was named Papa's executor and our guardian."

"I'm sorry for you." Shona's concerned frown became a scowl. "He is not a friend to the Indian."

"I imagine he's not, sir." She entwined her fingers and worked her hands together. With Jonah and Jed going away, she desperately needed help bringing in the harvest. "Mr. Everett sold some of our prime acreage, and now we have a neighbor, Captain Albright." She inclined her head toward the creek and to where the uppermost part of Mac's new barn could be seen from the road. "He's given us three-quarters of the harvest this year, despite the fact he now owns the grain fields and the fruit orchards." Lily sent up another silent plea to her heavenly Father. "Will you help me bring it in?"

"Not for a couple of weeks, but then. . ." He glanced at his tribesmen, who seemed agreeable. "We will return in a fortnight."

It was better than nothing and, if the weather held, the crops would stay. Meanwhile, she would do what she could with Aunt Hilda's help.

"Lily, come away from those savages at once!" Mr. Everett's shrill demand made her cringe.

"Your guardian may not approve of us bringing in your harvest," Shona remarked, his dark eyes assessing Mr. Everett's glower.

"It's not up to him. The arrangement was made between Mac and me—that is, Captain Albright and me."

"Is that so?" Shona tipped his head and his long black hair fell against his cheek. A curious glimmer entered his gaze.

Lily's face began to flame, and it wasn't from the evening sunshine. "We are neighbors, that's all. We're not even friends."

"Your neighbor puts color in your cheeks and a sparkle in your eyes." Shona and his men chuckled.

Embarrassed now more than ever, Lily strode toward the front steps. "I can expect you in two weeks, then?"

Shona gave a nod before sending a dark glare Mr. Everett's way. Moments later, the men continued their trek down the pike. Lily waved and watched them go.

"Lily, come here or I will come and fetch you myself!"

She clenched her fists at her sides and churned out a groan. One of the last native men passing by sent her a sympathetic glance.

It was then that Lily caught sight of Mac, leading his team of mules through the swath of orchard that he and Mr. Blake had been clearing on the far side of the creek. He'd need it to get to and from his barnyard, not to mention the drive his guests required as they drove their wagons to his upcoming party. He sent a sharp look toward Everett that seemed to slice through the remaining orchard on the edge of his property. Then his gaze fell on her. She lifted her hand in a tentative greeting. She didn't expect a reply.

He doffed his straw hat and surprised her.

"Lily!" Again Mr. Everett's voice commanded her attention.

"I'm coming." But she didn't care what he had to say—or who was present when he said it—she refused to marry the man!

Which meant somehow, some way, she and her family would need to survive on Papa's coins that were hidden away upstairs.

But how?

Sunshine burned into Mac's bare back, and perspiration trickled down the side of his face and his neck. After hoisting another log into place, he stepped back to admire his and Blake's work. The cabin was coming along faster than he expected.

Blake sidled up beside him. "Lookin' good, Cap'n."

Mac smiled, pleased. "I'd say we've got the knack of constructing barns and cabins, old man."

"Not much diff'rent than rebuildin' a ship after a good battering." Blake shook his head, and his graying hair fell across his shoulders. He gathered it and tied in back into a queue. "But I never thought I'd see the day when I built a cabin." He let go of a sigh. "Sure is a lot of work, but I'm not ascared of physical labor."

"I wouldn't have been able to get this far without you." Mac rapped his loyal friend between the shoulder blades.

"What will you do when I'm gone, Cap'n? The stage is expected to leave in three days."

"I'll manage." Disappointment coiled around Mac's insides. He'd grown accustomed to having Blake around. He was a good man to share ideas with and he always gave an honest reply. "At least I have shelter for the winter and an impressive barn for my animals come spring."

"I'm leavin' you in good shape then." Blake yawned and stretched. "But now methinks it's time for a nap."

Mac checked his timepiece. "It's only two o'clock."

"I know, but I'm tired."

Mac waved him off, and Blake headed toward the barn. Blake had said he enjoyed the woodsy smell of hand-hewn beams and planks.

Well, let him rest. They'd worked hard this morning. In truth, Mac could use some reprieve too.

Shirtless, he started toward the creek, intending to wash the sweat and grime off his body, when Lily pushed her way out of the brush. They stood only a few feet from each other, and Mac grinned inwardly as her flushed cheeks turned to crimson.

"As you can see, I was not expecting company." He couldn't keep the sarcasm from his tone.

"I'm here on official business." She cut her gaze away, but not before she'd given Mac an appraising glance. Did she like what she saw? Was she repulsed? "If you'll please don a shirt, Captain, I'll say my piece and be gone."

"Very well."

His mood was a mix of sweet and sour as he strode across the barnyard to where he'd slung his linen shirt across a fence rail. Official business. . . What was that girl up to now?

As he pulled the cotton garment over his sweating torso, he spied Lily watching him. She quickly averted her gaze, turning her attention instead to his two corralled mules. But not before he'd glimpsed the interest shining in her eyes.

Buttoning his shirt, Mac chuckled to himself. It wasn't the first time he'd noticed a woman's attraction to him, but with this particular woman it meant the world to him.

*Blast!* Was he becoming as much of a lovesick dolt as Blake?

Mac tucked in his shirt then made his way over to where Lily stroked his mules' necks. She pulled two apples from her apron pocket and fed them the treats. They nuzzled her for more, and she rubbed their noses.

Even his mules were falling in love with the woman!

"Miss Laughlin." Mac inclined his head. "How may I be of service?"

She whirled around. "As I said, I'm here on business. This is not a social—"

Her hand clamped down on her hat as the mules attempted to make it their next snack. Lily lifted her shoulders and giggled, a sound that turned Mac's heart inside out.

"Stop that," Lily chided the animals.

The mules voiced their complaints with their whinnied hee-haw snorts.

Lily faced Mac again, her face set in a serious expression. "I've come to speak with you about important—"

One of the mules nudged her, and Lily stumbled forward into Mac's chest. He instinctively caught her around the waist. A plume of lavender and fresh air drifted to his nose. She gazed up at him with dancing blue eyes, and her infectious laugh made him grin.

"I'm afraid your mules are partial to my hat and nibbling my neck."

*Lucky mules.*

He stared into her face, mesmerized. How simple it would be to lower his mouth to hers in the sweetest of kisses. . . .

With her hands splayed across his chest, she gently pushed him away. "As I said, I've come on official business."

"Of course." Mac stepped back and cupped her elbow, coaxing her forward. "I would suggest stepping away from my hat-hungry mules."

"What are their names?" Lily moved to Mac's right and stared at the pair. They tossed their heads in protest at the loss of Lily's attention.

"Names? They're mules. They don't have names."

"Are they yours?"

Mac inclined his head. "After renting them from James for a time, I realized what prized mules they were—for mules. James quoted me a fair price so I bought them."

"Then you must give them names."

"Why?"

"Because."

As if that was a good enough reason. Mac folded his arms. "What do you suggest, Miss Laughlin?"

She tipped her head, studying the animals. "A male and female."

"Correct."

"How about Diamond and Dusty? The female has a white diamond on her forehead and the male. . .well, he should have a name that starts with the same letter as hers."

"And why is that?" Mac rubbed the back of his neck. Female reasoning was always a curious thing.

"Because they are a pair, of course."

"Oh, of course." Mac still didn't see the connection. "So what is this official business that brings you over here?"

Lily's expression lost all brightness. "I have two points of business. Can we speak out of the hot sun?"

"As you wish."

They stepped over to the shade falling off one side of the barn.

"I saw Shona yesterday evening. He and his native tribesmen hire themselves out as farmhands. My father took them on the past few years, and they're hard workers. They promised to return in a fortnight to help me with the harvest. They work for a portion of what they bring in from the fields and pick from the fruit trees." She licked her lips, momentarily distracting Mac. "Would you like to include your portion of the crops? The truth is, I may not get to them otherwise."

Mac didn't see any harm in it. Besides, better he had some than none. "Yes, include my portion. Thank you."

"All right." She dipped her head. "For the next order of business, did Mr. Blake tell you that Jonah and Jed will be sharing the stage with him?"

"No." Mac wondered why his friend hadn't said anything.

"My brothers are traveling with Mr. Everett to Alexandria, where he has business. He's promised to show the boys the grand ships docked in the city's harbor. You can imagine their excitement."

"And you've allowed this?" Mac set his hands on his hips.

"I didn't have a choice. Mr. Everett is their guardian, after all." Lily looked away, her crystal-blue eyes turning stormy.

"And what does that have to do with me?" The words came out harsher than Mac intended. "Allow me to rephrase."

"No need. I understood the question perfectly."

"I didn't mean to sound cross."

"Yes, you did. You don't want me here. Unfortunately, this business involves you, otherwise I'd not be here."

"Proceed." Mac despised himself for his waspishness. If she only knew her effect on him, perhaps she'd truly understand and stay away.

"I want to invest in one of your family's merchant ships. Mr. Blake said a man could double, even triple his money, so I figured a woman could be equally as fortunate."

"I think you should hang on to your coins, Miss Laughlin."

"And I think I should invest them." She lifted her chin, and Mac almost grinned at her stubbornness. "Two hundred pounds."

Mac shook his head. "It's too much a risk and you're going to need that money." His chest constricted. "Unless you've decided to accept Mr. Everett's tyrannical rule."

"No, I have not accepted his rule or anything else. But my family and I cannot exist for long with only three hundred pounds. I must either find employment or invest. Marrying Mr. Everett is not an option. So, at this point in time, I've chosen to invest."

"I see, and I am sympathetic to your cause. But investing in merchant ships is a gamble that only the wealthy can make."

"My money isn't good enough?"

"It's good enough." Mac thought of his father and how much he'd appreciate another two hundred pounds to fund his struggling business. Last year's attack on Alexandria destroyed a couple of vessels, and Albright & Son Shipping lost a lot of money. "But there are factors beyond the best sea captain's abilities. A tempest could arise and sink the merchant vessel. Pirates are always a threat. A mutiny could occur and the goods might get stolen. Investors stand to lose far more than they make."

Lily's frown melted away and her features lit up, reminding Mac of sunshine breaking through the morning mist. "Oh, I'm sure none of those terrible things will happen. Each time I pray about it, the prompting grows stronger. Nonetheless, Mr. Blake said a woman's money might not be welcome and that's why I need your help. With a letter of recommendation to your family, I'm sure my two hundred pounds, as trivial as it might be, will be accepted."

"And if something happens, you will hate me forever."

"I will not."

"Surely you hate me now. I've been rude and cross and...plain old mean spirited."

"Yes, you have, and you should be ashamed of yourself."

A smile worked on Mac's lips but he dared not laugh. The woman was adorable, especially when her sky-blue eyes glinted with aggravation.

"It's not funny." She jerked her chin.

Mac couldn't hold back a chuckle.

"I can see I have wasted my time." She marched toward overgrown brush that hid the stone bridge.

"Watch out for the snakes."

She came to an abrupt standstill and Mac supposed he shouldn't have teased her. She pirouetted around on her tiptoes and faced him.

"Why did you have to remind me? I'd forgotten all about those awful creatures."

Mac traipsed toward her. "Snakes are in your flower and vegetable gardens. Have you never seen them there? Even the small garter snakes?"

"No. I ask God to get them out of my way, and He has not failed me."

"Well, send up a prayer right now, or doesn't God work at midday? Perhaps He, like Blake, needs an afternoon rest."

"You, sir, just proved how ignorant you are of God's ways. He never slumbers. He is ever mindful of His children."

"Then walk on, Miss Laughlin."

"I will." With another prissy thrust of her chin, she tiptoed back around within an inch diameter.

Mac released a peal of laughter. Oh, how his sisters would berate him for such taunting, but he couldn't seem to help it. Lily Laughlin was so much fun to tease.

"Would you like some assistance?" he asked between chortles.

"No, thank you." She didn't move.

Mac folded his arms. "Why are you not headed for your own side of the creek?"

"I'm merely giving God some time to get His creation out of the way, if that's all right with you, *sir*." She sneered the last word.

Mac heard that same tone when Lily spoke of Silas Everett, and it was sobering to think that he may have sunk to that level of animosity with her.

He walked to where she stood. "Lily, I was teasing, and I humbly apologize."

"Humbly? I daresay you don't know the meaning of the word."

Mac arched a brow. "I do, I assure you, and I'm sorry for teasing you."

"You may keep your apology, Captain." She scanned the grass, causing Mac to grin.

Moments later, he could stand it no longer. He bent over and took hold of her hand then tossed her over his shoulder like a sack of potatoes—a wiggling sack of potatoes.

"Put me down, you ogre!"

"I'm saving you from the snakes."

"You are a snake!"

"Then you should not have trespassed!"

"You are a despicable neighbor."

Mac made his way through the brush, ducking lower than usual beneath a thick tree branch to save Lily a whack in the back of the head.

She beat against his back. "How I'd like to darken your daylights."

"Would you, now?" Chuckling, Mac turned off the path to the stone bridge and headed for the creek. "Perhaps you need a bit of cooling off. I know I do."

"Don't you dare! You'll ruin my leather boots."

Despite her kicking, Mac held her around the knees with one arm and pulled off her boots. He tossed them to higher ground near the bridge.

"Would you like your stockings removed also? I would be happy to oblige you."

Her reply was a shriek of outrage and a pounding to the kidneys that made him wince.

Mac waded into the water and, when he reached the deeper swirls of what her brothers deemed the swimming hole, he tossed Lily off his shoulder. She hit the water, screaming what a cad he was, and Mac could hardly wait to hear the names she resurfaced with.

Except she didn't resurface.

Seconds passed and Mac grew uneasy. Had she struck her head on a rock, hidden just beneath the surface? Mac followed the slow current for a ways, hoping for a glimpse of Lily's citrine locks or blue apron. His heart drummed out a frantic beat when he saw only the creek's sandy bottom.

"Lily!" The desperation in his voice echoed back to him. The overhanging willows stirred as if equally troubled.

He circled the creek. Fear left him feeling oddly cold. Every second that she was injured and submerged meant less chance for survival.

"Lily, for the love of all that is decent, show yourself!" She had to. She must!

Mac wouldn't be able to live with himself otherwise.

## Chapter Sixteen

$\mathcal{L}$ily glided beneath the water's surface until she reached a familiar sandbar—one she knew was a good distance away from her loathsome neighbor. She surfaced and pushed her hair from her face, as the pins that held it in place only moments ago were long gone. Heaven knew which tree branch claimed her hat. She tipped her head, finding it odd that Mac's gaze was trained on the depths of the creek.

"You, sir, are ratsbane and a barnacle!"

"Oh, thank God. . ." Mac's expression registered relief. "I thought you'd drowned."

Lily's entire body tensed. "Was that not your intention? To drown me—so I don't trespass anymore, perhaps?"

"Lily, if you knew what a scare you gave me, you would not so flippantly throw out such an accusation."

"I should accuse you in all seriousness then?" She rolled her eyes. The man was impossible.

"I hope you would not accuse me at all." Mac dunked himself then floated on his back. "I decided we should be friends again."

"You are a presumptuous oaf. I will never be your friend. Never!"

"You wound me, Princess, but alas, I deserve it."

"Indeed you do."

Standing, Mac finger-combed back the waves of his short, ebony hair.

Water dripped from his bearded chin and turned his linen shirt transparent. It clung to his muscular chest. While Lily had seen bare-chested men before, they never resembled a living Zeus.

"Let's not be enemies." Mac came toward her. "It requires far too much effort."

"Too much effort. . .oh, pish!" Lily pointed her finger at him. "Know this, sir. I will never marry you, so don't even entertain the notion." She'd seen the way he'd looked at her when Diamond or Dusty had given her a playful nudge.

"I'm not asking for your hand in marriage." Mac's tone rang with amusement, fueling Lily's desire to slap his handsome face. "I'm merely proposing a truce."

"You are refused on both accounts." She blushed as his gaze lazily roved over her gown, now equally as plastered to her figure as his linen shirt clinging to his masculine frame.

"I will not dance with you at your party, and be warned, sir"—she worked her way toward the bank—"I will never kiss you, either." Clearly, the man was ninety-nine percent rapscallion and one percent rake. He'd even admitted it the first day they'd met. She was remiss in not taking him seriously.

"Never?" He arched his brows. "You'll never kiss me?"

"Never!" She hated the way her voice left room for doubt.

"Are you sure about that?"

"Quite sure."

Lily's backside came up against a large rock. Her folly flashed before her eyes. Mac was closing in and she had nowhere to escape in the knee-deep water.

He grinned like a wolf about to devour his prey. "Then, perhaps, being the pirate I am, I will steal a kiss."

"Keep your distance, sir." She held out her arm as if it alone would deter him.

It didn't.

He took a step closer, and her hand came in contact with the hard muscle covering his ribs.

"Come, now, Lily, you cannot throw out such a challenge and expect me to ignore it. Nay, my honor is at stake." He arched a brow and the corners of his lips formed a smirk. "Or should I say my *dishonor*."

"Dishonor is correct." So he planned to toy with her like a barn cat with a field mouse. Well, she wasn't about to get lost in that bushy beard of his. With both hands now she strained to push him away. Her efforts didn't budge him.

"Let me kiss you, Lily." His voice was husky.

"No." Her reply was but a squeak.

"One kiss."

"Well. . ." The man posed quite the temptation.

As if sensing her relenting, he cupped the sides of her head, holding her captive, and Lily braced for a scratchy, prickly encounter. He brought his lips to hers, moving across them in slow, deliberate measure, and causing strange, new sensations in her limbs that left her weak.

She fell against his chest, surrendering. But suddenly it didn't matter that he'd triumphed. All she could think about was the heavenly pleasure of his kiss.

A kiss that ended all too soon.

Lily stared up into Mac's face, feeling delightfully dizzy. She ran her palms up the corded muscles in his arms. He placed a kiss on the tip of her nose, and she smiled.

"That wasn't half as unpleasant as I imagined," she murmured.

His eyes widened, and she laughed at his wounded expression.

"I meant. . .the beard. I never kissed a man with a beard before." Feeling oddly brave, she slid her fingertips over its softness. Here she'd thought it would feel like the hedge lining the front walkway. "Truth to tell, I never kissed a man. Oliver doesn't count, as he was barely seventeen."

She felt Mac's amusement rumble in his chest before it left his mouth. "Then, since it was not displeasing, perhaps I shall steal another one."

"No need to steal, Captain." Lily couldn't fathom where her brazenness came from, but she wanted him to kiss her again. "It shall be freely given."

His lips met hers, this time with fervor that emboldened her. She locked her arms around his neck, reveling in the feel of him, pressed close. She felt cherished in his embrace.

He trailed kisses across her cheek and neck. She giggled when his lips found the tender, most ticklish spot just above her shoulder. Her pleasure only seemed to heighten his passion.

"Lily," he whispered into her hair. "I dream about you every night."

"Nightmares, then, Captain?" She lifted her chin and smiled. "We are not even friends, remember?"

"Because I have been an angry fool." Mac brushed his lips against hers and a chorale sung by nature's creatures filled the air. "Angry because I didn't plan. . ." His inky gaze searched her face, then glinted with something akin to unspoken mirth. "I didn't plan to meet you and be so easily taken up by your charms."

Lily jutted out her chin. "And I didn't plan to be captivated by a rapscallion."

"Captivated?" The corners of his mouth curved upward. "You flatter me, Princess."

Before she could respond to his quip, his lips claimed hers once more. . .

Until Jonah's voice broke through the euphoric madness.

Lily snapped back as her brother called her name again. Reality crept in as Jonah's voice grew louder. What had she done? Acted no better than a shameless hussy!

"I hope you won't think badly of me. . .I mean, since I enjoyed. . ." Her face felt suddenly sunburned. "You know. . ."

Mac's eyes twinkled. "Yet another secret I shall keep for you."

"Lily! Where are you?" Jonah sounded close enough to catch them both.

"Mac, please, don't let my brother find me like this." Lily's hands pressed against his firm chest. "He'll tell his friends, and you know how gossip spreads like wildfire through Middletown."

"I will protect you." His gaze wandered the landscape behind her. "Hide up there on those rocks. Jonah won't see you there if he crosses the bridge." His voice held a tender note that Lily hoped she'd still hear later today and tomorrow. . .forever. Had their kisses meant as much to him as they did to her?

Mac melted into the water, floating to the middle of the creek. Only his shoulders, neck, and head were exposed to the dappled sunlight spilling through the treetops.

"Ahoy, Captain Albright." Jonah must have instantly seen him.

"Greetings, Master Jonah."

"I see you decided to make use of our swimming hole and wash your clothes at the same time. That's what Jed and me do too."

Mac's chuckle reached Lily as she climbed the bank to shelves of uneven rocks, inhibited only by the muck that was certain to stain her white stockings for good. An ever-present reminder of lingering in Mac's embrace and passionate kisses.

Was it wrong to wish for more?

"I'm looking for my sister," Jonah called. "Have you seen her?"

She froze, hoping the leafy birch tree sufficiently shielded her from her brother's keen vision.

"Now why would I know where your sister is?"

Lily cringed. The bite in Mac's tone sounded all too familiar.

"Aye, Captain, I figured you'd say that, but I had to ask anyhow. Mr. Everett's at the house and wants to speak with Lily—and he brought her a bouquet of flowers. Right in the middle of the afternoon."

"Did he now?"

"I'll bet he's gonna ask Lily to marry him."

Her stomach pitched.

"Marriage, huh?"

"Yeah, so if you see Lily, tell her to keep hiding."

Lily smiled at her brother's attempt to protect her.

"Well, I suppose I can make an exception and talk to her today." Mac's casual gaze flitted to her then back to where Jonah had to be standing at the end of the stone bridge.

Her smile grew.

"I'd misbehave on purpose and get rid of him like I usually do, but Mr. Everett is taking me and Jed to Alexandria with him. We're gonna see some ships—maybe even like the ones you used to command."

Mac floated on his back once more. "I wish you a good time, lad," he said, sounding like a sailor.

"Aye, sir, but I'll see you before we leave. We're coming to your party Saturday night."

"Ah, yes, the party. Tell your sister she may attend in case she's had a change of heart. In fact, I will be personally offended if she doesn't."

"I'll tell her. She'll be happy. Lily loves the reels and country dances."

"Is that so?" Mac sent a discreet glance across the water, and Lily guessed he was having a bit of fun with her younger brother. "A pity I don't dance."

"A shame for sure. Plenty of girls in Middletown are squabbling over who will dance with you." A pause. "Personally, I think I'm a good dancer."

"I gather you enjoy high-stepping with members of the fairer sex, but is there one girl in particular you like best?"

"Yes, but don't tell Lily."

"I won't say a word."

Lily strained to hear Jonah's response.

"Evie Ashton is my girl, but Lily can't know, because Evie's older brother broke her heart."

"Something tells me your sister has moved beyond her infatuation with Mr. Ashton."

Her cheeks grew warm with his subtle reference.

Moving higher onto the rocks, Lily tried to get a glimpse of her brother. Surely he'd be on his way soon. Then again, if he was on a mission he didn't care about, he might decide to loiter with Mac until suppertime.

Her wet stockings caused her foot to slip, sending her careening forward. She caught herself by grabbing onto the upper plateau of rocks. It felt warmed by the afternoon sunshine, and Lily climbed higher up the bank. Had Jonah heard her? She still couldn't see him.

Sudden movement to her right claimed her attention. Only too late she spotted the thick coppery-brown viper. It sat coiled and ready to strike, its eyes fixed on her, copper with black vertical black slats. She jerked her hand away, but the creature lunged, and its fangs sank deep into her forearm. Lightning-white pain shot up her arm while her terrified screams flooded her ears.

♥

When Lily screamed, Mac rushed toward the creek bank with a hunch she'd encountered a snake. What else could make her thrash about? Reaching her, he spied the two-foot copperhead clinging to her flesh.

Pulling a knife from his boot, he killed the reptile and disengaged it from where it had gotten stuck in Lily's arm. He flung its body into the brush. Lily's shrieks subsided, but her knees gave way. Mac caught her before she landed on the stony creek bank.

"Lily, you must stay calm. You've been bitten by a poisonous snake." He tucked his knife back into the top of his wet boot. "The more upset you become, the faster the venom will take hold of you."

Jonah came nearer, his expression one of fear mixed with curiosity. But there was no time for explanations now.

"Jonah, run and tell your aunt that Lily's been bitten by a copperhead."

"Aye, Captain." He took off running.

Mac scooped Lily into his arms and hiked up the bank. He called on his experience in order to gauge his next move. Lancing the bite and bleeding the area would affect nothing and risked infection. Wrapping the limb must be done at once before it swelled.

Reaching the orchard, Mac gently set Lily down beneath the canopy of apple trees.

"Stay sitting up and take slow breaths."

She held her arm. "It hurts, Mac."

"I'm sure it does." He retrieved his knife and made a cut in the bottom of his shirt. He then tore off a swath of material, large enough to bandage her arm. Immobilization was paramount. Soon her arm would swell and she'd not be able to move her fingers and elbow until the poison left her system.

If she survived.

He wrapped the wet cloth tightly around her arm until he reached her wrist.

"Am I going to die?" Tears glistened in Lily's large blue eyes.

"No, of course not." He cupped her sweet face, wishing he could promise her the world. The truth of it was he couldn't promise her next breath. "This particular snake's bite is rarely fatal for adults," he said, more to assure himself than to calm her. "I've seen many a sailor get snake bit. Vipers often hide in cargo holds and feast on fat rodents. Sailors find them when they unload."

"Rodents and snakes? What awful passengers." Lily wrinkled her pert little nose, and Mac grinned.

But all humor quickly died away as he finished bandaging. "I will be forthright and predict that you will be ill for a while. Ten days, I'd guess. It depends on how your body reacts."

"I'm strong and healthy."

"Yes, you are." Mac stroked her cheek with the backs of his fingers. "And that is to your advantage."

"My head hurts, Mac." She brought her hand to her forehead. The color in her cheeks drained away. The venom was already at work.

*Please God, let her survive this. . .*

Mac chided himself as he gathered Lily in his arms and stood. Why would God deign to hear from a sinner such as he?

"Stop. I'm going to be sick."

Mac set her feet on the grass and held her around the waist as she vomited. When she finished, he wiped her mouth with the remaining ends of his moist shirt, keeping one arm firmly around her midsection.

"You would make a fine doctor, Captain." An audible breath left her. Her eyes rolled back, her lashes fluttered closed, then her legs gave way.

Mac held her close for a few precious seconds. "You're going to be all right, Lily," he whispered against her forehead. How lovely she looked even as the snake's poison wound its way through her veins. How delicate, even fragile she appeared, resting in his arms, her long, golden hair cascading over his arm—and how very unlike the woman who flung taunts at him not even an hour ago.

Delicate and fragile, yes, but, Mac chose to park on Lily's remark about her strength and good health.

He lifted her limp body and carried her across the meadow and to the house. As he reached the entrance of the kitchen, he found none other than Silas Everett waiting for them, arms folded, his toe tapping impatiently. The man's darting gaze traveled from him to Lily, taking note of her damp hair that lost its pins somewhere in the creek. Jonah and Jed gazed at their sister's unconscious form with worried lines creasing their foreheads.

"Is she dead?" Jed pushed past his brother to get a closer look.

"No, she merely fainted. She's had quite a shock." Neither boy seemed appeased, so Mac added, "She'll be very sick for a time, but then she'll be all right." He wanted so badly to believe it.

Mrs. Gunther entered the kitchen, a glint of purpose in her gaze. "Bring her to the daybed in the sewing room. I've prepared a poultice and found a splint to immobilize her arm to control the swelling." She glanced over her shoulder. "I see you managed to bandage it."

"Yes, ma'am." Relief washed over him. Mrs. Gunther obviously knew what she was doing.

He carefully maneuvered the turns in the hallway until reaching a femininely papered room. Lily had told him it doubled as a ladies' drawing room for formal affairs.

Mac laid her gently on the divan. A soft moan escaped her despite his efforts not to jostle her afflicted limb. After smoothing Lily's hair off her face, he stepped back so her aunt could take over.

"Will you need the doctor?" Mac placed his hands on his hips.

"No, Captain, I've tended to plenty of snakebites in my life. Only one was fatal." Mrs. Gunther met Mac's stare. "You're sure it was copperhead and not a water moccasin? The latter's bite can be more severe."

"I'm sure. I killed the snake and got a good look at it."

She gave a nod.

"You both are wet and disheveled." Everett's tone could grind stone. "What on earth happened, and how did Lily acquire a snakebite?"

"It's a long story." Mac remained focused on Lily's care. He'd feel much better if she'd awaken.

"How dare you return Lily in such a state?" Everett arched a brow as he looked her over. "Her stockings are ruined. Her hair is a tangled mess. And she is wet from her head to her muddy feet."

Lily's eyes opened. She stared at Mac and he breathed easier.

"I demand to know how this occurred!" Everett's fist came down hard on the sideboard, rattling the lamp.

"Yes, Captain, do tell," Mrs. Gunther said, unwinding the makeshift bandage.

Jonah and Jed had taken places beside Mac. "It's very simple, really." He sent Lily a wink. "Lily fell in the creek."

"Was she on the stone bridge?" Jed asked. "She does lots of thinking there."

"She probably fell over the side—or slipped." Jonah folded his arms, looking as though he'd solved all of life's mysteries.

Mac concealed a grin. The boys were making his alibi easy. "When she didn't resurface, I assumed she'd struck her head and needed rescuing." That much was true.

"Aw, Lily never needs rescuing." Jed chuckled.

"Yes, so I discovered."

Lily's face contorted with pain when Mrs. Gunther moved her arm. "Forgive me, dearie. I'll be done soon enough."

Lily's pained features dissolved into her smooth complexion, so Mac continued the tale. "When I learned she was all right, I decided the water felt nice and cool on this hot, muggy day, and that's when Jonah found me. I was merely taking a quick dip before returning to my work."

"By then Lily was coming up the bank, right Captain?"

"Right." Mac clamped Jonah's shoulder in the manner offered to a few favorite sailors.

"Is that where she got snake bit?" Jonah asked. "On the creek bank?"

"The very place," Mac said. "So you boys take extreme care next time you go fishing."

"What happened to her shoes?" Everett folded his arms and shot a glare Mac's way.

The question caused Mac to remember his boots were filled with water. He glanced down at the puddle accumulating beneath his feet.

"Well? No answer for the loss of Lily's shoes?"

"Did they fall off when she fell in the creek?" Jed asked with wide, innocent eyes.

Mrs. Gunther cast Mac a doubtful glance, but didn't voice her suspicions. He would be more than happy to reveal the truth—most of it, anyway—once Everett was gone. However, it struck Mac as odd that Lily's well-being didn't take precedence with Everett. Instead, he was consumed by her bedraggled state.

Except she looked as lovely as ever to Mac.

"I should stop dripping on your floor, Mrs. Gunther, and get my boots off before my feet start pickling." His remark sparked chuckles from the boys.

Lily's gaze, however, pinned him in place. Questions filled her eyes.

He guessed her thoughts. "I will return to check on you."

"Don't bother," Everett grumbled. "I have severe doubts about your character, sir, and I dislike your poor influence on my wards."

"My apologies." Mac dipped his head then turned to Jonah. "Will you please mop up the puddle I made?"

The lad snapped to attention. "Aye, Captain."

"Thank you, sir, for rescuing my niece," Mrs. Gunther said while smearing the muddy-looking poultice over Lily's forearm. "You have our undying gratitude."

Pain swarmed in Lily's eyes—pain Mac wished he could take on himself. He'd rather have received the bite than see her suffer.

"Take your leave already, man!" Everett's face reddened.

"Of course." With one last glance at Lily, who gave him a brave smile, Mac left the room. His boots squeaked and squished with each step.

However, despite Everett's request, Mac didn't intend to stay away for long. He would be back.

## Chapter Seventeen

The sound of her own whimpers awoke Lily. She opened her eyes and drank in the familiar papered walls of the sewing room. A small fire glowed in the hearth, and moonlight as bright as lamplight spilled into the chamber. She tried to sit, but pain exploded through her right arm and spread through her entire body. Every muscle rebelled at even the slightest movement.

The snakebite. Lily recalled it vividly now. All her life in the Shenandoah Valley and she'd only glimpsed the slithering reptiles from afar. The closest she'd been to a viper was when that black racer slithered across the tips of Mac's boots. Never had she been eye to eye with a snake before it struck, and she didn't think she would ever forget its soulless stare. Ever since she could remember, she had swum in the creek with sheer abandon, never bothered by dangerous water snakes or those like the coppery serpent that bit her. Her brothers, of course, had caught garter and king snakes and shaken the wiggling bodies at Lily, hoping for a startled reaction. But she'd always pretended not to be afraid. This last encounter, however, made her fear snakes all the more.

Especially since God had allowed it. But why?

"Are you awake, dearie?" Aunt Hilda appeared from out of the shadows. She laid her cool palm on Lily's forehead. "Your fever seems to have passed." She let go of an easy breath. "Glory hallelujah! I can't tell you how relieved I am. Goodness, you've been in and out of consciousness nigh unto two days now."

"Have I?"

"Indeed." Aunt Hilda leaned closer to Lily's ear. "The captain comes by to check on you every thirty minutes or so." She snorted a laugh. "He's as bad as a clucking hen."

"He is?" Lily found it even hurt her jaw to push the words from her tongue. "Why does every muscle pain me, Aunt?"

"It's the venom. It affects muscles, especially those close to the bite. 'Tis why I've bound your arm to your midriff. It seemed the most suitable position for it to heal in. The less movement the better, so be still."

Lily wasn't about to argue. Aunt Hilda sifted a spoonful of white powder into a tin cup. "What is that?"

"Laudanum for your pain, mixed with my blackberry cider." She put the glass to Lily's parched lips. "Take a drink."

At first Lily didn't want it, but after a sip, a powerful thirst grew and could no longer be ignored.

"Easy now." Aunt Hilda pulled the glass away and replaced it with a tiny bit of biscuit. "Here, eat this. You love my butter biscuits, Lily, now don't you?"

Lily attempted to bob her head while baked deliciousness dissolved in her mouth. Its buttery, rich flavor brought her appetite to life. She opened her mouth like a baby bird awaiting another morsel.

"That's my girl. You get something substantial in your stomach and the laudanum won't come back up on you." Aunt Hilda urged her to drink the rest of the drug-laced cider. "You'll be feeling no pain soon enough."

"Thank you." Lily's voice cracked, and she cleared her throat. Coziness enveloped her like Mac's embrace.

"Did he really come to check on me?" Lily wanted to hear it again.

"The captain? He certainly did." A smile punctuated Aunt Hilda's words. "He was particularly concerned, as were we all, when you didn't wake up after twenty-four hours. But now I'm feeling like dancing a jig."

Lily smiled.

"Do you hear the music?"

Aunt Hilda strode to the window and lifted the sash. The faintest musical notes wafted in on the cool breeze.

"Mac's party... Then it must be Saturday night."

"That's right. John said the captain's got a fine turnout."

"Which means Cynthia Clydesdale is most likely there." Envy nipped at Lily's conscience like a rabid pup. "Why, she is an expert at batting her lashes at poor, unsuspecting men."

"Captain Albright is hardly unsuspecting." Aunt Hilda chortled while tidying the room. "You needn't worry about him, dearie."

"Well, he is only human."

"True enough."

Lily watched her aunt flit around the sewing room like a hummingbird and remembered Mr. Blake's marriage proposal and his plans to leave the day after tomorrow.

"Aunt, you ought to be enjoying the party next door."

"Nonsense. I'm needed here."

"I'm feeling better now. Besides, Mr. Blake is probably lonesome. You have precious little time to enjoy each other's company."

Aunt Hilda stood quietly beneath a shaft of moonlight, her gaze never wavering from Lily. Was she considering a jaunt next door?

"Truly, I don't mind if you go."

"Well..." Aunt Hilda untied her apron strings. "I should probably check on the food. It wouldn't do if we ran out."

"It would not do at all. Besides, my pain is subsiding by the minute." Lily wiggled the fingers on her right hand then stretched her toes. Indeed, the agonizing soreness had been sufficiently muted. "In truth, I would feel worse, Aunt, if you were deprived of Mr. Blake's company on account of me."

"Oh, bah!" She straightened the many blankets and quilts piled on top of Lily. "Well, perhaps I'll go over and make sure your brothers are behaving."

"Please do, otherwise Mrs. Kasper might change her mind about accepting them into her classroom." Lily caught her aunt's wrist. "I don't mean to complain, but I'm overly warm, Aunt. Perhaps fewer coverings."

"Another sign you're improving." One by one, Aunt Hilda peeled off the layers, folded them, and set them aside. "Earlier today, I couldn't keep you warm enough."

Lily scooted higher up on the daybed. "May I attempt to rise and use the chamber pot?"

Aunt Hilda sailed from the room and returned with the porcelain container. With her aunt's assistance, Lily rose from bed and relieved herself. Aunt Hilda took the contents and tossed them out the side window, opposite the direction of Mac's property. Then she brushed Lily's hair and helped her walk back to the daybed.

Lily collapsed onto it, her limbs as weak as a newborn foal's.

"Better?"

"Yes, thank you." The minor exertion had exhausted her and she vowed never again to take for granted the inconsequential ablutions of her daily toilette.

Lying back on the daybed, her head slightly elevated due to its slope at one end, Lily was more than happy to allow Aunt Hilda to situate her. She had done amazingly well thus far. Somehow nightclothes covered her instead of the gown that she recalled wearing. . .

When Mac threw her into the creek.

And then their kiss. And then their next one. . .

Lily was suddenly grateful for the darkness that concealed the sudden flush in her cheeks. She hoped her aunt wouldn't question her about how she happened to tumble into the creek. Or had Mac already provided answers? Her foggy memory told her he had.

"All right, then. I'll go next door." Aunt Hilda filled the tin cup on the table beside Lily with liquid. "Water," she explained as if sensing Lily's unspoken query. "It's my belief that the more you drink, the faster the venom will wash through your veins."

"Then I will drain my cup by the time you return."

"I hope to find you fast asleep by the time I return."

Lily smiled at her aunt's militant tone. "Yes, ma'am." She yawned. "See, I'm drowsy already."

♥

A slam. Lily jolted awake. Had it been a dream? In her present state it was difficult to differentiate the earthly from the ethereal. But perhaps the wind blew the door shut when Aunt Hilda left.

She gazed at the open window. The moon's glow had waned since her previous glance, indicating the passing of time. Perhaps Aunt Hilda had returned home, although the heavy footfalls in the hall didn't belong to Aunt Hilda, and they were too slow and deliberate to be her brothers or even Mr. Everett.

Lily inched herself upward on the daybed as an imposing shadow filled the entryway.

"Lily?" came the whispered voice. "You awake?"

"I am, Captain." She spoke in her normal pitch.

"May I come in?"

"Yes, of course." She smiled as he crossed the room. "Are you sorry you tossed me into the creek?"

A sharp, quick chuckle split the darkness. "Not a bit."

Her laugh turned to a moan when Lily inadvertently jiggled her right arm.

"Are you in very much pain?"

"Evidently, yes, although the laudanum my aunt gave me reduced it to tolerable."

Mac folded his frame into the chair Aunt Hilda had vacated.

"I understand your party is a success."

"Yes. . ." He sat forward, his forearms on his thighs. "So I've been told."

"And have Middletown's young ladies been swarming around you like honeybees around their hive?"

"I can't be certain. Thus far I have managed to evade them."

"Even Cynthia Clydesdale? She possesses charm enough for any man."

"Not this man." He sat back. "Besides, I don't know which of the. . . *honeybees* she is."

"She's the one who buzzes the loudest."

"Ah." Mac stood, closed the distance between them, and touched the backs of his fingers to Lily's forehead. He then hunkered beside the daybed and a piney, masculine scent made its way to her nose. "Your aunt told me your fever abated. It appears it's still gone, which is good news."

"My headache has vanished too." Lily noticed his abrupt change in subject. Then again, Aunt Hilda said he'd been concerned. "I'm feeling much better."

"Which is a relief, to be sure."

Lily pondered his remark. "I hope you don't blame yourself. I've been swimming in Cedar Creek and climbing those rocks practically all my life. I've never encountered a snake face-to-face. God always kept them at bay, like in Psalm ninety-one, where He promises that we will tread on lions and serpents and they won't harm us." When Mac didn't respond, her curiosity grew. "Why do you think God didn't protect me this time?"

"I'm hardly an expert on God, but if forced to answer—"

"Consider yourself forced." Curiosity gripped her.

He grunted a laugh. "Then I'd say that God did protect you. It could have been so much worse, but here you are, back among the living, breathing, talking to me. Your aunt called it 'answered prayer.'"

"And what do you call it?"

"A miracle."

Lily would have called it a curse or, at the very least, punishment for sharing intimacies with Mac in the creek.

Mac's shadowed features were indiscernible, but the breath that left his lungs spoke volumes. "I feared the worst, Lily. I thought you would perish like—"

"Like Mary?" Lily stretched out her hand to him.

Mac captured it between both his palms. "For the first time in a very long while, I felt something, something more powerful than life itself. I tasted it, smelled it, and it was all too familiar."

"What was it?"

"Fear. Raw, unadulterated fear."

"For me?"

"Yes." He brought her hand to his lips, sending a current up her arm.

"Then may you fear no more. As you can see, I'm much improved."

"Words cannot describe the happiness in my heart at the news."

"Then go and enjoy your party, Mac. I will be well soon enough."

He stroked her cheek and Lily noted something different about him. She touched his jaw and smiled. "You shaved off your whiskers."

"So to make nothing about me unpleasant."

Lily's smile lingered. "I believe I acclimated, sir."

"Indeed."

A blush worked its way up her neck and warmed her cheeks. Lily was grateful for the darkness between them.

Strains of music competed for her attention—and won. "I wish I had been able to attend your party. You wouldn't have escaped me. I would have made sure you danced." She churned out a sigh of longing. "I do so enjoy the fiddlers. And I presume Mr. Blake is playing along on his squeeze-box."

"He is—and doing a fine job of it."

"Oh, how I long to be there. I've only been hearing faint strains of the music. Is Mr. Crocker playing his fife?"

"I believe so, although I didn't catch his name. I met most of Middletown tonight. It'll take me a while to remember everyone's name."

"Then you, of course, are forgiven." Lily tried to hear more of the music, but it got lost in a gust of wind.

"Allow me to make your wishes come true, Princess."

Her pulse quickened when she guessed his intentions. "I cannot go. I'm in bedclothes with my right arm tied up tight, and my legs feel like Aunt Hilda's mint jelly."

He kissed her forehead and got to his feet. "I shall return shortly."

"No, wait. . ." Lily reached for the tails of his frockcoat but missed. The attempt left her feeling exhausted. "Mac, please come back!"

## Chapter Eighteen

As if possessing the strength of ten men, Mac lifted the wrought iron bench from the yard and set it down in a secluded area in the orchard. When Mrs. Gunther had shown up at his party and exclaimed that Lily's fever was gone and that she was awake and talking, Mac had to come and see the miracle for himself.

And now he'd make her wish come true.

He set his hands on his hips and scanned the yard. Buzzing insects, croaking toads, and tree frogs sang dissonant night songs while the fiddler's foot-stomping tune carried across the creek. Perfect. They wouldn't easily be seen and Lily would hear the music.

Satisfied, Mac strode back to the house. Entering the sewing room, he rubbed his palms together. "Are you ready, Princess?"

"Ready for what?"

Hearing the suspicion in Lily's tone, Mac grinned. He crossed the room and carefully helped her stand. Then, after gently wrapping a quilt around her, he scooped her into his arms.

"Feeling all right?"

"So far." She giggled and set her forehead against his jaw, obviously intoxicated with the medicine's effects. "Funny, but I seem to always end up in your arms, Captain."

He smiled. "Irony at its best."

"But please don't take me to the dance. I'm sure I make a disastrous sight."

"You're beautiful, Lily." Mac meant every word. If she only knew how frightened he'd been the past couple of days. Somehow he couldn't imagine the world deprived of Lily's gift of song and his life devoid of the light she brought to it. "However, I don't intend to share your company tonight, so rest easy."

Her head lolled against his shoulder as if it proved too heavy for her to hold up. Well, he'd only keep her out for a few minutes. Just long enough for her to enjoy a song or two.

Mac reached the bench and gently set Lily on her feet.

"Are there snakes in this grass?"

"Most likely. But they won't bother us." He wrapped the quilt more tightly around her, mindful of her injured arm, then sat and pulled her onto his lap.

"I don't want them to creep up into my covering. And what if another poisonous viper finds me?"

"Shh, Lily. Someone might hear us."

She collapsed against him.

"You must not allow your fear to affect your common sense." Mac kept his voice to a whisper. Perhaps she'd bury his advice deep in her subconscious and recollect it tomorrow, after the medicine wore off. "Snakes are more afraid of us than we are of them."

"Not the viper that struck me. He was aggressive. . .and evil."

"On the contrary. You most likely startled him, and he reacted on his instinct to defend himself." Mac readjusted the precious burden on his lap. "Besides, how do we know that serpent was a *he*?"

She responded with a soft laugh that sent a measure of amusement coursing through him. He'd successfully steered her away from her fear.

A burst of music resounded through the orchard, followed by several shouts of "yip!" and "yeehaw!"

"The musicians sound good tonight." Lily pressed her left forearm into his shoulder and drew herself upright. "Oh, and I can hear chords from Mr. Blake's squeeze-box."

Mac's heart grew double its size. Such a simple, yet sweet success to bring her a measure of happiness after what she'd gone through.

Again she rested her head against his shoulder and hummed along with the tune. Pleasing Lily certainly had its rewards. Mac rested his head against hers.

She moved slightly. "I love you, Mac."

Her words wrapped around his soul, claiming him for all time. He didn't mind—not anymore, not since he'd glimpsed into the dark abyss that was his life without love. Without Lily. True, it hadn't been his plan to succumb to such binding emotions, but fate would have its way. In a desperate plea earlier today, he'd promised God his own life if only the Almighty would spare Lily's.

The stars above glinted with shining victory.

As for his need to succeed, well, somehow he'd figure out a way. While in India on a voyage with Taylor Osborn commanding the frigate, he'd heard a saying; "Everything works out in the end. If it hasn't, it's not the end." Memories of his studies of the Holy Bible as a boy rose to the surface of his mind and recalled something similar. God was sovereign. He was in control.

Yes, everything would work out in the end.

"Did you hear me, Mac? I love you."

"I heard every word, Princess, and once you're feeling better, we'll discuss the matter at length."

"I feel fine."

Mac chuckled. "I'm sure you do, with snake venom, laudanum, and your aunt's cider coursing through your veins."

"A powerful drink, my aunt's concoction. My pain is practically gone."

"Good." Mac cupped her head and pressed it against his shoulder. "Rest now, Lily, and enjoy the music."

She stilled, and a warm breeze brushed over them. Mac set his shoulders against the back of the bench. He sat through the rest of the tunes. The small group of musicians did, indeed, sound quite good. When the music died away, activity spilled from the barn. If Mac wasn't mistaken, his guests availed themselves of the food tables. Such an array of delectables he hadn't seen in a long while.

Female laughter near the stone bridge reached his ears. All evening lovers had been strolling across it, but from what Mac saw, no one ambled into the orchard. Even so, it was time to get Lily back to her bed.

"Lily," he whispered against her cool forehead.

Soft, steady breathing was his only reply. She'd fallen asleep.

Had it only been dream?

Lily's foggy memory conjured up images of herself in Mac's arms. Had they been in attendance at the party?

No. Except she recalled hearing music. She glanced down at her nightgown. How could that be? She'd worn this same nightwear since last evening when she awakened from her fevered state. Alas, it truly had been a dream—but a marvelous, beautiful dream, to be sure.

Scuffling boots directly above her signaled Jonah and Jed's activity in the chamber they shared. Most likely they dressed for church. By the continued sound and occasional thud, followed by Jed's wails, Lily guessed the two were quarreling.

She attempted to sit up. She'd give those boys an earful for picking at each other on the Lord's Day. Her feet touched the carpeted floor as pain tore through her right arm. The room swam and Lily's stomach pitched.

She sat unmoving for a moment and held her forehead in her left palm. Oh, if the world would only right itself.

The door creaked open. Lily lifted her gaze to find Aunt Hilda's disapproving frown above the large wooden tray she carried.

"Trying to get up, were you?" The hem of her plum gown brushed softly against the tops of her black laced boots. She set down the tray and helped Lily back onto the daybed and tucked the quilt around her. "Now, here, eat some porridge and a biscuit. You need to rebuild your strength."

Lily allowed Aunt Hilda to arrange the tray on her lap, but the smell of food caused a knot to form in the back of her throat.

"One bite at a time, dearie," Aunt Hilda said, as if reading Lily's thoughts.

She complied, taking a spoonful of the porridge over which her aunt had drizzled honey. One bite did, indeed, lead to another.

"That's a girl." Her aunt smiled obvious approval then she bustled around the room, opening draperies and straightening furniture.

"Did you enjoy the party last night?"

Aunt Hilda glanced over her shoulder. "Very much. But I'm especially grateful that your fever is gone."

"Thanks to your nursing."

"Thanks to the Almighty!"

"Indeed!" Lily watched her aunt move about. "And Mr. Blake—did he have fun?"

"Did he ever." Aunt Hilda's eyes twinkled. "I'd say the captain's barn is now properly christened."

"You'll miss him after he leaves, won't you?" Lily lifted the biscuit to her lips. She hated to think her aunt might be heartbroken in the days to come.

"Aw, yes, but he'll be back. It's like I've been telling John, if the good Lord wills our union, then so it shall be."

Lily found much comfort in those words, especially when she thought of Mr. Everett and whatever diabolical plans he had in mind for her family. "Aunt, do you really think Papa gambled away our *Haus am Bach*?"

"It's possible, I suppose, and I won't call Mr. Everett an outright liar on mere suspicion, but more's the chance he's up to no good."

Lily's sunny mood vanished behind a cloud of doom. "Oh, Aunt, how remiss I was to allow him so much control after Papa died."

"You didn't have a choice, Lily, and you were in a state of shock. We all were." Aunt Hilda stood over her and frowned. "Come, now, another spoonful of that porridge."

"Was Mr. Everett at the captain's party last night?"

"Yes, surprisingly. And I saw him shake the captain's hand in the most cordial of ways." She quirked a brow. "Made me wonder what Mr. Everett's up to next."

Lily wondered too, although Mac was far too wise to be hoodwinked.

Aunt Hilda hovered. "One more bite of your biscuit?"

"No, thank you."

Her aunt took up the tray. "Any pain in your arm?"

Lily nodded. "When I try to move."

"Then you'd best stay still." Her features softened. "I'll bring you a bit of laudanum when I return."

Lily gently touched the tips of her swollen digits. "My fingers resemble the sausages you cook with cabbage."

"It'll be a while before the swelling goes down. Your joints will ache like you're ninety-five years old, but you're on the mend and that's what matters." Aunt Hilda kissed her forehead. "Now I'll go fetch a cup of tea and medicine for you and then, while the tea is cooling, I'll help you to the chamber pot. I'll even brush and braid your hair before I take the boys to church. But after that you must stay put and rest."

"Yes, Aunt." Lily sank into the end of the divan. Her strength waned from the simple task of eating. "Perhaps I can be moved to my own bed-chamber."

"In due time." Aunt Hilda made purposeful strides toward the door.

While Lily waited for her return, her mind whirred with questions. Would Mr. Blake still carry her two hundred pounds with him to Alexandria tomorrow? Was she doing the right thing by allowing Mr. Everett to take her brothers on the trip? To that end, she carried little influence. Mr. Everett was their court-appointed guardian and Jonah and Jed wanted to go.

Lily worked her lips together as she continued her ponderings. And what about that dream last night? It seemed so real. However, her lack of strength surely proved she had only fantasized of being in the protective confines of Mac's arms while lively music danced across the orchard's leafy overhang. . .

She frowned. Or had she?

"So your decision is final, eh, Cap'n? You're returnin' to Alexandria?"

"It is and I am." Mac glanced to his left and eyed Blake while their boots crunched the gravely road as they walked home from church. "I hate to leave Lily, but I distrust Everett more." Mac inhaled the mild autumn air, perfumed with the wildflowers, mint, and sage growing along the road. "Besides, the fact that I've not heard from my father is troubling. The builders he promised to send should have arrived by now. Before long, the weather will turn."

"I'm sure Miss Lily will be sad to hear you're leavin'."

"Perhaps, but she needs to concentrate on her health at the moment."

Blake nudged him with his shoulder and sent Mac several paces into the road. "You're besotted. Admit it."

"All right, I admit it." Mac figured he deserved the ribbing.

"I never seen you so worked up over a woman, Cap'n. It's love fer sure."

"Oh, and now you're an expert, I presume?" Mac hurled a gaze toward the heavens.

"Just observin'. Ain't no crime in that."

Mac let the remark die away. He had more pressing matters occupying his thoughts, Lily being the mainstay. He wondered how much of their conversation, if any, she recalled today. He'd sent up a prayer in church that, should she remember, she wouldn't regret uttering words of love.

A southwest breeze drifted down from the Alleghenies, cooling the valley, although the sun's warmth caressed Mac's face. He'd been uplifted at church, a strange and radical occurrence for him. Lily's survival turned even Everett's stony expression to one of joy. Reverend Kasper gave thanks to God. From his place in the pew beside Jed, so did Mac, albeit in his own way. He would not forget the vow he made to God during the hours he'd feared for Lily's life. Now, for the first time in many years, Mac deemed another's existence more precious than his own.

He swatted at a swarm of gnats. Had his spiral into selfishness begun with the seizure of his merchant vessel? Somehow the event heightened Mac's instinct for survival, and it hadn't subsided, even when the fighting stopped. Mac supposed he had little defense for his selfishness prior to the conflict. But something happened recently. He felt different.

Reaching his property, Mac eyed the mess of bark chips and tree stumps which would eventually be his barnyard's drive. He certainly had his work cut out for him. Perhaps he couldn't afford to leave right now.

Again, he weighed the pros and cons. He and Blake had made great strides in the past few weeks, but there was so much more to accomplish, and bringing on a crew of men was essential.

Mac kept on walking, keeping time with Blake's determined strides toward Mrs. Gunther's kitchen. The dear lady had invited them to dinner after church and neither he nor Blake refused. Their bellies were as hollow as deadwood, even though they'd dined on food from the party at breakfast time.

However, Mac's visit held a dual purpose. He wanted to speak with Lily. He couldn't leave for Alexandria without an understanding between them. He'd made that mistake with Mary and lived to regret it. She'd died without a word from him. He'd been too self-focused and, yes, too ashamed to write.

But this time, such a foible would not be repeated.

# Chapter Nineteen

ily gauged her response when Mac entered the room. Elation or embarrassment, which should it be? She feared the blush creeping up her neck and blooming in her cheeks would choose for her and reveal what she dared not express.

"How are you feeling?" He paused near the doorway.

"Better, thank you." She took in his dapper attire—white shirt, necktie, brown waistcoat, and tan trousers, tucked into knee-high black boots. Aunt Hilda had said both Mac and Mr. Blake attended church this morning.

"Are you up for a conversation?"

"Yes, of course. Please come in." Before the last words left her lips, Lily's heart drummed out an anxious rhythm. If her sweet dream had been reality, she owed Mac an apology for her forward behavior. "Anything in particular you'd like to discuss?"

"Yes, actually." He grasped the cane-backed chair, flipped it around, then placed it close to the daybed. He sat and crossed his legs. "Do you recall my taking you to hear the music last night?"

Her heart fell like a brick. Her face burned as if her fever had returned. "About that..."

He cocked his head, waiting for her to continue.

She winced. "I may have said some things that...well, that might be construed as bold and ever so forward."

"Yes, you said *some things*." His inky gaze darkened.

"Did you take them seriously?" Part of Lily prayed he did.

"Should I have?"

Would he admonish her if she confessed? He'd made it clear he did not desire courtship, love, marriage, children—all blessings that Lily longed for.

"Do you regret the words you spoke last night?"

"I regret the delivery of them, yes." Lily couldn't be disloyal to her heart.

"But not the message itself?"

"No." She dropped her gaze to the quilt that covered her to the waist and traced the pattern with her finger.

"Hmm. . ."

"Hmm, you say?" Lily frowned. "It's your fault I freely spoke my heart. You must know you're terribly charming."

A smile quirked the corners of his mouth. "Then I shall take full responsibility."

"How gallant of you." Varying emotions stung behind her eyes. Hurt. Anger. Irritation. What a horrid reaction to her declaration of love. "I suppose you're glad you have yet another of my secrets to add to your collection."

He pursed his lips. "I hadn't thought of that, but yes, I am glad. Very glad."

The man was impossible!

Mac glanced at the empty doorway. "And I would enjoy teasing you all the more if I wasn't so concerned about Silas Everett barging in, preventing me from having my say."

Lily felt suddenly deflated. "You were teasing me? About such an important matter?" A sorrowful sheen clouded her vision until she blinked it away.

"Forgive me." Mac left the chair and knelt on one knee by the daybed. His palm swallowed up her unrestrained hand. "The truth is, I wish to discuss that very topic." His woodsy, spicy scent enveloped her. "I simply went about starting it off all wrong." He aimed a gaze at the doorway. "But there's no time to waste now. Your aunt and Blake are distracting Everett."

"I see." She pulled her hand away, immediately wishing she hadn't broken contact. "Aunt Hilda is aware, then, that you are on your knee and speaking to me about an *affaire de coeur?*"

"Yes, she knows, at least in part. You see, it's my turn to share a secret with you."

Curiosity held her fast. "What is it?"

"You have won my undying affection, Miss Lilyanna Laughlin, which probably isn't much of a secret, come to think of it." His brow rippled and tiny lines appeared around his eyes. "Nonetheless, I have nothing to offer you—yet. But in a year, I hope to be in a position where I can ask for your hand." A tiny smile hiked up one side of his mouth. "If you'll have me. By then you'll know me better than anyone."

She gaped at him. "You are, indeed, a wicked tease. I suppose this is another joke."

"The only joke is on me." His eyes darkened. "What a fool I've been these last weeks, fighting my feelings, believing I could be happy living isolated and alone. You and this entire community have shown me otherwise—and in short order." He took her hand again. He stared at their entwined fingers. "I also made a solemn vow to God." Mac lifted his head. "I gave the Almighty my life."

Lily smiled at the news. "You believe?"

"I'm beginning to. Six weeks ago I would have denounced religion as foolishness. However, I'm certain I saw the hand of God work these last few days."

"You've opened your heart to God, and that's a marvelous first step."

"The next, Reverend Kasper told me, is reading the Bible, studying short passages at a time."

"And will you?"

Mac wet his lips. "I think I'm up to the challenge." He dropped his gaze to their clasped hands.

Happiness bubbled up inside Lily, spilling out in her smile.

"Now, what I want from you, what I'm hoping for, is acknowledgment of my intentions."

Lily giggled. "Oh, I acknowledge them, but I can't decide whether to kiss you or slap your face."

"The former, please." Mac ran his thumb along Lily's lower lip, sending shivers of expectancy up her spine. "But not now. I expect Everett to charge in at any moment."

At the mention of the man's name, Lily snapped from the hypnotic-like state Mac so easily evoked. She straightened the coverlet on her lap to hide her wayward emotions.

"Everett is no fool," Mac said. "He senses our attraction to one another and he doesn't like it. I suspect he has much to gain if he marries you."

"I'd rather die." Lily held tightly to Mac's hand as humiliation filled her being. "He deceived me. I realize that now. But after my father died, I thought Mr. Everett had my family's best interests at heart. He was, after all, one of my father's most trusted friends." She lifted her gaze. "Don't be taken in by him, Mac."

"You needn't worry." He kissed her fingers, stood, and reclaimed his chair before craning his neck for a better view outside the door. "Lily, I'm leaving for Alexandria in the morning, so I'd like to hear that we have an understanding—if you agree, of course."

"Leaving?" One by one the puzzle pieces clicked into place. She recalled his regrets for not stating his intentions to his beloved Mary before she passed. "Why are you returning to Alexandria? You will come back, won't you?"

"I will return, yes." Mac grinned and sat forward, his forearms on his thighs. "I need to complete a business transaction. I will also invest your two hundred pounds," he whispered, "if that's still your wish."

"It is!" Perhaps the gambler in Papa had manifested itself in her. After all, there was no guarantee she would be any more successful than he had been. It frightened her to think she might be about to squander the funds and lose everything. "Do you think it terribly unwise?" She lifted her hand, palm side out. "Allow me to rephrase. Would you make the investment?"

"I would, yes, but I don't have a family—yet." He sent her a devilish wink, setting Lily's face ablaze.

Alas, it was not quite the assurance she'd hoped for.

"Sleep on the idea. I've already told the boys that Blake and I will collect them in the morning so as not to inconvenience Everett. Instruct your aunt to give me the coinage at that time if investing is what you wish."

"Good advice. Thank you." She would revisit the matter later with Aunt Hilda. "And I accept your. . .*understanding*."

Mac's features broke into a smile. "It will give us ample time to get to know one another. As I said before, you may change your mind."

Lily doubted it. "I'm grateful that you're willing to travel the distance with my brothers. I fear they'll misbehave and sorely try Mr. Everett's patience."

"Blake and I arrived at the same conclusion. Besides, I need to settle business with my father."

Reality reached out from its sphere and gave her a shake. How correct Mac had been. Her knowledge of him could fill a thimble. "I look forward to learning about your family."

A shadow tiptoed across his handsome face—

And then Mr. Everett marched into the room.

♥

Mac patted the inside pocket of his coat containing Lily's money and surveyed the large red-brick structure across the street that he once called home. After two and a half long days of travel with nonstop chatter from Jonah and Jed, the stagecoach pulled up to the inn where he, Blake, the boys, and Silas Everett disembarked. They parted ways, Blake heading to the docks to inquire over a job, Everett and the Laughlins to the hotel, and Mac, to his parents' house.

He surveyed the scene around him. Ladies strolling, shielded by their parasols, maidens scurrying off on chores, and men hurrying past, packages tucked beneath their arms. Buggies and wagons clamored down the street. Odd how he could forget the hustle and bustle of the city in such a short time. Where once he'd preferred wide open waters, where the sky seemed to bow to the sea, he now appreciated the slower, amiable pace of Middletown.

It had been a long while since he called Alexandria "home."

Shifting his valise from his right hand, he crossed the street then climbed familiar stairs to the front door. Who would be home this time of day? Mother, perhaps. His four younger sisters had married and would, no doubt, be caring for their own families. Father and Prescott were presumably attending business at the office and warehouse on the river's edge. He faced the gleaming brass doorknocker and, feeling more of a stranger than part of the family, decided to use it.

Mac rapped three consecutive times and waited. He gave the neighborhood a glance, searching for a familiar face, and found none. Relief caused the knots between his shoulder blades to unwind. Given the scandal last year, anonymity suited him.

The door opened, revealing the longtime housekeeper's priggish scowl. "Hello, Pearl."

She blinked, then her brown eyes widened and she cupped the sides of her face. "Mercy!"

"May I come in?"

She opened the door wider and bid him enter.

Mother's honeyed voice wafted in from the parlor. "Who is it, Pearl?"

"Why, it's none other than Blackbeard himself, ma'am."

Mac chuckled and set down his valise. With three days' growth on his jaw, he probably deserved the jab. "It's nice to see you too, Pearl."

Her scowl deepened, and she marched off.

Mother sailed around the corner, spotted him, and broke into a wide smile. "Mac! You're home. Why, I barely had time to get a letter off to you."

He wrapped his mother's pudgy figure in a warm embrace. The tangy jasmine and spice scent of her imported perfume gave his fondest memories free rein. Mother had always been his true supporter.

"I didn't expect you."

"There was no time to send word." Mac stepped back. "Besides, this is an impromptu visit, mostly business."

"Ah. . ." Mother patted the sides of her coif but nary a single strand of her silvery locks had come unpinned from Mac's exuberant greeting.

"Of course, I realize it's best not to advertise my arrival."

Mother expelled a long, weary sigh. "I suppose not, although the scandal is no longer foremost on wagging tongues."

"I'm glad." Mac meant it. The angry accusations and disgraceful perpetrations by citizens and solicitors alike had resulted in a mockery of American justice. Mac was lucky not to have been hanged. Unfortunately, the damage to the Albright name had been significant.

He followed his mother into the parlor. Nothing in the sunny yellow room had changed in the past month and a half.

"What sort of business brings a Middletown farmer back to Alexandria?" Mother sat on the edge of the settee and arranged the skirt of her deep-blue printed gown. "Have you tired of the countryside?"

Mac grinned. "Hardly. Things are moving along quite well. With the help of my new community, my barn is up, and Blake and I built a cabin where I plan to winter until my home is built."

"Oh." A tremulous smile played on Mother's mouth.

"Did you wish to hear that I abandoned my farming ambitions and have returned to Alexandria for good?"

She heaved a sigh. "I suppose I did."

Mac crossed the room and kissed her cheek. "I missed you too, Mother."

She waved him away, and pink spots plumed in her powdery cheeks.

"Actually, my visit here is twofold. My neighbor asked me to invest two hundred pounds in one of Albright Shipping's merchant vessels."

"A welcome investment. Your father will be pleased."

"Yes, I think he will." Mac took a seat beside his mother. "I've also come to inquire about the construction crew Father promised. The men have not shown up, but the lumber for my home has been ordered."

"Oh, dear. . ." Mother's dark brows knitted a heavy frown.

Mac perceived problems. "What is it, Mother?"

"Nothing, dear. Nothing."

"It's something." Mac arched a brow as an uneasiness crept over him. "Tell me, Mother."

"Very well. I won't mince words." She inhaled deeply. "Our family is facing hardships."

"What?" Mac jerked back. "How can that be?" He paused to think on it. "Certainly, there were losses last year when the British sailed in and occupied Alexandria, but the books were in order when I left."

"Ask your father and Prescott, dear. I don't know all the particulars."

"Please." He took his mother's hand. "Tell me what you do know."

"We've dismissed all our household staff except for Pearl." Sorrow and disappointment weighed down her features, and her dark eyes lost their gleam. "She's an average cook, and I'm learning. Your father said it's never too late for a woman to learn her way around a kitchen."

Mac couldn't believe his ears. His mind failed to grasp his mother's words. "Is this due to the vessels Albright Shipping lost last year when the British invaded Alexandria?"

"Partly."

The truth pressed in on him. "And due to the scandal I caused when I returned home from war."

"No one blames you, son." Mother's cool fingers gave his hand an affectionate squeeze. "However, you may just be our family's salvation."

"Me? How?"

"We should wait to discuss this until your father and older brother are present."

"I'd rather hear it from you than Prescott to be sure!" Father usually left the dirty work to Mac's older brother.

"Gwyneth has a younger sister," Mother began, referring to Prescott's wife. "She's a pleasant enough girl, and—"

"Stop." Mac held up a hand. "I know where this is heading."

"She has a large dowry." Her tone indicated she meant to tempt him. "Twenty thousand pounds."

He shook his head. "No."

A little pout pulled at her mouth. "But you'd rescue our family's shipping business and marry into a family with a good name. Your reputation will be restored. The Albright name will be restored."

Mac pushed to his feet. "Mother. . ."

"I know you miss Mary. We all do. We loved her too."

Mac closed his eyes and steeled himself for the guilt soon to shower over him.

"Rarely do people marry for love. Marriage is a business arrangement. A partnership. I've heard you say so yourself."

It was true. Hadn't he told Lily the same thing not too long ago?

"I have changed my views on marriage, Mother." He walked to the cold hearth and propped his elbow on the rich walnut mantel. A breath of early autumn blew in through an open window, fluttering the gold draperies. "I've decided I will marry for love. For richer or poorer."

"Oh, my soul. . ." Mother pulled out her fan and waved it frantically in front of her face. "You're our only hope, Mac. Our salvation."

"I'm sure we can find hope elsewhere."

"Your father and Prescott have been over and over all our alternatives."

"And marrying me off was the best they could come up with?" Mac regretted his harsh tone. "Mother," he began again, reclaiming his seat beside her. "Don't upset yourself. Prescott has never been a creative thinker, but now that I'm home, I will help him and Father develop a suitable solution. One we can all live with."

Still working up a wind with her silk fan, Mother gave a stiff nod. "I hope so. Our very existence depends on it."

# Chapter Twenty

What have you been doing with the company's funds?" Mac ceased his pacing and paused in front of his older brother.

"None of your business." Bringing his brandy snifter to his lips, Prescott slammed its contents down his throat.

Mac's patience frayed. What the tiring journey from Middletown hadn't achieved, his older brother's arrogance was about to. "If I'm to be the company's 'salvation,' as Mother put it, I think I deserve to know why."

"You deserve?" Prescott's hazel eyes darkened. "Ironic that you should choose those words." He rose from the brown leather chair, a sneer on his lips. "Many in this city think you *deserve* to hang."

"A moot point." Mac's blood began to boil. "I was acquitted of all the ridiculous charges the prosecuting court jester dreamed up."

"Except they weren't that ridiculous." Prescott arched a well-groomed brow.

Mac turned to his father who, until this moment, had been sitting mutely behind his desk. "I refuse to be tried once more, Father. And by my own brother."

"That's enough, Prescott." Father's tone lacked its usual zest. His brown eyes looked dull, and his forehead seemed to espouse permanent worry lines.

Mac faced his brother once more, taking note yet again of how different they were—always had been. Where Mac possessed dark features, Prescott's were light. Blond hair, neatly combed back, hazel eyes, a clean-shaven jaw. Expensive attire covered his willowy frame. Throughout their growing-up years, Prescott had been their mother's pet. Mac, on the other hand, bonded with their father.

Mac folded his arms. "Where did the money go?"

"A good deal of it went to you." Resentment flashed in Prescott's eyes. "Here you stand, the prodigal son, returning to ask for more funds because, ah, allow me to guess, you deserve it."

"Unlike the prodigal son, I have not squandered my inheritance."

"Nor have I. So we're even." Prescott crossed the imported Persian carpet, refilled his snifter, then returned to his chair. "And it is I who feels as though he's on trial."

Mac wouldn't stand for his brother's self-pity. "We're not quite even. I can account for every coin I've spent. So far, Prescott, you cannot."

From out of the corner of his eye, Mac caught his father's movement. He looked over in time to see him, once a bulwark of a man who possessed all the answers, run a shaky hand through his graying black hair.

"Father, why did you give me the money to begin anew in the Shenandoah Valley if Albright Shipping was experiencing financial difficulties?" The question had plagued Mac since he learned the news of his family's hardship.

Father's eyes shifted to Prescott. "I was unaware of any financial difficulties."

"Just as I presumed." Mac struggled to remain even tempered. This didn't involve him directly, and he had no intention of marrying his sister-in-law's sister. "Well, Prescott, what have you to say for yourself?"

"If you must know, I deserved equal compensation. I have a wife, after all. You, Mac, have no one to consider but yourself. Therefore, I purchased a home just outside the city."

"A sprawling tobacco plantation on four thousand acres," Father added, "with at least one hundred slaves."

"Tobacco plantation?" Mac hung his head back and guffawed. "You don't have the slightest idea what's involved with being a planter. Why, you were the only boy who disliked getting his hands soiled at playtime."

"Scratching in the dirt is what my slaves are for."

Mac's moment of amusement fled. The idea of owning another human being sickened him. After being impressed into service for the British, he had been forced to do menial tasks aboard the frigate, an attempt by the captain to humiliate his American captive. When Mac dared to disobey, which happened on one sorry occasion, he was flogged in front of the entire crew.

Yes, he'd gotten a taste of slavery then.

"How can you sleep at night, Prescott?"

"I sleep very soundly. Thank you." He drained his snifter again in one gulp.

"Our parents don't have a cook. They have dismissed their household staff due to their poverty while you reign like a king over your plantation."

Prescott crossed his legs. "I have offered them slaves, but Mother doesn't want those people in her house."

Mac closed his eyes and rubbed his forehead. "Fine. Let's stop bickering. Instead, let us put our minds together and come up with a solution."

"We have a solution." Prescott cocked his head. "Father and I decided you should marry Samantha Eden. My father-in-law is desperate to find the girl a husband, and she's worth twenty thousand pounds."

"Yes, Mother told me of your cockamamy scheme." Mac slid his gaze to his father. "And what have you to say about this idea?"

"Your mother and Prescott deserve all the credit for it."

Just as Mac suspected.

"Thank you, Father." Prescott's haughty expression reminded Mac of Silas Everett's highbrow ways. "At least we agree that I *deserve* that much."

Mac longed to take his brother outside and show him just exactly what he deserved. "Understand this, brother. I'll not marry Miss Eden or any other female of your choosing. As it happens, I have decided whom I shall marry and when."

"Really? And your choice of a wife is. . .who? A commoner then?" Prescott lifted his chin, taunting Mac further. "A farmer's daughter, perhaps?"

"America has no commoners. Thomas Jefferson wrote that all men are created equal." Mac bent to meet his brother's gaze. "That goes for your slaves."

"Spare me. Jefferson, himself, owns slaves."

Frustration pumped through Mac's veins and knotted at the base of his skull. This conversation failed to move forward even an inch. It seemed to go around and around. Massaging the area that pained him, he strode to the bank of windows which overlooked the street. The sun had begun its descent in the western sky, and activity outside had died away. He thought of Lily and wondered about her recovery. He hoped—no, he prayed—that she was up and about by now.

"Do we know the young lady you've decided upon?"

Mac turned and faced his father. His understanding with Lily wasn't a secret, although he had said nothing about it during the journey here from Middletown. He would have spoken up, however, if Everett mentioned his intention to marry Lily.

"No, you don't know her. She's my new next-door neighbor, and we have but an understanding. I'm in no financial position to ask for her hand yet. But I shall."

A snort came from Prescott.

"My hope is that in a year's time I'll be ready."

"Planning is crucial." Father dipped his head in approval. "You are wise to set future goals."

"I learned well from you, Father."

"Indeed." The older man smiled for the first time since greeting Mac earlier.

"Shall I take my leave so you two can enjoy your slobbering reunion?"

Mac glanced at Prescott. "Green with envy, are you?" One brotherly jab for another seemed fair. "Or perhaps your verdant complexion is due to a bad crop of tobacco." He chuckled, and even Father snickered.

Prescott's face reddened. "Go to the devil, Mac."

"I have been there, brother, and have changed my ways." Mac regarded his father. "But I digress. What I intended to say is that Miss Laughlin, my next-door neighbor and subject of my interest, has asked me to invest two hundred pounds in one of your merchant vessels. Have you any ready to set sail?"

"We have a ship moored on the River Thames," Prescott muttered. "She'll be setting sail soon."

"Good." Mac rubbed his palms together. The information proved positive.

"Unfortunately, any earnings we make on the wares in her hold," Prescott said, "will go to pay the captain and his crew their salaries plus back pay, as we were unable to pay them for their last undertaking. We also owe suppliers."

"So you will break even?" Mac set his hands on his hips.

"More or less."

"Which is it?"

"Less, if you must know." Prescott helped himself to a third brandy, not that Mac was counting. "We have been running on a deficit for some time now. I'm afraid it's finally caught up with us."

"There's more." Father pushed slowly to his feet. "We were unable to hire a crew for our merchant sloop *Ariel*, which is scheduled to sail for Massachusetts, and the goods in the hold spoiled."

"In order to garner business, we guaranteed the shipment. Now we owe our consigners."

"That was a mistake," Mac said. "You cannot guarantee shipments. Captains and their crews encounter any number of calamities at sea."

"I tried to tell Prescott that." Father walked around his desk and to the sideboard where he filled a brandy snifter for himself.

"Yes, well, it's not my fault the Albright name cannot be trusted in this city." Prescott downed his brandy.

"*Ariel* was set to sail for France with a cache of weapons, musket balls, beaver pelts, gunpowder, and whale oil." Father sipped from his glass. "However, one of the barrels of oil somehow burst, soiling the furs and making our loss all the greater."

"A devastating loss," Prescott added.

"I am sorry to hear of your misfortune," Mac said. "Truly, I am. However, I fail to see how my marrying a woman for her dowry would help. Yes, you could pay your consigners, but that would only plug one crack in a leaking dam."

"Ha! That's where you're wrong." A slow smile spread across Prescott's face. "If you marry Sam, the Albright name will be salvaged. Her father, my father-in-law, Jethro Eden, possesses much clout, not only in Alexandria, but in all of Virginia. He has been a guest at Monticello numerous times."

"Then why hasn't such grace been given to you?" Mac still failed to understand the fix. "You've already married an Eden daughter."

"And I've blown through her fortune trying to save our family business."

"Family business?" Mac frowned. "Albright Shipping is your business, Prescott, entrusted to you by our father."

"I am not to blame!" Prescott shot to his feet.

"And I am not your salvation!" Mac tensed, ready to take on his brother if necessary. Oddly, Reverend Kasper's words rang in his memory: *"Only Jesus imparts salvation...."*

Father moved between them and faced Mac. "We are in desperate need of a capable sea captain." His gaze pleaded. "I was never keen on the marriage scheme, but this, I know, will help us." Father turned to Prescott. "We can salvage what's left in *Ariel's* hold and bid her bon voyage to France."

"As much as I sympathize, gentlemen—and I do sympathize—I'm adamant about not returning to the sea." Mac refused to give in to the pressure he faced and seated himself in the chair adjacent to Prescott's. "I would ask that you respect my wishes."

"From renowned master and commander of a seafaring crew to humble farmer." Prescott wagged his head. "You are a pitiful fellow."

"You will not endear your brother to us with name-calling." Father spoke through a clenched jaw before his dark eyes slid to Mac. "Please consider my request as a personal favor to me."

Icy dread crashed over Mac. He didn't expect his brother and father to understand his decision. But what he'd experienced at sea during the war, he would never forget, and he longed to put his past behind him.

"You can do both, you know?" Father stood in the center of the richly paneled room and sipped his brandy. "Captain a ship and farm your land in the Shenandoah Valley. Why not?"

"But why would I take a chance of being impressed again? The war with Napoleon may have ended, but Britain still claims the right of impressments if necessary, and they consider any captured merchant vessels their prizes. Spoils of war."

"The war with England is over too, son." Father moved back to his seat behind his desk.

"Not to the British." Mac knew that firsthand. Taylor Osborn, after all, was a captain in the Royal British Navy. "Americans are still viewed as traitors to the Crown."

"Perhaps you have another suggestion." Prescott's voice beheld an unmistakable edge.

"I haven't got a single idea." Mac hated the way his father's shoulders slumped forward as if in defeat.

A sturdy *rap-tap-tap* behind the mahogany door drew Mac's attention. "Enter," Father called.

The door opened, revealing Pearl's dour face. "Someone to see Captain Mac," she growled.

Mac stood and stepped forward, wondering if his guest was Blake, Silas Everett, or even the boys. He'd given them his parents' address.

A solid figure dressed in blue walked out of the shadows and into the study.

"Taylor Osborn. Well, blow me down." Mac chuckled and hurried to greet his old friend. "I was only minutes ago thinking about you."

They clasped hands.

"Mr. Blake told me you were back in Alexandria." Taylor's weather-lined face crinkled with his smile. "I just had to come by and say hello."

Mac turned to his father and brother. "I trust you remember Captain Osborn."

"Yes, of course, come in." Father shook Taylor's hand.

Prescott gave only an acknowledging nod.

Mac supposed his brother was entitled to wariness. Taylor was a Brit, after all, and the war's end hadn't stopped Americans from remembering the conflict. Taylor, on the other hand, had been granted immunity from any charges stemming from the war in exchange for his testimony in court. He'd sworn to Mac's and Blake's impressments into the Royal British Navy and had gone on to describe England's perspective of the conflict. Simply, its intent was twofold; to prevent America's trade with France and to keep America from overtaking Canada.

Taylor accepted the snifter of golden liquid from Father, who, clearly, didn't hold a grudge.

"What are you doing back on American soil?" For the first time Mac noticed that, although he was dressed in blue, Taylor wasn't wearing his military uniform. "Are you here incognito?"

"Hardly."

Taylor's rumbles of laughter brought back fond memories to Mac. He and Blake had gone from abused prisoners to respected guests aboard the *HMS Victorious*, and, yes, at times they'd lent helping hands to the crew. They took up arms against pirates—and, yes, Americans.

*God forgive me. All I could think of was saving myself. . .*

"As it happens, I've been honorably discharged."

Mac snapped back to the conversation at hand.

"My military exploits are over." Taylor fingered his thick brown mustache. "Now I find myself rather persuaded by the American experience, thanks to you and Blake, and I'm looking for a business endeavor."

"Are you?" Mac couldn't believe his ears. Another miracle. If he hadn't been persuaded of God's existence days ago when Lily battled for her life, he would be convinced now.

"Father? Prescott?" He placed a hand on Taylor's shoulder. "Say hello to Albright Shipping's real salvation."

Chapter Twenty-One

*L*ily smiled and waved to Mr. Martin as he drove his wagon down Mac's creekside pathway to the pike. Mac's cabin now boasted of three chairs and a large, round table.

From her place on the wagon bench, she turned to Issie, who bounced baby Amanda in her arms. "I'd never set eyes on this cabin until two days ago," she said. Even so, she hadn't yet seen the inside of it. She had only been moving about without pain for a few days.

"The captain intends for it to be a future bunkhouse for hired hands." Issie spoke with confidence. "But he'll reside in it this winter. Wouldn't you like to have a look around inside?"

"No, thank you." It meant crossing a grassy lane. "I've wondered about Mac's intentions for the near future." In fact, for the better part of two weeks, pondering was about all Lily managed to do as she recovered from her snakebite. The fever had returned the day after Mac, Mr. Blake, and the boys left Middletown, but it disappeared by the next day and, though the pain in her arm was better, it still required a sling. "James's donation idea is a good one."

Issie bobbed her head, and the rim of her bonnet rippled like a soft current. "I thought so too. And if each of our church families gives one piece of furniture, the captain will have his winter home completely furnished. By spring, he'll be building Fairview, his impressive manor on the hill."

"You know of his building plans?" Lily tipped her head.

"Oh, yes." Issie pushed the bonnet up off her forehead, and her hazel eyes danced when they met with sparkles of sunshine. "He was taking supper with James and me quite often, and we became very well acquainted. Of course, James was helping the captain build his barn and all. Talk of building was their favorite topic at the table."

"It's a beautiful barn, indeed." The entire yard was evidence of Mac's tireless efforts. The grass and weeds had been cut or cleared, and sturdy snake-rail fences enclosed various pens and corrals. "I've never seen the barnyard look so well groomed. Papa would be impressed, I think."

"I think so too." Issie smiled. "James promised to come over and look after the mules in the captain's absence. That's when he got the idea for furnishing the cabin." She lifted her shoulders and giggled. "Won't the captain be surprised?"

"I'm sure he will be." Lily felt a little left out of Mac's life. It seemed her best friend knew more about the man she loved than she did. Then again, Mac had been rudely avoiding her—until the day they kissed in the creek.

Lily hid a secret smile. Her cheeks flamed at the memory. What in the world had she been thinking? Any number of people could have happened upon their disgraceful behavior.

"Are you all right?" Issie leaned closer. "You look a bit feverish again."

"It's nothing." Lily pushed out a smile, hoping it concealed her chagrin. If she and Mac were to have an understanding, then she would insist on propriety at all times.

But was that even possible? Somehow Mac possessed powers that set her common sense askew.

Issie tugged on Lily's left elbow. "If you don't want to tour the cabin, let's sit in the shade by the barn."

"I'd prefer to stay here on the wagon."

Issie tipped her head. "But the sun is withering the flowers in your straw hat."

"The blooms are silk, you goose." Lily rolled her eyes. However, the truth was that she didn't venture far these days and when she did, it was by buggy or wagon. Her horrifying encounter had left her overly cautious, and she avoided walking through meadows or sitting in the grassy shade.

"I promise to chase away any snake that dares to approach us."

Lily swiveled and met Issie's smiling face. "How do you always guess what I'm thinking?"

"I've known you all my life. You're my second best friend."

"Second?" Lily drew back. "Who has taken my first place?"

"Why, James, of course." A knowing little gleam entered Issie's eyes. "And soon I will be replaced as your first best friend."

"No, never." Despite her reply, Lily had a hunch what was coming.

"I'm prepared to hand off my position to a certain former sea captain in whose yard we are sitting."

"Are you, now?" Though Lily feigned insult, a wide smile gave her away. "Well, as a matter of fact, that certain former sea captain and I have an understanding between us." She'd only told Aunt Hilda, who wasn't a bit surprised by the news. She even approved, although she thought a year was too long a wait. Young love must have its way, she'd said, adding that Mr. Everett could inflict much damage in all that time, particularly if he did, indeed, own *Haus am Bach*.

"What sort of an understanding do you and Captain Albright have?" Issie placed Amanda over her shoulder and patted her back.

"An understanding that we'll take time to get to know one another. Exclusively."

"Like a courtship?"

"I suppose so, although he didn't use those exact words."

"I've never heard of such a thing as an understanding. Is it popular in Alexandria?"

"Must be."

Issie adjusted her bonnet. "Sounds like one of those stuffy British formalities."

"Perhaps it is." Lily lowered her chin and traced the pattern of her dress with her forefinger. "I told him I loved him."

Issie gasped. "You barely know him."

"True, but that's the purpose of our understanding—to get to know each other."

Confusion settled on Issie's brow. "Then it's a courtship, you goose."

"Whatever it is, I know what I feel in my heart."

Issie smiled. "Then it must be love."

Lily leaned closer. "I never felt this way, Issie. Not even about Oliver Ashton."

Issie churned out a groan. "Why must you always bring up that man's name?"

"For a comparison, is all." Lily hurled a glance toward the azure sky.

Issie pursed her lips and narrowed her gaze. "I don't believe you really love the captain."

"What?" Surely Lily hadn't heard her friend correctly. "I know how I feel."

"Prove your love then."

Lily rose to the challenge, her chin held high. "What would you have me do?"

"Climb down from this wagon and walk to yonder shady spot." Issie pointed toward the barn.

"But I saw a black snake there." Even as she spoke the last word, the recollection of being held in Mac's strong arms overshadowed the reptile sighting.

"You cannot be a farmer's wife if you're frightened of harmless black racers or rat snakes. Now, climb down, Lily." Issie's voice took on a pleading note. "The sun is baking me, and I must think of my child. It's not good for Amanda to get a sunburn."

"No, of course not." Still, Lily hesitated, surveying the yard for the slightest movement in the short grass.

"I'll go first." Issie set the baby in Lily's lap.

Lily held Amanda fast with her left arm while Issie climbed down. Scooting carefully to the edge of the bench, she leaned over so Issie could reclaim her precious bundle.

"Your turn."

Even with one arm in a sling, Lily easily made her descent off the wagon. It was hardly a foreign activity, and yet it left her feeling slightly dizzy.

"First, you must tour the captain's cabin."

"Well..." Fingers of trepidation slithered down Lily's spine. She glanced at the wagon.

"Stop fretting. We will be fine."

Issie led Lily along like a second child. They tramped across the grassy area. Not a single reptile in sight. They reached the cabin and stepped up to what resembled the beginnings of a front porch.

Issie opened the door and waved Lily inside. The scent of hand-hewn wood and tar filled the place. A stone hearth occupied the wall at the far end of the L-shaped cabin. Off the one main room was a bedroom.

"Mrs. Butterworth donated her late husband's bed. As you know, he fell while hunting last November."

"Yes, I recall the accident. It happened just before Papa died."

"And, look. . .she made it up with linen sheets and a quilt." Issie sat on the edge of the bed and bounced. "Comfortable."

Lily rolled her eyes at her friend's antics. "Some folks never grow up."

Issie rolled out her bottom lip, feigning a pout.

"It's easy to see where Amanda gets her good looks." Smiling, Lily walked back into the single sitting room, wondering where Mac intended to cook his meals. In the hearth most likely. Would he want his table and chairs on that end, or would he prefer them on the other side? She tapped her chin with her forefinger in indecision. If Mac placed the table and chairs by the hearth, then he'd forfeit places near the fire to sit and read on cold, snowy days. But if he placed the table and chairs near the entrance to the bedroom, he would have room enough to invite guests for supper. . .

Would Mac have guests? He didn't seem the type. However, if he had a wife, she might invite folks, and they'd all sit down and eat and talk.

"Are you decorating Mac's cabin in your mind?" Issie grinned.

"No." Lily considered her petite friend and decided to shock her. "I'm imagining myself as mistress of this cabin."

Issie's eyes grew wide, and Amanda squawked. "Why, Lilyanna Laughlin, you're as forward as Cynthia Clydesdale."

"Except, unlike Cynthia, Captain Albright and I have an understanding."

"Indeed." Issie cradled the baby and tickled her tummy. Amanda giggled.

"And he kissed me."

Issie's mouth fell open. Her eyes grew as wide as one of Papa's silver coins. Lily held her head high. There. She'd gotten the best of her friend at last.

This time.

James shadowed the open entrance before stepping inside the cabin. He removed his hat then used his sleeve to wipe the perspiration off his brow. "I thought I saw you two walk in here." He turned to Lily. "So what do you think?"

"It's very cozy." She moved to the corner of the cabin near the hearth. "I think Papa's writing desk would look just fine here. It will be my donation."

"Lily, you'd give away your father's desk?" Issie's russet brows knit together. "Are you sure that's wise?"

She nodded. "Papa would want Mac to have it." Dare she shock her friends with another admission? "And it's not like I'll never see it again. I hope to marry Mac one day."

James broke out in a hearty laugh that hurt Lily's feelings.

"How dare you laugh at me like that, James Hawkins."

"I'm not laughing at you, Lil. I'm laughing at Mac." Another chuckle. "He sure did try to fight his feelings for you. He gave up the day after that snake bit you. He said God was the only hope, and the two of us knelt down in the barn and prayed together."

"You never said a word." Issie approached James, who gave a shrug.

"It was a personal matter, dearest."

"Oh, I suppose it was." Issie huffed anyhow, and Lily smiled.

"Besides, Mac's feelings for Lily wasn't my news to tell." James flicked a glance at Lily. "But now that the secret is out, I can say it."

"Lily says she and the captain have *an understanding*." Issie inclined her head toward Lily.

James shrugged. "Courtship, eh?" He dipped his chin in approval.

"Mac says I'll change my mind when I find out more about him, but he's wrong."

"There's always a chance, I suppose." James raked his hand through his sandy-brown hair.

"No, I will always love him." Lily ran her fingertips along the tabletop. "Even if it means living in this cabin for the rest of my days. As long as I'm with Mac, it will feel like home."

"And he kissed her, James." Issie appeared almost indignant over the matter.

"Issie!" Lily felt a blush work its way up her neck and into her hairline.

"I'd say a kiss makes the courtship official," James remarked, seemingly unaffected. "I know that's what Mac wanted."

"He told you?" Now it was Lily's turn to be surprised.

"Not in so many words. We men have our own way of expressing ourselves. But I can say this. Mac is captivated by you, Lily, so don't ever assume he doesn't care about you. He does."

"The feeling is mutual." A thrill passed through Lily.

"But, for now, we'll get you back home and into bed." James pressed his hat onto his head. His brown hair peeped out from beneath it. "You look feverish again."

"I'm fine."

James lifted Amanda from Issie's arms. "Help Lil to the wagon, will you, Issie?"

"Of course. But I think she's more lovesick than sick."

Lily smiled and stared down at the cabin's plank wood floor. She was impressed by Mac's hard work and found the cabin a little retreat from the busy manor, although with the boys gone, there wasn't much commotion. Lily sent up a quick prayer for her brothers' safety. Were they behaving themselves?

At the wagon, James helped Issie up, then passed her the baby. He next assisted Lily up to the bench before climbing into the driver's seat and taking up the reins.

"Everyone ready?"

"We're set." Issie exchanged glances with Lily. "Are you all right?"

"I think so, but I'm suddenly exhausted."

"We'll get you home right quick," James said, snapping the reins above his horses' behinds.

The wagon jerked forward, and soon the sound of the horses' hooves and jangling harnesses filled the air. Lily took a last glance at Mac's barn, yard, and cabin. Pride swelled in her chest and somehow reassured her of any doubts that Mac would settle here in the valley. Soon he'd be back from Alexandria—and she couldn't wait to see him again.

❤

Mac surveyed his brother's tobacco plantation as he drove the carriage up the drive. Impressive. No other word came close to describing it. The mansion was of red brick and boasted twin two-story white pillars and a wraparound veranda. However, the black men and women slaving in the surrounding fields despite the humid air and hot sun looked more like raisins than human beings. The sight prompted Mac to do something about it—but what?

He pulled on the reins and the horses halted at the top of a wide, circular drive. His parents alighted from the buggy, Father helping Mother down. Mac jumped from his perch and tied the reins to the carved iron hitching post.

"I know what this dinner is all about," Father grumbled. "Your brother has a notion that Mother and I will move into this ostentatious manor with him and Gwyneth."

"I must admit"—Mac said, climbing the stairs to the veranda—"the idea did cross my mind." He'd had an entire week to contemplate Albright Shipping's fate. He'd been at the dock twice to assist Taylor with securing a crew, and he'd rolled up his sleeves with the best of them to clean up the spill in *Ariel's* hold.

"I must be near my business," Father grumbled. "Things can change like that"—he snapped his fingers—"and I must be able to reach the wharves within minutes."

"Ah, yes, but that's Peter Canfield's job." As operations manager, Mr. Canfield was awarded an apartment in town free of rent and brought in a nice salary—yet another expense, but Mac supposed a necessary one. "Allow him to perform his duties."

"But I must supervise."

Mother churned out an exasperated sigh and gave the brass front doorknocker a few hard raps. "Can we please enjoy this dinner without the shadow of Albright Shipping looming over us for once?"

Mac exchanged glances with his father. At times Mother forgot that Albright Shipping was the family's bread and butter, so to speak.

The door opened wide, and a plump, dark-skinned woman wearing a black dress and white apron appeared in the entryway.

"We're the Albrights and are expected for dinner." Father pulled back his shoulders and tugged on his black frockcoat.

"Yes, sir." The woman opened the door wider and collected Mother's shawl and the men's hats, hanging them reverently on the hall tree. "I'll let the missus know yous arrived."

She hurried off.

Father leaned close to Mother. "Now, see there, Olivia? That Negress is an apt maid. Surely one of Prescott's slaves will make us a fine cook."

The muscles between Mac's shoulder blades wound tight. "Slaves are not the answer," he said to his parents. "We'll find you a cook. Someone, perhaps, willing to work for room and board."

"Well, I suppose. . . ?" Mother jerked her chin.

Gwyneth sashayed into the foyer wearing an ivory gown and sapphire shawl. Her complexion was reminiscent of freshly-fallen snow, and her eyes were so bright a blue they were nearly translucent.

She dipped a curtsy. "Welcome." She held her hand out to Mac and he placed a perfunctory kiss upon it. "How good to see you again, brother dear."

Mac smiled. "My pleasure entirely."

Gwyneth greeted his parents and then turned to the woman directly behind her. Mac hadn't noticed her until now.

"Allow me to present my sister, Miss Samantha Eden. She's visiting us for the week."

Irritation reared up inside of Mac. A trap, and he'd sailed right into it. He should have been wary at the onset of this dubious dinner invitation.

He did his best to conceal his annoyance and gave the curvy woman with bark-brown hair a courteous bow. "Miss Eden."

She curtsied. "Captain." Her voice mimicked sandpaper over rough wood, and her small eyes resembled two nail heads. "I've heard much about you."

He pushed out a smile.

"Please, let's sit in the parlor." Gwyneth led the way. "Dinner will be in an hour, but I expect Prescott and Captain Osborn any time now."

Mac was glad to hear Taylor would be in attendance.

"But Mother Albright and I decided there will be no discussion of business at the dinner table." Gwyneth gave Mac a pointed look.

"As you wish." He almost chuckled aloud. It wouldn't be he who brought up business, and Gwyneth may have a difficult time hushing her husband and father-in-law.

Miss Eden stepped in beside Mac. "You're quite infamous in most

Alexandria circles, you know."

"I thought by now the tongue waggers would have found new morsels to nibble on."

"Indeed they have, but none have been as scrumptious as the traitor pirate, Captain Albright."

Oddly, her amused tone put Mac at ease.

She swung around and blocked his entrance to the parlor. "You are as devilishly handsome as I've heard, but know this, I will not marry you nor any other man for that matter, especially one in need of my dowry."

A grin pulled at the corner of Mac's mouth. "You can't imagine how relieved I am to hear it, Miss Eden. You see, I have entered into an understanding with another young lady, and not even your dowry can tempt me hither."

Her gaze narrowed. "Not even if it means rescuing your family's business and restoring the Albright name?"

"Not even then." Mac locked his hands behind his back. "I believe there are other ways of accomplishing those goals." He gave his opulent surroundings a sweeping gaze. "Downsizing may be an option." Prescott was, after all, the one who ran Albright Shipping aground.

"My thoughts exactly!" Miss Eden's features brightened and she appeared almost pretty.

Mac smiled. Perhaps this evening wouldn't prove torturous after all. He lifted his hand, indicating the room that seemed to have swallowed up the rest of their family members. "Shall we?"

Chapter Twenty-Two

*A* word, Mac?"

At Taylor's nod toward the veranda, Mac followed him through the open French doors and into the cool evening air. "What is it?"

Taylor seemed somewhat breathless and notably distracted ever since he'd walked into the house minutes ago.

"Blake said he saw a gentleman by the name of Everett at the wharves with two lads. Blake said you'd know to whom I referred."

"Yes, I do."

"Evidently, Everett indentured the boys."

"What?" Mac straightened. "Indentured?"

"Blake claims to have overheard the deal go down between Everett and Captain Curt O'Malley. Blake seemed quite frantic about getting the news to you. I promised to relay it immediately."

"Madman O'Malley?" Mac rubbed his fingers against his jaw. While a decent fellow, O'Malley earned the moniker at the gaming tables, where he placed outrageous bets that he never seemed to lose. "And the boys were indentured to him? For what purpose? Money?"

"I don't believe so. It wasn't a monetary exchange, according to Blake. Everett said he just could no longer afford to care for the two lads."

"More's the truth that Jonah and Jed were in Everett's way." And their absence left Lily vulnerable. As for the boys. . .

"Has O'Malley set sail?"

Taylor shook his head. "First thing in the morning."

Mac's mind raced to find a solution. "I've got to get those boys back."

"Then let's go."

Turning, Mac saw that Prescott had arrived. Dinner would be served within minutes.

"After dinner?" Taylor suggested. "The lads are in no imminent danger, and perhaps we'll be more inspired with full bellies."

Mac felt as edgy as a thoroughbred at the racing gate. Sitting at the dinner table would be torturous. Besides, there were business matters for Taylor, Prescott, and Father to iron out, despite the ladies' request not to discuss Albright Shipping.

"You stay, Taylor. Enjoy the evening and get better acquainted with my family. You are, after all, in the throes of deciding whether to work for my father and brother."

"Oh, I've made my decision." Taylor gazed out across the yard, no doubt admiring the well-groomed lawn and garden.

"And?"

"And I've got a business proposal for them." Taylor gave Mac a side glance. "I want to buy into the company and become a co-owner."

Mac mulled it over. Certainly the buy-in would help Albright Shipping's financial concerns. "Then it's crucial that you stay here. I'll go to the wharves and speak with O'Malley."

Taylor inclined his head. "If you feel the need for assistance, Mr. Blake is at the Sunken Vessel Tavern."

*Figures.*

"He's got reason to celebrate." A slow smile spread across Taylor's face.

"I suppose I should inquire as to the reason."

"Blake has agreed to be my first mate on my maiden voyage as captain of the merchant ship *Ariel*."

"An excellent choice. Blake won't disappoint."

"Oh, I'm aware of that." Taylor tucked errant strands of brown hair behind one ear as they didn't quite reach his queue. "I'm also in need of a cook, and Blake mentioned a woman—a German woman with whom he's half out of his mind in love."

"The widow Mrs. Gunther." Mac chuckled. "Yes, Blake is besotted."

"But can she cook? Is she capable of delivering a meal to the masses?"

"Yes on both accounts." Mac leaned against the railing. He had already put the pieces together. Blake and Mrs. Gunther—soon to be Mrs. Blake—sailing off into the sunset, happily ever after. "One of the first things Blake and I learned about her is she enjoys cooking for hungry men."

"That's all I need to hear." Taylor sported a crooked smile. "Blake said you'd give a good reference."

"Indeed, I will vouch for the woman's capabilities in the kitchen, and once she learns her way around a galley, she will impress your crew with her skills."

"Good to know."

Mac inhaled the fragrant air, a mix of drying grasses, tobacco, and late-blooming flowers.

"I've given Blake two weeks to fetch the lady. We'll have a chaplain on board, as usual, and he can perform the marriage ceremony."

Mac smiled, recalling his friend's superstition about never sailing without a man of God aboard. And Mac had to admit, there were times the chaplain's words were downright comforting, not to mention inspirational.

"Besides, it'll take me at least that long to finish cleaning the hold and ready *Ariel* for our voyage."

Mac mulled over the timetable. The trip was doable for Blake, although Mrs. Gunther's absence left Lily alone in the manor, and that caused an uneasiness to seep into his bones.

Although, Lily claimed to know how to use that pistol she first waved at Blake and him.

The memory of their initial meeting tempted Mac to grin, and he would if he weren't so troubled over Jonah and Jed's indentation.

"If I take my leave, will you make my excuses to my family?" Mac imagined he'd get tangled in Mother's and Gwyneth's disappointment and complaints and never get out of the house.

"Certainly."

After a friendly rap between his friend's shoulder blades, Mac descended the brick stairs from the veranda and made his way around the mansion to the horses and buggy still hitched to the post. Within minutes, he was on his way to the riverfront.

His played out several scenarios in his mind, keeping the fact that O'Malley enjoyed a gamble in the forefront. How badly did O'Malley want to keep Jonah and Jed aboard? What if he refused to release them? Lily would be heartbroken—no, worse than heartbroken. She'd be devastated.

Anger surged though Mac, tensing every muscle in his body. Everett, that devil's spawn. What had he done?

Mac flicked the reins, urging the horses into a faster gait. The last of the sun made a glorious exit in the western sky while darkness hungrily gobbled up the remaining daylight. By the time he reached the wharves, night had settled, bringing cooler air. Fog hovered over the Potomac.

Mac pulled the team to a halt near the Sunken Vessel Tavern and climbed from the buggy. The smell of fish, rum, and every kind of waste permeated the air. He tossed a coin to the guard standing over tavern patrons' mounts and vehicles. Making his way down the walk, the heels of his boots kept time with the beat of a bawdy tune hailing from the place. If he wasn't mistaken, that was Blake's squeeze-box in the background.

Mac entered through the establishment's open doors. He glanced over the heads of male customers. Several of them leaned against the bar and eyed him with wary expressions. Others played cards at a nearby table.

Walking farther into the place, Mac strained to see through plumes of smoke. When he spotted Blake, off to the right, singing at the top of his lungs, he headed toward him.

Blake's gaze landed on him a couple of times before the old man paused. "Am I hallucinating or do I see my best friend, standing before my eyes in a dump like this?"

Mac moved to the door and motioned for Blake to follow him.

Blake did so, instrument in hand. "Glad you got m' message, Cap'n."

"Yes. Thanks for it, but I need your help. Point me toward O'Malley's ship."

Blake pointed down the dock. "He's aboard the *Sarabella*. I was there just today inquirin' about a job. That's when I learned Everett's rotten plan and bumped into our ol' pal Cap'n Osborn. He's the one who gave me work."

"Yes, I heard." Mac tamped down his impatience. "I understand you're to be his first mate. Congratulations."

"Aye, thank you." Blake squared his shoulders. "And at dawn, I'm off to claim m' bride and get back in time to set sail."

"Good for you. I hope Mrs. Gunther agrees to cook for an entire crew."

"Oh, she will. I got that feelin' in m' bones."

Mac clapped him on the shoulder and started toward O'Malley's ship.

"Wait, Cap'n. I'm coming with you in case there's trouble."

Mac waited while Blake stashed his squeeze-box behind the bar and under the tavern owner's watchful eye. Then they traipsed down the dock. At last they came upon the *Sarabella*. Her masts stretched upward and disappeared in the fog. Lanterns glowed both near the hull and on deck. Sailors rolled large barrels of supplies or cargo up the gangway beneath a slew of orders, shouted from the supervisor on the dock.

A brief inquiry revealed that the sailor in charge was the boatswain, a man named Mr. Darby. He informed Mac and Blake that O'Malley was not abed for the night and gave them permission to board.

"Ahoy, Captain Albright and Mr. Blake!" Jonah's unmistakable voice cut through the fog. The boy jumped off a tower of thick rope. "What brings you aboard tonight?"

"Sounds like a reg'lar seaman, he does." Blake turned to Mac with an amused grin. "And he don't look no worse for wear."

"No, he doesn't." Mac gave the boy a once-over and glimpsed Jed standing in the shadows. "Come on out, Jed."

"He's scared," Jonah said.

"No, I'm not!" Jed stepped forward. "See?" He walked out of the shadows and tripped over a piece of rope.

"He hasn't found his sea legs yet." Jonah set his feet apart and placed his hands on his hips as if he were an experienced deckhand.

"Mr. Everett blundered terribly when he indentured you boys." Mac looked from one to the other. "But Blake and I are about to speak to Captain O'Malley about the situation."

"But I want to stay on board and be a sailor." A pleading note rang in Jonah's voice. "It's what I was born to do."

"Me too," Jed said, standing beside his brother.

Blake chuckled, and Mac quirked a smile.

"Maybe. When you're older," Mac said. "For now you belong in school. Besides, your sister will be upset by your absences. What have you to say about that?"

"I say that with the money Jed and me can send to her, Lily won't have to marry dumb ol' Mr. Everett."

"I'm afraid you've got this all wrong. Being indentured means hard work, and you'll have to obey the captain or face painful consequences. There's no pay involved."

"Slavery is what it is," Blake added.

"But Captain O'Malley told us we'd be treated well if we didn't cause trouble," Jonah said, "and we might earn a few coins if our shipment arrives in the West Indies on time. I'll save every coin I get for Lily."

"Me too," Jed parroted.

"That's very noble of you boys."

"But being indentured is a serious matter. I'm afraid I must speak to Captain O'Malley about this. . .arrangement."

The boys hung their heads but didn't argue.

Mac chided himself for not suspecting foul play sooner.

Blake stayed with the boys while Mac asked a passing sailor the whereabouts of the captain's quarters. Getting his answer, he grabbed a lighted lantern and descended the ladder.

At the pungent smell of tar, memories flooded in, reminding Mac of all the reasons he gave up his life as a sea captain. The dank smell of the effects of the salty seawater on wood filled his nose and made him long for his sweet-smelling orchards and the fertile land of the Shenandoah Valley.

And Lily's lovely face.

He arrived at O'Malley's cabin and rapped several times on the door.

"Enter!"

Mac walked in and O'Malley gave him a moment's glance, then looked up again after recognition set in. A wide smile inched across the older man's face.

"Well, well, if it's not my ol' friend, the infamous Captain McAlister Albright." He rose from his chair, situated behind his desk, and chuckled. "To what do I owe this unexpected pleasure?" He narrowed his gaze and pointed his finger at Mac. "You'll not tempt me with a card game or suggestion of a chess match. I can't be persuaded. I set sail in the morning, as soon as the fog lifts."

*Chess.* . . Mac recalled Lily's quick win the day they met and an idea began to form.

"State your business, Captain Albright."

Mac squared his shoulders. "It's about the two indentured boys." He planted his feet firmly apart and clasped his hands behind his back.

O'Malley's features lost all traces of hospitableness. "What about them?"

"What will you accept as a trade for them? They were wrongly indentured, and I want them back."

"Can't have 'em." O'Malley walked around his oak desk. Maps covered its surface. "I need a cabin boy, and the eldest of the two will do nicely in that position. The younger one"—O'Malley shrugged—"he's small enough to clean cannon, and he'll learn to climb the ratlines and be a lookout in the crow's nest if nothing else."

Mac forced himself not to cringe. A fall from the crow's nest meant certain death. Jed wasn't up for that task.

"About that chess match. . ." Mac spotted a leather case across the room which looked similar to others which harbored chessboards and game pieces.

"I said I won't be persuaded. I have work to do."

Mac crossed the room and lifted the case, and, despite his earlier resolve, O'Malley stared at it like a drunk in need of a bottle of brandy.

"Come now, O'Malley. What's one game between old friends? I've got nothing better to do tonight." Mac moved to the long table and opened the rectangular box. His suspicions were confirmed.

"No chess game, Albright. And you'll not get those boys either." O'Malley sat on the corner of his desk and folded his arms over his wide chest. His face was a combination of stony planes and angles, and his mouth curled as if fixed in a permanent sneer. Even so, his gaze never left the chess pieces that Mac went ahead and set up on the board. O'Malley appeared transfixed.

"If you win," Mac said, "I'll give you two of my experienced crewmen, handpicked by Captain Taylor Osborn. Then, of course, you keep the boys too."

"Handpicked, you say?" O'Malley worked his thick tongue between his lips as if thirsting for the competition.

"Handpicked, and you know how fussy Taylor is about his crew."

"I know..."

"And if I win, I get the two indentured lads."

A slow smile worked its way across O'Malley's weathered face. "If I win, I get you as my first mate, two of Osborn's finest deckhands, plus the two lads."

Mac opened his mouth to protest, but O'Malley raised his hand, palm side out.

"I'll not have it any other way, Albright. I'll give you two minutes to decide."

Two minutes? He didn't even need two seconds. If Mac lost Jed and Jonah to this indenture it could ruin those boys' lives forever or get them killed. What's more, Mac might lose Lily's affection.

But he wouldn't fail this time. He couldn't. The stakes were far too great.

Another kink in his well-laid plans. But hadn't he recently witnessed a miracle? Surely God was in control of this situation too.

"I accept your terms, O'Malley."

The old captain laughed and rubbed his palms together. "Then let's get to it!"

Mac took a seat at the table while O'Malley grabbed two glasses and a bottle of rum. He then poured them both a swallow and set the bottle within an arm's reach.

"Since it's my ship," O'Malley began, "I lay stake to the white pieces, and I'll make the first move."

"As you wish."

O'Malley moved a pawn out two spaces.

Mac slid his pawn opposite O'Malley's.

O'Malley moved another pawn.

Mac slid a pawn forward. He rubbed his jaw, never taking his eyes off the board.

A laugh bubbled out of O'Malley as he brought up his knight and poured more rum into his glass.

Mac studied the board, considering his next move. He recalled Lily's remark about leaving his royalty unguarded. She'd believed him a patriot from the start.

And, by heaven, he was an American patriot!

*Lord, I just have to win.* Thoughts of losing the boys and Lily plus returning to sea paralyzed him. Perspiration tickled his temples.

O'Malley took another swallow of rum. "I'm about the best chess player on the high seas."

Mac gave a grunt of acknowledgment and continued eyeing the chess pieces.

"Move, already!"

Mac complied. If his opponent was as good as he claimed, he'd already lost. . .

*Lord, please. . .I simply must win!*

"Don't tell me you're not an expert chess player."

"Expert?" Mac lifted a shoulder, then decided to be honest. "No, no, I'm not an expert by any stretch of the imagination." He rubbed the back of his damp neck and shrugged out of his jacket.

"Gettin' worked up, are you?" O'Malley's booming laugh filled the cabin. He made his move, then leaned over the chessboard. "Tell you what, Albright. If you win this game, I'll give you my ship."

Mac narrowed his gaze. The man wasn't called Madman O'Malley for no reason.

O'Malley refilled his glass. "So what do you say?"

The offer blew over Mac's head like an ocean breeze. All he wanted was the boys—and a chance to return to the Shenandoah Valley.

"Do we sweeten the pot or not?"

"Yes, sure. . ." Mac rubbed his jaw again, and the biblical account of David and Goliath flashed across his memory. He'd heard the Bible story as a child and then again throughout his formal Christian education.

*Lord, O'Malley is my Goliath. . . .*

Another gulp of rum. "Quit stalling and make your move."

"Patience, my friend." Mac moved his bishop.

O'Malley captured one of Mac's pawns.

The temperature in the cabin seemed to escalate with each passing minute.

And then. . .

"Checkmate!"

"What?" Snarling, O'Malley examined the board. "It can't be."

Relief spread through Mac's entire body. Another miracle.

O'Malley pounded his fist on the table. "You insufferable blackguard, get off my ship!"

"I believe *Sarabella* is now my ship." Mac stood.

O'Malley pushed to his feet so fast he knocked over his chair. He punched the air with both fists.

"But I'll tell you what I'll do, seeing that we're old friends. I'll forfeit ownership of *Sarabella*, but I will take the lads."

O'Malley's rage-contorted features regained a measure of normalcy. "Collect them and go."

"Fine. And I'll take any paperwork that goes with the boys, too." Mac placed his hands on his hips.

O'Malley grumbled and stomped over to his desk.

Minutes later, with a smile on his lips and spring in his step, Mac left the captain's quarters. He climbed to the first deck and found the Laughlin boys sitting beside Blake's sleeping form. Jonah and Jed would be his guests while Mac perused the contents of their indentation papers and consulted his family's solicitor. If the papers were straightforward enough, perhaps the boys could ride back to Middletown with Blake tomorrow.

"Good news, fellows." He set down the lamp and gave Blake's boot a kick.

The seasoned sailor grumbled and muttered, then clambered to his feet.

The boys broke into laughter at the sight.

"How'd it go, Cap'n?" Blake rubbed his eyes.

"Yeah, Captain Albright." Jonah moved forward. "Do I get to sail?"

"We'll have that discussion later. For now, you're coming with me to my parents' home. You'll be my guests while I study the arrangement Mr. Everett made with Captain O'Malley."

"But—" Jonah looked ready to stand his ground.

"Show me you're ready to sail by obeying your captain. I am now in possession of your indentation papers."

Jonah backed down.

"Good news, Cap'n." Blake smacked him on the back, nearly causing Mac to lose his balance.

"Go gather your things. Hurry up. Mr. Blake and I will wait here."

"Aye, sir." Jonah shuffled off like a pup with his tail between his legs. Jed followed, running ahead of his older brother.

Mac breathed easier, although he wouldn't relax altogether until he got the boys safely to his folks' home and read the documents. The boys' future still hung in the balance. However, if the indentation was impossible to break free of, there was a chance that Taylor could use a cabin boy and swabbie.

Mac, of course, hoped for the former—prayed for it. For Lily's sake.

## Chapter Twenty-Three

*M*ac offered his arm to Miss Eden, and she slipped her gloved hand around his elbow.

"This is getting to be routine, Captain Albright, but I appreciate the escort."

"My pleasure." Something about the woman's hoarse voice raised the compulsion in Mac to clear his throat. Oddly, Taylor found the scratchy sound part of Miss Eden's charm. He'd fallen for the woman nearly a week ago, the night Mac left the dinner party to rescue the Laughlin boys.

Unfortunately, he hadn't been able to save them from indentation. The Albright family solicitor pronounced the documents unalterable, as the court retained a copy along with Everett and O'Malley. The lawyer petitioned the court for a transfer of deed and received it. However, it was all the magistrate would allow. The boys would remain bondservants of a sea captain, as Everett claimed the boys refused to attend school—and the boys confirmed it. But at least their education was now in Taylor Osborn's capable hands. Taylor promised to "torture" the boys with books and mathematical problems during their voyage. Those two rascals would likely receive the education of a lifetime, seeing the world aboard a merchant vessel. Consequently, it would be two years before Jonah and Jed saw their home in Middletown again.

But how to break the news to Lily. . .

"Alexandria will soon be abuzz with rumors, you know."

Miss Eden's raspy voice pulled Mac from his muse.

"Especially since my sister mentioned her idea of a match between you and me to certain tongue waggers."

"I care not about this city's rumor mill, although I wouldn't want you to compromise your reputation by being seen in my company."

"Oh, pshaw! I delight in being the topic of gossip." Miss Eden lifted her bonneted head high, revealing the wide beige ribbon beneath her chin.

Mac gave in to a small grin. However, his thoughts were still on Lily. While he was certain that the boys would be safe, his heart crimped to think she'd be upset by the news of their indentation.

"I can't wait for news to make it up the ranks that I board a vessel each day and take lunch with a retired British sea captain in his private quarters."

Again, Mac pulled himself to the present. "Take care, Miss Eden. A good name is hard to revive once it's been dragged through a pigsty of backbiting."

She shrugged off the warning. "I understand you'll be leaving us shortly and taking twenty of Prescott's slaves with you."

"Yes. While I disagree with many of Thomas Jefferson's writings, I find much reason in his philosophy of gradual emancipation."

"What do you mean?" Miss Eden gazed up at him with a curious frown that added years to her young age.

"I believe in teaching slaves to read and write along with teaching them skilled trades so that when they are manumitted by deed, they can become productive citizens who are able to care for themselves." Similar to Jonah and Jed's situation, although the boys were never slaves.

"And you plan to manumit your brother's property."

"They were Prescott's gifts to me." Mac despised the way he'd just described human beings. *Gifts.* Surely not! They were men and women, no better or worse than he was. Once his manor was constructed, Mac's hope was that they would see it as not only his shining accomplishment, but theirs too.

When he posed his idea to his *gifts*, it was met with much optimism. Those who wished immediate freedom would get it. Mac refused to keep any man against his will.

"You and I are opposing thinkers, sir." Miss Eden waved to a well-dressed woman across the street. "I believe the British have it correct. Everyone serves a purpose within society according to their rank and file."

"Rank and file?" Mac guffawed, turning a few heads. "I see you have been influenced by Captain Osborn in more ways than one."

"Oh, hush."

Mac pushed out a small smile.

"If you must know, I find the captain's recount of his military detail quite interesting."

"I'm sure." And Taylor's versions never lacked flare and grandeur.

They reached the *Ariel,* and Mac gladly handed Miss Eden over to Taylor, who eagerly received her. The pair strolled aft, their heads close, as if they conspired together.

"Ahoy, Captain Albright." Jed waved from where he stood topside with a mop in hand.

"Swabbing the deck, are you?"

"Aye, sir. Not my favorite of chores."

Mac chuckled. "Any news of Blake's return?"

"Should be any time is what I overheard Captain Osborn say."

Mac nodded. "Carry on."

"Aye, sir."

Jed swung the mop from one side to the other and backed up as he did so. Mac wondered if Lily had heard the news. Had Everett told her? He'd left for Middletown the same day as Blake. In fact they shared the same stagecoach. Surely Lily suspected something was amiss when the man returned home without her brothers.

Gazing toward the cloudless September sky, Mac breathed a prayer that Lily would digest the news without much distress. Was that even possible? And would she feel like Mac failed her? Despite the possibly bright outcome, he felt like he'd failed both Jed and Jonah.

How he wished he were home in the valley now, where he could assure Lily that the Almighty had His hand in the chess game with O'Malley—

Most of all, Mac wished he wholly believed it.

Lily stepped into the kitchen and peeled off her bonnet. After recuperating for the better part of a month, it felt good to be outside in the sunshine, helping Shona and his men bring in the harvest. Shona had fashioned a long "snake stick" for her to swing back and forth in front of her footsteps. If any snake didn't hear her coming, it would be prodded to slither away by a whack of her stick. Now Lily didn't feel so frightened about strolling through the meadow to the orchards.

She crossed the room and inhaled deeply. Aunt Hilda's sweet cinnamony apple brew tantalized her senses. "What are you cooking up, Aunt?"

"A batch of applesauce." Aunt Hilda tasted a sample, then stuck her wooden spoon back into the boiling pot. "Needs another dash of nutmeg."

"You and your nutmeg." Lily smiled. "You put dashes of nutmeg in all your sauces."

"Are you complaining?" Aunt Hilda's gaze tossed out a challenge.

"Hardly, Aunt." Lily took another whiff of the bubbly apple mixture. "I wish I knew how to cook and bake as well as you do."

"I had many years of feeding a husband before I came to live with your family, so chalk up my talent in the kitchen to God's grace and life's experiences."

"You're saying there's hope for me, then?" Lily sent her aunt a coy smile.

"Dearest, there's hope for you—and your brothers too. No reason they shouldn't learn to cook for themselves."

"Now there's a frightening thought," Lily teased. "Jonah and Jed in the kitchen, preparing a meal..."

Aunt Hilda's features scrunched. "Well, maybe there's no hope for those two troublemakers in the kitchen after all."

Lily giggled.

"Ahoy! Anyone home?"

Lily froze at the sound of Mr. Blake's unmistakable boisterous voice. Had Mac returned also?

Aunt Hilda's eyes widened. "John?" She set down her wooden spoon and wiped her hands on her apron as she made for the open doorway. "John Blake, is that you?"

"In the flesh, madam." He stepped in and swept off his hat. Whips of shoulder-length silvery hair flew in all directions, though the majority of it remained tied at his nape. "I've brung good news."

"Is Mac—I mean, Captain Albright with you?"

"Nay, Miss Lily." His gaze flitted to her arm, now free of its sling. "Good to see you up and around. The cap'n will be glad to hear it. But, alas, he'll remain in Alexandria a while longer. Helping his family business find its sea legs again."

"Oh." Disappointment fell over Lily.

However, Mr. Blake's grin never wavered. He took Aunt Hilda's hand. "And it's Albright and Osborn Shipping I'll be working for now. First mate to Cap'n Osborn who's both a friend of mine and who recently became co-owner of Albright Shipping. He walked in and saved the day, you might say. And the cap'n needs a cook, Hilda. Will you be our cook?"

"Cook?" Aunt Hilda withdrew her hand.

"And my wife." Mr. Blake's face reddened. "I forgot that part about you marrying me." He seemed to recover from his blunder, and confidence shone on his tanned features. "We'll see the world together. And you couldn't be part of a better crew than what Cap'n Osborn's puttin' together."

"Marry you? Be a part of a captain's crew?"

Mr. Blake gave a nod. "We'll marry aboard the *Ariel*. Capn' Osborn never sails without a chaplain. Says it's bad luck if he do."

Lily watched the exchange with a mix of horror and delight. What an opportunity for her aunt, and how romantic to be married on a ship's deck in the middle of the ocean. But what a loss for Lily and her brothers.

"What do you say, Hilda? You'll be my bride?"

Lily stepped back, hating to intrude on this private moment.

"Oh, yes, I'll marry you, you old sea biscuit."

The couple embraced and then smooched as if they'd forgotten Lily stood only several feet away. She tried not to stare—or giggle.

Mr. Blake pulled away. "Well, go get packed, woman. The stage what brung me and that maggotpie Everett here leaves for Alexandria at three this afternoon."

"Mr. Everett has returned?" Lily perked up. She wouldn't be completely abandoned, although she wanted to travel to Alexandria and see her aunt get married. "So my brothers are home?"

"Er. . ." Mr. Blake suddenly wore a sheepish look. "No, Miss Lily. But the cap'n, that is Cap'n Albright, gave me clear instructions. He said it's Everett's news to tell."

"News?" Lily's insides did a nervous flip. "Did he pack my brothers off to a boarding school, as he's been threatening?"

"Nay, miss. But I can't say. You must learn it from Everett."

Aunt Hilda huffed. "There'll be no secrets in this family, John, and if you want me to start packing so as I can run off and marry you, then you'll spill the beans—or go without eating them."

Mr. Blake's weathered face seemed to weigh his options. He grimaced as his alternatives pressed in. "It's a kind of boarding, yes."

"Oh, that rat!" Lily stomped her foot.

"Silas Everett needs to tell you the entire story, miss."

"And he will." Lily licked her lips, hating the idea of rattling around this manor alone. "I wish I could go with you and watch you two get married."

Aunt Hilda's shoulders slumped. "It's harvesttime, Lily." She looked at her beloved Mr. Blake. "I can't leave the girl, John. Every year we have a festival where we sell our crops, and that money buys us the little extras we women need."

"Don't be silly, Aunt Hilda." Lily's voice felt faraway, belying what she felt in her heart. She longed to beg her aunt to stay. "Of course you'll go get married, and you both will sail off to a lifetime of happiness." Would she ever see them again? Lily quickly blinked away the emotion gathering in her eyes. "Shona is here. He and his men will help me. I can handle the harvest by myself."

Aunt Hilda tipped her head and arched a brow as if in silent argument.

"Let's get you packed." Lily took hold of her aunt's elbow. "Come. There's no time to waste if you intend to be on that stagecoach."

Mr. Blake lifted a halting hand. "Your friend Mr. Hawkins, the blacksmith, offered the use of his wagon for this auspicious occasion. He wouldn't let me rent one, and I'm too old to carry a woman's trunk to town."

Lily grinned at the image and couldn't resist teasing him. "But you'll carry it to the wagon, won't you?"

"Aye, that I will."

As she led Aunt Hilda from the kitchen, Lily glimpsed the gratitude brimming in Mr. Blake's eyes and it stoked her resolve. She would see the couple off. Indeed, there were never two people more deserving of each other's love than Aunt Hilda and Mr. Blake.

And once the stage pulled away, Lily had every intention of visiting the Stony Inn and discovering what Mr. Everett had done with her brothers!

## Chapter Twenty-Four

With her eyes still moist from a tearful farewell to Aunt Hilda and her future Uncle John, Lily stomped into the Stony Inn. Several pairs of eyes landed on her like probing darts, and she caught a curious look from a dark-skinned woman sweeping the floor, but still she marched on to Mr. Everett's office. She rapped on the door and turned the knob even before the words "come in" met her ears.

"Lily." Mr. Everett stood from his desk chair, his face a mask of surprise. "As you can see, I have returned."

"Yes, I see." She slammed the door, causing Mr. Everett to flinch.

"I planned to come over for supper tonight and check on you and your aunt."

"My aunt is gone."

"Dead?" Concern fell over his aging features. Whether it was genuine, Lily could only guess.

"No, Aunt Hilda is not dead." Lily tried to inject a note of happiness in her tone. "She's on her way to Alexandria with Mr. Blake. They will be married aboard a ship christened *Ariel*." Lily recalled the way Aunt Hilda's eyes lit up as Mr. Blake further described their impending adventure to France. The two barely took note of Lily, sitting in the back seat of the wagon, on their way to town to meet the stagecoach.

"Married, you say?" Mr. Everett wrinkled his nose. "To Blake? How shocking. He never mentioned it during our journey."

Lily jerked her chin and surveyed the paneled room. "If you cared any-thing for my family, you would know that my aunt and Mr. Blake fell in love almost immediately." She stared at Everett and folded her arms. "Now where are my brothers? I understand that you have news for me that only you can share."

"Ah, yes. . ." Everett reclaimed his seat and indicated that Lily should sit in the black leather monstrosity nearby.

She shook her head.

Everett sighed. "Very well. Your brothers, Lily, are hellions. Your father, though a good friend to me, and a man I respected, spoiled those boys—and spoiled you too."

Lily let the insult go while her heart drummed out a frantic beat. "So what did you do to cure my brothers of their waywardness?"

"I contracted. . .tutors."

"In other words, you sent Jonah and Jed to a boarding school?"

"Yes. By now, they're sailing away to unimaginable adventures. I've been guaranteed they will learn to obey without complaint. They'll return home in twenty-four months."

"Two years?" Lily felt sick. "I won't see my brothers for two long years?"

"Yes, and it will be good for both them and you. You're now free to con-centrate on learning to be the genteel lady of the manor."

"Your manor. That you won from my father at the gaming table."

"Now, Lily. . ." His voice held a note of warning. "I have new slaves that arrived from Richmond while I was away. They're learning their places here. Like them, it's time you learned yours."

"As your slave?" She let go of a laugh. "Never!"

"We'll talk more about this tonight. You're emotional and in no condi-tion to carry on a conversation."

"I know your vile plans for me. Mac told me. But I will never marry you. Never!" Lily whirled toward the door.

"Funny you should bring up Captain Albright's name—and in such famil-iarity. While in Alexandria I learned quite a bit about him and his family."

Lily paused, her hand on the iron knob. Standing with her back to Everett, she waited for him to continue.

"His family is bankrupt."

"So? The captain moved here to begin a life of his own."

"And you never pondered why a sea captain would leave behind a good occupation to be a farmer?"

Lily turned to face Everett. "Mac was fed up with the sailing life."

"Did he say why?"

"Yes. Because of the war. He was impressed."

"He is a traitor, Lily." Everett stood. His eyes suddenly resembled cold, hard, creekside pebbles. "The man fought against Americans. The impressment story is just that. A fable." He opened a suede file and removed a document. "Here is proof."

She took it and scanned the newsprint. "This is dated last year and states that Mac was acquitted of all charges of treason."

"Yes, but only because his father swayed the judge with money—money he didn't have. Now Albright Shipping is sinking in debt." Everett chuckled. "Sinking. . .the shipping company."

"I do not find this amusing."

"No, I didn't imagine you would." His smile vanished. "But you may be interested to learn that in order to save his family's business, the captain has asked Miss Samantha Eden to marry him. It's rumored she's worth a goodly sum."

"You make the lady sound like a prized racehorse."

Another wicked-sounding chuckle passed Everett's wormy lips. "Consider this document," he said, sliding another piece of paper toward Lily. "It's a sworn statement made by Mrs. Francis Delacroix, whose husband owns the largest and most prosperous hotel in Alexandria. We've been acquainted for some time, as we share similar businesses."

Lily resisted the desire to roll her eyes. The Stony Inn was a far cry from a luxurious hotel in a thriving city.

"Mrs. Delacroix moves in all the important social circles, and she was told by Mrs. Prescott Albright that the captain would marry her sister in order to relieve the family's debt, brought on by the captain's treasonous acts and the judge's stiff payoff."

"I don't believe you. I don't care who gave a sworn statement, it's still hearsay."

"No, Lily. It's the truth. Captain Albright and Miss Eden have been keeping company. I saw them together the day I boarded the stage for home, walking down King Street, arm in arm."

Lily set her jaw against the jealousy nibbling at her confidence.

"Miss Eden is a handsome woman and, as I said, of considerable wealth."

"I'm glad for her then."

"Doubly glad, hmm? She's betrothed to Captain Albright." Mr. Everett's words stung like a slap.

But they weren't true. "The captain and I have an. . .understanding. In a year's time, when his farm is functioning, he'll ask for my hand."

Everett threw his head back and laughed while humiliation stormed into Lily's face.

"And where will you and your traitorous husband live? In his shanty? Or, perhaps in the barn?" He chortled again. "Why, I daresay the pigs and sheep won't mind your presence too much."

Lily turned for the door once more. Oh, if she only had something akin to a brass candlestick to throw at Everett's head. . .

"You, my dear, have been badly taken advantage of, I'm afraid."

"No, sir, you are misinformed."

Wicked laughter met her remark.

Lily twisted the doorknob, but the rustling of documents behind her brought to mind thoughts of Papa's will and the deed for *Haus am Bach*.

She gulped a breath and prayed for courage, then slowly faced Everett again. "In your passel of papers, might you have a copy of the deed to my father's manor?"

"I'm sure I do." Everett didn't meet her gaze as he opened his ledger. "Now, be a good girl and run along. I'm a busy man."

"I'll wait." Lily strolled to the black leather chair and sat down.

"Wait for what?" His brow puckered and deep lines collected on the bridge of his nose.

"I'll wait for you to produce a copy of the deed."

"Don't be impertinent. It's most unbecoming."

"Mac doesn't think so. He thinks I'm beautiful."

Everett snorted. "Taken in by pretty words from a practiced charmer." He clicked his tongue. "A shame. But you're young. You'll get over it soon enough."

"I want to see the deed to *Haus am Bach*."

"Run along, Lily. I mean it." Again, he buried his gaze in his account book.

"Of course if you can't produce it, I'll petition Mr. Rosemont. As Papa's solicitor, he'd no doubt have a copy."

The muscle in Everett's jaw seemed to throb. "Go home."

"Or what? You'll send me off to boarding school?" Lily pushed out one of her sweetest smiles. "Except I'm not a little girl, and I won't allow you to manipulate me, especially if the ownership of my home is in question."

"It's not."

"Prove it."

Everett slammed his fist on his desk, giving Lily a start. "I don't have to prove anything to you."

"Yes, I'm afraid you do. I believe Papa meant for my brothers and me to own our manor. I think you're lying."

"After all I have done for you?" Everett was on his feet again. "I have seen to your every need this past year. I have shown you my deepest care in your time of mourning. And this is how you reward me?"

"You've sold our horses, carriage, animals, and our orchards, our wheat and corn fields. You dismissed our housekeeper and cook. Can you account for the sum you've collected over the last year? I highly doubt our needs equaled it."

"Why, you spitting little shrew." Everett's voice sounded as deadly as an ambush. "How dare you call my integrity into question when I have so faithfully looked after you—as your father would have wanted."

Lily refused to be cowed. "I take it you cannot produce the deed I've requested." She stood and strode to the door.

Everett hurried around his desk to block her path. "You will apologize at once."

She pressed her lips together.

"Apologize, Lily." Everett's eyes became two slits.

"For what? Demanding to know the truth?"

Everett lifted his arm and backhanded her. Pain exploded in her cheek. She stumbled back, knocking over a vase and side table as she fell to the hard wooden floor. Fire erupted in her bottom lip. She tasted blood.

Persistent knocking on the office door reverberated inside Lily's head. She heard a familiar male voice, saw a looming shadow, and then a pair of giant hands lifted her to her feet. Scents of wood smoke and hot iron penetrated her fuzzy brain. Lily blinked and stared up into the blackened face of Issie's husband.

"James!"

♥

"We will make camp here tonight."

"My thanks." James shook Shona's hand.

"It's not necessary." Lily removed the cool, wet compress from her swollen cheek. "I can take care of myself."

James's gaze widened. "Like you took care of yourself by thundering into Everett's office, calling the man a liar, and making demands without so much as another man's protection?" He sucked in a breath, doffed his hat, and wiped away the droplets of perspiration—or perhaps exasperation—dotting his brow. James had driven her home in his wagon, and Lily had listened to his chastening for an entire mile, although it seemed like twenty.

"I suppose I got what I deserved." Tears clouded her vision.

"No." James took hold of her chin and forced her to look at him. "No woman ever deserves abuse. There is no excuse for what Everett did."

"Among my people, it is a crime to strike a woman, and it carries with it much shame."

"A pity my people aren't that smart." James released Lily and let his arm fall to his side. "If I notify the authorities, Everett will merely get a scolding—if the complaint doesn't get completely ignored."

Shona's gaze bore into Lily. She took to studying the tips of her leather boots.

"Me and my men will camp here. That is final." The sternness in Shona's voice left no room for debate.

Lily swallowed any remaining protests. In truth, she felt more embarrassed than hurt. "Thank you."

"I still say you ought to stay with Issie and me," James said. "She'll have a conniption when I tell her what happened. You can bet I'll get some kind of tongue lashing for not insisting you come to our house tonight."

Lily smiled, then winced and fingered her fat lower lip. "Issie knows how stubborn I am. Let the truth be your alibi. I'm determined to sleep in my own bed tonight."

"So be it." James lifted his shoulders. He sent Shona a parting nod and climbed up to his wagon.

Lily lifted her hand in farewell. Then she wished Shona a good evening.

"If there is anything you need, please knock on the kitchen door. I'll hear it."

Shona dipped his head in acknowledgment. "And if there is anything you need, call out and we will hear you."

The promise filled Lily with a sense of security, and she was grateful Shona had his way. "Thank you," she repeated.

Then, opening the front door, she entered a much-too-quiet house. An instant wave of misery crashed over her. Her brothers' shenanigans didn't seem so terrible now, and what she wouldn't give to hear Aunt Hilda scolding them and smell one of her delectable meals bubbling in the kettle or her delicious bread baking in the oven.

Removing her bonnet, Lily strode into the empty kitchen. She spied Aunt Hilda's recent batch of applesauce. A recipe lay beside the jars, left there for Lily's benefit, as Aunt Hilda knew how to make and preserve fruit by heart.

Lily reverently lifted her aunt's apron. What a blessing to find a task to occupy her mind. She thought of how happy, even giddy Aunt Hilda seemed as she packed her belongings while spouting off a list of directions for Lily.

She would begin tomorrow at first light.

And in the days to come, God willing, Lily would figure out what to do with the rest of the harvest.

She released a wary sigh. If only Mac would return. She didn't believe a word of what Mr. Everett had said, and she refused to even consider the matter until she heard from Mac's own lips that he was betrothed.

Again, jealousy threatened, but she collected her wits and turned her thoughts to her brothers. As much as she loathed admitting it, boarding school wasn't the worst thing for them. Mr. Everett had been correct about them acting like hellions at times. But away from home and in a disciplined atmosphere, they would be forced to study.

Lily decided to read for the rest of the evening. She strode toward Papa's study to get a book and paused in the hallway. She'd forgotten to ask about the boarding school's location. Mr. Everett said the boys were sailing off. . . but to where? England?

Her shoulders drooped along with her resolve. She dare not inquire of the pompous man further. She'd acted on her anger instead of approaching him with a clear head. Rather than getting the answers she sought, she'd started a battle—another war of independence, such as it may be.

And there was no turning back now.

# Chapter Twenty-Five

$\mathcal{M}$ac snapped the reins, and his mules quickened their gait. He could see his orchards in the nearing distance and couldn't wait to arrive home.

He swiveled on the wagon bench and signaled to Rogan, one of the freed Negroes who agreed to build his home in exchange for room and board and a chance to learn life skills—or practice the ones he already knew. While Mac drove the supply wagon, Rogan drove the wagon filled with dark-skinned men—freedmen—and a host of additional supplies.

Upon leaving Alexandria with twenty slaves, Mac concluded that dangling their freedom in front of their faces in a tradeoff for work was a sort of blackmail. He wanted men willing to build Fairview. He wanted builders who shared his vision. Hence he gave each man his walking papers, so to speak—losing seven men in the process. Mac let those men go. But the thirteen remaining were dedicated to the job and ready to begin their lives on the far side of the Blue Ridge Mountains, in a lush valley known as Shenandoah.

Each time they'd stopped for the night on this week-long journey, they had begged Mac for stories of the wide open spaces of the valley. They asked what freedom felt like, what it tasted like. Mac answered their questions the best he could, and their nighttime discussions allowed him to become better acquainted with the men.

He marveled at their experiences and knowledge. To think Prescott deemed them simpletons, capable of only manual labor. How very far from the truth. Gerald played the fiddle like a professional musician. Marcus read aloud from the scripture every morning. And Thomas cooked almost as well as Mrs. Gunther, considering he possessed only basic utensils. Mac stood back in awe and gratitude.

Then, as darkness had settled over their camps these last six days, Mac relayed everything he knew about the Shenandoah Valley. Homesickness enveloped him with every word he spoke.

Homesickness and thoughts of Lily. Blake said she'd recovered and looked healthy. Mac was eager to see for himself.

He slapped the reins again and the mules strained against their harnesses. He dared not overwork the poor creatures. After all, the wagon bed was piled high with limestone and lumber.

Lily's *Haus am Bach*, as she called it, came into view. Mac caught a glimpse of movement in the orchard, then to his left in the wheat field. The men Lily spoke of the day she was snake bit had obviously made good on their promise to return and help bring in the harvest. Mrs. Gunther expressed concern over Lily's probable attempt to manage more than she was physically able, but it seemed Lily had things under control.

Mac pulled to a halt, then jumped down from the wagon and tethered his mules. He waved to Rogan, and the man reined in his team.

"Go on ahead of me, and drive the wagon up the swath on the other side of the creek."

"Yes, sir." Rogan gave a nod.

Mac issued several more instructions before turning toward the manor. He took the stairs two at a time, then rapped on the front door.

No answer.

Additional knocks produced the same result.

Mac walked around the house. He heard Lily singing before he saw her in the orchard, standing on a ladder and gathering apples. He waved and caught her attention.

"Mac!" Her exclamation wafted across the wildflowers on a tepid breeze and made him smile.

Then she jumped down and smoothed her coral gown before taking hold of a stick. She resembled a blind man with his cane as she hurried across the grassland. Worry rose up inside of him. Had she lost some of her sight?

Mac jogged to meet her. She dropped her stick and peeled back her wide-rimmed bonnet as she reached him.

He took her hands.

"I'm so glad you're home." Her blue eyes gleamed like sapphires, and she smelled like fresh air with a hint of bergamot.

Mac lifted her hands to his lips and placed a kiss on the backs of her fingers. "I'm doubly glad to be home and to see that you have recovered nicely."

"I feel perfectly fine now." Her smile lit his soul.

However, he wanted more of a welcome than the offer of her hands. He cupped Lily's face and touched his lips to her sweet mouth.

She pulled away. "Mac, no. . .Shona is watching."

"Who?"

Lily hung her head to the left, then slid her gaze in the same direction. Mac saw a brown-skinned man with long black hair making purposeful strides their way.

Reluctantly, he released Lily. She looked as disappointed as he felt.

The man named Shona reached them, and Lily made the introductions. Mac stuck out his hand, and the valley native gave it a shake.

"Shona and his tribesmen have not only been working steadily to bring in our crops," Lily explained, "but they've been so good to camp nearby and offer me their protection."

"After her rout with Silas Everett," Shona said, "I felt it was necessary. My men agreed."

"What rout?" Mac folded his arms across his chest.

"It was nothing." Lily focused on the tips of her black boots.

"Hardly nothing." A deep frown weighed Shona's features. "Everett struck Lily and nearly knocked her senseless."

"He did what?" Fire erupted inside of Mac. He clenched his fists.

"It's not hard to believe. Everett is a cruel man. It was a good thing the blacksmith saw Lily enter Everett's inn and followed."

"Really, it wasn't as bad as all that." Lily's cheeks turned pink. "Besides,

I purposely infuriated him when I learned he sent my brothers to boarding school."

"Boarding school!" Mac reined in his temper when Lily took two steps back. "Is that what Everett said? He sent Jonah and Jed to. . .boarding school?"

"Yes." Lily worked her lips together as if frightened by Mac's show of anger.

He tamped it down for her sake, but he'd love to darken that man's daylights for hitting Lily. How dare he? And then he had the gall to lie about the boys.

"Everett did not send your brothers to boarding school, Lily. He indentured them to a sea captain for two years."

She gasped, and her eyes widened. "Indentured? Oh, no!"

"Blake found out and alerted me. I managed to persuade Captain O'Malley to turn the boys over to me."

"Thank God." Lily looked about ready to collapse.

Mac took hold of her elbow.

"Did they come home with you?" Her gaze seemed to plead with him, and Mac cursed Everett for his deception.

"No, Lily. I tried. I even took the matter to my family's solicitor, who petitioned the court. The indenture stands, although a good friend of mine, Captain Taylor Osborn—"

"I recognize that name. He's Mr. Blake's employer and now my aunt's too."

"Correct. And he accepted the boys on the *Ariel*, promising to teach them navigation skills and insist they practice reading, writing, and mathematics. They'll come away with more of an education than any boarding school can offer."

"But what if there's a storm and they're drowned?" Fear filled Lily's gaze. "Or what if they're attacked by pirates?"

"What if they are snake bit?" Shona's lips formed a half-grin. "What if a wicked innkeeper abuses them?"

Lily huffed. "All right, you have made your point, sir."

Still, a little pout lingered on her mouth, and Mac longed to kiss it away.

She bent and retrieved her stick. The wood was smooth and it had been fashioned with two prongs.

"What have you there?" Mac folded his arms.

"My snake stick." She wielded it with a proud tilt to her head. "Shona made it for me. If the snakes don't hear me coming, they'll feel the nudge of the stick and get out of my path."

"Hmm. . ." Mac glanced at Shona, who shrugged.

"Lily required a, um, crutch of sorts," he said.

"With my stick in hand, I'm no longer afraid to cross the meadow, or any grassy yard, for that matter."

Mac recalled her fear and questions about the Almighty on the night of his community barn-christening party. Did she really think God failed her by allowing the snake bite?

Three of his men hailed him from the orchard. No doubt they wanted to know where to unload and where to make camp for the night.

"I must get over to my property. I have thirteen able-bodied men waiting on me."

"Your construction crew?"

"Yes. Freed black men." Mac didn't say they were gifts from his brother. It was more offensive to him now than ever.

"May I come with you?" Lily looked up at him in a way which rendered Mac unable to deny her request.

"Of course."

"We have a surprise for you." She bounced on the balls of her feet as obvious excitement got the better of her. "And if you wouldn't mind, Mac, I'd like to know more about my brothers' situation. Were they terrified or discouraged to be indentured?"

"Not at all. They have Blake, your aunt, and Captain Osborn keeping watch over them. Jonah, of course, was in his element."

"I imagine so."

Shona bid them farewell and returned to whatever task he'd been doing before Mac's arrival.

Lily slipped her hand around Mac's elbow and they crossed the meadow. Pink and white daisies seemed to bow in deference as they passed.

"Mr. Everett also told me you're betrothed to a woman named Samantha Eden," Lily said when they reached the stone bridge. "Is that true?"

"What do you think?" Mac stopped short, earnestly wondering if Lily had fretted over the lie or, God forbid, had lost any sleep over it. Surely, she could tell how he felt about her. He placed his hands on her shoulders so she faced him. "I'm curious, Lily. Tell me."

"I think Mr. Everett is a liar, and I told him so." Her features softened, and Mac glimpsed the faded bruise on her right cheek.

He clenched his jaw.

"Don't be angry with me for asking, Mac."

"Angry with you?" He shook his head. "I am not the least bit upset with you. It's Everett I want to pound into the ground."

"Please don't." She placed her palms on his chest while a pained expression pinched her features. "I'd rather forget it."

Mac kissed her cheek and gathered her in his arms. "I have missed you so. You are always in my thoughts by day and in my dreams by night." He kissed her temple.

"I've missed you, too."

"And I promise you this, Lily. . ." He held her at arm's length and stared deeply into her eyes. "No matter how angry I may get, I will never hurt you. Never."

"I believe you." A tentative little smile worked its way across her ruby lips. "But you didn't answer my question."

Mac hated the vulnerability that clouded her otherwise sunny disposition. Surely she wasn't frightened of him. He'd just vowed never to harm her. And she couldn't possibly have entertained the idea that he was betrothed when the two of them had an understanding.

Then, again, Lily had been heartbroken before.

"I am not betrothed to Miss Eden. She is my sister-in-law's sister."

Mac took her hands and explained the circumstances involving Miss Eden. He told her of his family's misfortune and how Taylor's decision to buy in and become a partner elevated the shipping business from debt and financed the voyage on the *Ariel*.

"I invested your funds."

"Thank you."

"Are you satisfied now?"

"Completely." Lily stepped closer. Not a trace of hesitation, worry, or fear showed on her face. She lifted her chin. "If you hurry, you can kiss me while no one's watching."

Mac needed no further invitation and gathered her in his arms. He pressed a kiss on her lips and took his time tasting her intoxicating sweetness. He knew then—as he'd known before—that he loved her. Loved her beyond belief. He wanted to make her his own for all time.

"I love you, Mac." Her voice was a breathless whisper.

"I love you, too." He'd never spoken those words—not even to Mary—and he'd never felt them as passionately as he did in this moment.

Reality pressed in. He had nothing to offer Lily. Not yet. But soon, and when he was ready. . .

She slipped out of his embrace and took his hand. "Come and see the surprise we have for you."

Lily held her breath as Mac inspected the furnished cabin. He said not a word, and she wondered if he liked it. Of course, much of the furniture had chips or scratches, but as temporary items, they were suitable.

Mac halted at her father's writing desk and placed his hands on his narrow hips. "This is a fine piece." He swung his gaze to her. "Your father's? The one from the parlor?"

She smiled that he remembered and nodded. "I thought you should have it."

"I will cherish it."

That was all Lily needed to hear.

"And all these furnishings. . . I'm entirely grateful to my neighbors for their generosity."

Relief rushed through her. He was pleased. "You are well liked here in Middletown."

"The feeling is mutual. Middletown is my home."

But how would the good citizens of this town feel about him if Mr. Everett spread those vicious lies around about Mac being a traitor?

Lily worked her bottom lip between her teeth and approached him. "Mac, I hate to bring up another matter, but I fear I must."

"Of course." Mac took her hand and led her to a wooden chair. He sat in an adjacent seat. "Speak your mind."

"Mr. Everett claimed that you were never impressed into the British navy, that you fought against Americans because you chose to. Is that true?"

A shadow crossed his face.

Lily rushed to his defense. "But you *were* forced to take up arms against us, weren't you? Oh, Mac. . .please tell me."

"I was impressed, Lily, but that doesn't make me feel less guilty for what I did. Impressment is a strange thing. It causes men to lose sight of right and wrong and forces them to act on their survival instincts."

"Of course. That makes perfect sense to me." Indeed, he had been *forced*, as in *against his will*.

"Listing out at sea for weeks, a man gets to know his comrades. At that time, I was under the command of Taylor Osborn."

"Your friend?"

"Yes. It was he who rescued Blake and me, in a manner of speaking. The same way he accepted Jonah and Jed aboard his ship. He's a good man, and once I gained his trust, I didn't want to betray him. Blake felt the same."

"Again, it all makes perfect sense."

Mac sat forward, his forearms on his thighs. "When my merchant vessel was overrun by a British frigate, every man on my crew, with the exception of Blake, was forced to walk the plank. Mary's brother was one of them. When I returned to Alexandria, I found her parents heartbroken by the loss of their children. They wanted revenge. Someone to blame. That someone was me."

Mac stood and pivoted toward the window. He gazed out over his barnyard. Somewhere in the distance, a man's deep voice called to another as the crew of freed men unloaded supplies.

"They charged me with treason and murder, then garnered sufficient support for a trial. In the end, I was acquitted, but the Albright name took quite a hit."

Lily stood and came up behind him. She touched his suede waistcoat, noting its softness. She ran her fingertips across his shoulder until she reached the sleeve of his white shirt. Then she captured his hand in hers.

He gave her a sorrowful smile. "It wounded me deeply. The people I held dear to me, those who I thought should be glad to see I'd survived the war, wanted instead to watch me hang."

"Oh, Mac. . ." Lily felt wounded for him. There were no words to express how much she longed to comfort him.

But, perhaps, starting anew in Middletown would prove all the solace he needed.

He possessed her heart.

And he loved her.

What more could a girl want?

## Chapter Twenty-Six

$\mathcal{M}$ac woke up and stretched. His muscles protested the movement. This past week's journey had obviously caught up to him. But how grateful he was to have come home to a soft bed, made up with linens and a quilt. This community had won his affection.

He pushed off the bedcovers and swung his legs off the straw mattress. His feet touched the cold plank floor, and he was tempted to hop back into his warm bed. Instead, he padded to the well-worn chest of drawers and glanced at his timepiece. Church service began in one hour, and Mac didn't want to miss it. Already the congregation seemed like family.

Pulling on black trousers and donning a clean shirt, Mac stepped from the cabin barefoot and headed for the recently dug, brick-lined well. It had been started years ago by Lily's father, but never completed. Together, Mac and a local mason renewed the project the day Lily fell ill from her snake bite. Mac had been glad for physical labor in which he'd worked out his fear for Lily, although the well hadn't been completed when he left for Alexandria.

Yet another surprise from his friends here in Middletown. The well was finished, except it was still poorly marked. Mac would have to work on it in the days to come, and, perhaps, build on a well room for easy access in the winter.

After collecting water, Mac washed up and finished dressing. He walked north, toward the back of his property where Rogan and the others had made camp. He paused, hearing their joyful song of worship, punctuated by heartfelt praise, and decided he wouldn't interrupt.

Coming back around to the front of his yard, Mac walked down the wagon-rutted pathway to the pike, made a right, and headed for church. He arrived and noticed no one stood in the churchyard chatting. Buggies and wagons filled allotted spaces, and horses and mules munched on tidbits of drying grass and leafy branches.

Music drifted through the church's open doors. Mac straightened his waistcoat, then made his way inside. Dread sliced through him. He'd arrived late, and he had no wish to make a spectacle.

Standing in the shadows, he clasped his hands behind his back and felt the autumn breeze that cooled the perspiration on his neck. He looked over bonneted heads and thought he spied Lily sitting in the second pew from the front. He wasn't about to dash up the center aisle in order to sit with her. But when the congregation stood, he hurried toward the first vacancy he saw in the third pew from the last.

He stepped in and immediately realized his blunder. Beside him stood a starry-eyed brunette by the name of Candy...no, Cindy. Cynthia. Yes, that was it.

She gave him a coy smile.

Mac inclined his head politely, then trained his gaze on the altar. They sat, and three older women marched to the front of the altar. The piano accompanied their practiced warbles and, at the end of the song, Reverend Kasper stepped up to the pulpit.

"All rise." His voice boomed through the country church.

Mac pushed to his feet.

"Let's pray as the Lord Jesus taught us. Our Father which art in heaven..."

Mac lowered his head, but before his eyes closed in prayer he glimpsed Lily leaning out of her pew. She met his gaze and motioned him forward. He glanced around at the many bowed heads, then stepped out and quietly made his way up the aisle.

"And forgive us our debts, as we forgive our debtors..."

Mac reached her pew and she moved over to make room for him.

"For thine is the kingdom, and the power, and the glory, forever. Amen."

"Amen," Lily echoed, along with the rest of the congregation.

"Please be seated." The reverend made a downward motion with his hands.

Mac sat and slid a glance to Lily. She nudged him, and he swallowed a grin.

"And now for our message today." Reverend Kasper opened the large, leather-bound volume in front of him. "As we reach another Sabbath, let us reflect on—" He sucked in a startled breath, his eyes grew wide, and his jaw dropped.

Mac twisted around to see what had captured the reverend's attention. A young man, with thick blond hair and a winning smile, walked slowly up the aisle. Horrified wheezes, grunts, and fluttering fans followed in his wake. Women fainted in their pews.

Beside him, Lily gasped. Mac turned. Her eyes appeared voluminous against her suddenly pale complexion.

"Who is that man?" Mac whispered.

"Why. . .it's Oliver Ashton!"

Lily remained in her pew, her head bowed, long after the rest of the congregation sprang up and shuffled to the courtyard. Oliver's easy tone carried to her ears, followed by happy voices and exclamations. She wiped the moisture from her cheeks, hoping to conceal her emotion from Mac. He sat like a bulwark beside her, but he needn't have stayed.

She let out a ragged breath that likely gave her away, but she couldn't walk out of the sanctuary now, couldn't face Oliver.

"Do you still love him, Lily?" Mac's breath tickled her cheek.

"I despise him." She hiccupped, and more tears leaked from her eyes. Why couldn't she seem to stem the flow? Her heart was as cold as a slab of limestone, yet she cried like a child.

Mac's palm encompassed her hand, and warmth spread through her glove.

"But perhaps I despise myself more." Lily turned aside and slid her damp hankie across her eyes. "The reverend's message was about forgiveness, but all I can think of is how I'd like to see Oliver Ashton drawn and quartered. Then publicly flogged. And then—"

"Lily, if you don't love him, you should feel nothing."

"Should I?" She lifted her head so she could see Mac, unencumbered by her wide-rimmed bonnet. "But I'm certain it's not love I feel at the moment."

Mac's features softened, and he fished out his handkerchief. "Here."

Lily accepted it, breathing in his rugged scent. It seemed to calm her nerves. "It's just such a shock."

"I'm sure."

"And I don't believe he was held on a prison ship for years. He looks far too healthy, so he's lying."

Mac pushed out his bottom lip and quirked his brows. "Good point."

"What's more, the experience hasn't humbled him one bit. He's as cocksure and full of himself as the day he marched off to fight the British."

"So what, exactly, will appease you, Lily—other than a lynching?"

"How about an apology?"

"Mmm. . ." Mac's gaze darkened with a new understanding. He leaned closer. "I believe you'd have better luck organizing a lynching."

A laugh bubbled out of nowhere, and Lily felt decidedly better. She worked her fingers in between his.

"Ready to head for home?"

Lily's upturn swirled downward. "I'm not ready to face Oliver—or anyone else."

"Then perhaps you shouldn't. Is there another way out of the church?"

"Yes. Through the reverend's study chamber."

Mac stood and pulled her to her feet. "Lead the way. No one is about."

Lily strode toward the altar and around the pulpit. She'd actually been amazed that Mr. Everett had kept his distance. But, of course, even he had more sense than to approach while she was in Mac's presence.

Lily pulled on the door, which opened to the narrow hallway that saw them to the reverend's study chamber. The wooden floor creaked beneath their feet, and Mac's boots kept time with Lily's heartbeats.

At last they descended the stairway that opened to the side yard.

Lily halted, teetering on the last step.

"What's wrong?" Mac stepped onto the long grass.

"I forgot my snake stick." She hadn't needed it, walking up the pike where she could see if a viper lay ahead.

"Are you asking me to carry you home?"

Imagining the sight, Lily burst into a giggle. "No, of course not."

"Do you truly believe God can't keep a measly little snake away from you, that you need a stick instead of His hand of protection?"

"When you put it that way. . .no." A blush worked its way up her neck and into her face.

Mac helped her off the last stair and folded her hand around his elbow. Together they walked through knee-high overgrowth that pricked Lily's legs right through her stockings. Despite her pleas, Mac took her on a meandering path as if he dared a serpent to show itself. By the time they reached the pike, Lily didn't know whether to sock him in the arm or thank him. He proved she didn't require the snake stick, although it did provide a measure of comfort.

"God keeps revealing Himself to me," Mac confided, "ever since that copperhead bit you. On my journey from Alexandria, I listened at dawn to one of the freed men read from the Bible. Jesus said He is the Way, the Truth, and the Life. I know that's so." He gave her a side glance, and Lily smiled. "So what have you to say about that?"

"I say it's quite a change from the man I first met some six weeks ago."

"Well, I'd say God intended for you to get snake bit."

"What?" Lily stopped. "How can you say such a thing? God wouldn't want me to be injured."

"He allowed his Son to be crucified."

"But. . ." Lily found it difficult to argue.

Mac replaced Lily's hand in the crook of his arm. "I was very frightened over the thought you might die. I'd never felt that way before. In my helpless state I turned to God, and He met me in my hour of need."

His words warmed Lily's heart. "As I recollect, you promised Him your life."

"I did, yes, and I never go back on a promise."

They continued walking, and she hugged his arm. "How unfortunate for me if I'd married Oliver Ashton and missed out on falling in love with you."

"You are quite bold, Miss Laughlin."

"Yes, I suppose I am."

"I'll overlook it this time."

She flicked a glance heavenward. "Now you sound like Mr. Everett."

"Such insult!" Mac put his hand over his heart. "You wound me, Princess."

Lily smiled, enjoying their banter and the autumn weather. Had the sky ever been any bluer? Had the turning colors on the foothills of the Massanutten looked any more aflame?

Suddenly Oliver Ashton's arrival in Middletown seemed very far away and oh, so meaningless.

## Chapter Twenty-Seven

*L*ily handed jars filled with Aunt Hilda's delectable applesauce to Mac, who packed them safely into the wagon bed. Jams came next, followed by preserves. The pies and cakes were loaded last. In another wagon, Mac's crewman, Mr. Rogan, loaded up barrels of fruit, wheat, and corn. The harvest had been plentiful this year.

Lily wiped her hands on her apron. "That's all of it." At Mac's nod, she strode into the kitchen. She took one last look around. It seemed they'd remembered everything.

She unpinned the white smock from the bodice of her blue-printed gown and untied it at the waist. After tossing it onto the worktable, she snatched her shawl and gloves, then left the house, pulling closed the kitchen door behind her.

"Ready for the festival? Mac jumped down from the wagon.

"Ready."

A giddy sort of anticipation bubbled up inside of her as Mac assisted her ascent to the wagon bench. He climbed up beside her, then took hold of the reins.

As they bounced along the pike, with Mr. Rogan following a safe distance behind, Lily noticed the azure October sky and imagined an ocean of the same hue.

"Do you think my aunt and brothers like their lives aboard the *Ariel*?"

"I presume so." A side glance and a grin. "If not, they'll have plenty of time to adjust their attitudes."

"Will you ever adjust your attitude about the sea?"

"Most likely not."

Lily turned to him. "Will I ever meet your family?"

"Ever? Certainly."

She smiled. "Soon?"

"I don't know." He pushed his hat higher up on his forehead. "You're full of questions this morning."

"Begging your pardon, Captain." She rubbed her gloved palms together. "Nerves."

"Mm. . ."

"But it's not that you're ashamed of me, a poor country girl, are you?"

Mac flicked an annoyed glance her way, and Lily grinned. His wicked humor must have been contagious.

"No, of that I'm quite certain. I'm not ashamed of you. It's my family, Lily. My folks, my brother Prescott, and his wife, can be overbearing. They plot and plan others' futures when they ought to mind their own instead."

"But you forgive them for their attempt to marry you off to Miss Eden."

"Yes, I forgive."

The statement sounded unfinished, but when more was not forthcoming, Lily decided not to press.

The wagon hit a bone-jarring rut that threatened to unseat her. She clung to the bench's side rail and decided to change the subject before Mac requested it.

"How proud Aunt Hilda would be." Lily only had to close her eyes to see her aunt's nod of approval. "I followed her recipes to the letter."

"Award-winning treats is what my palate tells me."

Lily thought so, too. However, year after year, Mr. Everett laid claim to a position on the judges' panel, and this year she didn't expect high marks from him.

Mac turned off the pike and drove into the churchyard. Many wagons had already arrived and more trailed in behind the one Mr. Rogan manned. Once parked side-by-side along a stretch which promised much-needed shade once the sun moved higher in the sky, Lily arranged both wagon beds in a manner sure to attract buyers and barterers alike. In years past, Aunt Hilda performed the setup. The festival had always been more of a social event for Lily and an excuse for pranks by her brothers and their friends. This year, it was up to Lily to bring home the blue ribbon, and if such a prize was won by determination alone, she'd have it.

The morning grew busy as patrons and sellers filled almost every spot of the churchyard. By noon, laughter and music strayed over from a favorite picnic spot on the grassy knoll closer to the church. By midafternoon, the judges made their rounds, sampling wares and jotting down results on slates with pieces of chalk.

Mr. Everett paused at Lily's display. He seemed as detached as in previous years, although he wrinkled his nose at Lily's pear preserves. "Much too sour."

Lily cared little about his opinion. She'd presumed she wouldn't get his vote anyway.

He moved on and other judges took his place, tasting and testing Lily's fruity offerings. Then a sort of horrified hush wound its way through the crowd, and all eyes seemed to lock on the eastern sky. Turning that way, Lily glimpsed what others evidently saw too—thick curls of black smoke, rising into the cloudless sky.

"Fire!" someone shouted.

The festival goers parted like the Red Sea. Mac and Mr. Rogan, along with droves of other men, took off running in that direction. Lily guessed the location to be in the vicinity of Mac's property or *Haus am Bach*. But perhaps it was farther on down the pike than that.

"Barn fire!" A boy tore through the crowd. His next words sent a dagger slicing through her heart. "Fire at Captain Albright's farm!"

Mac, Mr. Rogan, and scores of other men took off running. Lily hurriedly packed up their goods and belongings. She'd leave the wagons here and Mac and one of his freedmen could come for them once the crisis passed.

She sprinted down the pike, her lungs burning while the black smoke continued to climb into the air. When she arrived in Mac's barnyard, his glorious barn was beyond saving. The men turned their attention to the cabin's blaze. Smoke as dense as coiled rope blotted out the sun's evening rays. A pall settled over the bystanders, comprised of mostly women and children. Within minutes, the hungry flames proved too much for the volunteers. They stepped back and helplessly watched it devour two months' worth of sweat and tears.

Lily found Mac near the corral. The two mules that weren't used to pull wagons to the festival made their long whinnied hee-haw noise as if crying over the loss before them.

She neared, longing to say something that would ease the anguish etched in Mac's features. No words came. She smoothed his shirtsleeve, then slipped her hand around his elbow.

Mac shook her off.

Lily stumbled back, insult added to the wounds she, too, felt. Her father's desk had gone up in flames along with Mac's cabin, although the nostalgia was nothing compared to his greater loss.

"I only meant to give some comfort."

His dark gaze slid her way. The animosity she thought gone with the snake venom in her body had returned. The corners of his mouth seemed to curl in a sneer.

"Can you not see that I've lost everything?" His voice increased by decibels with each word.

James and Issie turned their way, wearing curious frowns.

Lily stepped back. "You have not lost everything, Mac. You can rebuild. God has not abandoned you. I have not—"

"God?" He whirled on her, and Lily forced herself not to scamper off like a frightened rabbit. "You dare speak to me about God? My entire life is quite literally going to the devil."

She stared at him as the barn's roof collapsed with a shower of sparks and a belch of black smoke. The mules became unsettled and Mac assured them by stroking their noses and patting their necks. In that moment, it seemed to Lily that he cared more for his mules and possessions than he cared for her.

But of course that was absurd. Wasn't it?

"You have lost a barn and a cabin, Mac. They can be rebuilt. And look around you. Your friends are here. I'm here. And, yes, God is here too. Remember what you said not but a week ago Sunday. . ."

"Are you so thickheaded that you cannot understand simple mathematics? I have no more funds with which to rebuild."

Lily held herself around her midsection. His words hurt twice as much as Everett's slap across the face.

"There is nothing in Middletown for me now."

"No, I daresay you are right about that." Lily whirled around and marched toward the pike. A chill passed over her. She'd left her shawl at the festival, along with Mac's wagons and whatever was left of the sellable harvest. She'd return there now and collect it and whatever else was light enough to carry home.

Tears stung, but she refused to succumb to the sadness knocking at the door of her heart. God had shown her a monumental truth. The man she loved, or thought she loved, considered her nothing more than a burdensome, chattering magpie, although a bird would probably receive more respect from Mac than she did.

Lily reached the festival and found Mr. Everett near Mac's wagons.

He removed his hat. "May I be of some help? I kept my eye on your wares while you were away."

"Thank you." Lily wouldn't lash out like Mac had done, although she disliked Everett and Mac professed to love her.

Obviously, he did not.

"It appears you've done well today."

Lily found her shawl and wrapped it around her shoulders. "Not as well as you might think."

Her heart began to crack, leaving an irreparable schism. She gathered the remaining jars of jams and preserves and filled her arms.

Then an idea struck, although if she weren't so upset and, yes, confused, she wouldn't dream of inquiring. But it seemed most practical, given the circumstances.

"Might you have your carriage, Mr. Everett?"

"Why, yes. Shall I bring it by and take you home?"

Lily nodded. "Thank you."

She located a couple of wooden crates and unpacked, then repacked her things. On the way home, she stared at her folded hands in her lap and forced herself not to look toward Mac's property. How grateful she was to have glimpsed this warped side of him before they married. But he'd warned her and predicted she might change her mind.

Well, she had!

♥

The fire had stopped smoldering and now, twenty-four hours later, Mac walked through the ruins of what had been the beginnings of his new and bright future. James Hawkins walked beside him, and Mac did his best to receive the fellow's advice with a tolerant ear. However, James, like practically everyone else in Middletown, tried to console him with talk of rebuilding. They couldn't seem to wrap their minds around the fact that it cost money to rebuild and Mac had nothing left.

"Even the Son of God didn't have a place to lay His head during his short ministry." James placed his hand on Mac's shoulder as they surveyed the cabin's ruins.

The muscle beneath his friend's palm convulsed. Mac stepped out of James's reach.

"Believe it or not, Mac, plenty of us men have stood in your boots."

"Really?" Mac set his hands on his hips. "And did you return to your families a failure? Prodigal sons who squandered their inheritance?"

Deep lines wrinkled James's forehead. "Well, no. . ."

"Then stop trying to make me feel better with weightless remarks and meaningless advice."

"Very well." James inclined his head. "But only if you'll stop feeling so pathetically sorry for yourself."

Mac's shoulders slumped in final defeat. No one understood the extent of his suffering. Not a single soul. Most of the freedmen had packed up and left. Only Rogan and Marcus stayed around, but Mac suspected they'd soon depart. Nothing was keeping them here.

"Have you seen Lily since the fire?" James asked. "Of course you haven't. You've got tunnel vision that only goes one way—to yourself."

"Go home, James."

"Fine, I'll leave. But you broke her heart when you yelled at her."

"My entire future was aflame!" Mac raised a fist to the heavens. "I have a right to my own black moods."

"Black moods?" James grunted a laugh. "Sinful response is what I'd call it."

"Of course you would." The man needed to shut his mouth and go on his way.

"Selfishness, self-pity. . ."

"Are you about through?" Mac balled his fists, longing to knock that smirk off James's face.

"I reckon I am. . .for now." He pointed at Mac. "Just remember, friends don't abandon each other, even when one of 'em's being a mule-headed jack-anapes."

"That does it!"

Mac swept the hat off his head and threw it down on the dirt before charging James and throwing a punch. James ducked and slammed his fist into Mac's gut, then his jaw. The side of Mac's face exploded, and when the silvery stars stopped swirling before his eyes, he realized he lay prostrate on the ground, gasping for a breath.

"More advice, my friend." A winning smile rang in James's voice. "Never pick a fight with a blacksmith or the Almighty. You're sure to lose on both accounts."

# Chapter Twenty-Eight

aptain Albright seems to have vanished since the fire a couple of days ago. No one has seen him since. I suspect he's taken his leave, and I am sorry. You deserve better than that treasonous scoundrel."

Lily turned away from Everett's feigned empathy and strode toward the parlor's hearth. Embers from the low-burning fire took the damp chill from the room. Thunder rumbled in the distance and pulled her deeper into despair. Mac hadn't even said goodbye. Of course, she'd only wished for a final meeting so she could slam the door in his handsome face. Perhaps he figured as much.

"You're young, Lily. Time will heal your heart."

"No, I'm afraid it won't."

"Well, in any case, love is rarely the basis of a good marriage."

"So I've heard." Hadn't the same words spewed from Mac's mouth? But how could she have been so stupid as to fall for all his shallow words of love? She'd allowed him liberties and believed his whispered intimacies.

"Lily, I dread bringing up the subject, but the time is at hand." Rustling paper captured her attention. She watched Everett unfold the documents in his hands. "The deed to *Haus am Bach*. It took me a while to procure it from the courts, but here it is at last. As you can see, it names me as owner of the manor."

Lily took the proffered document and scanned it. "Yes, it does." If she wasn't so emotionally numb, she'd be shocked and angry.

"So I have an ultimatum for you. Marry me and remain here in your comfortable home, or refuse my offer and face immediate eviction."

"But I will require time to find another place to live."

"Those are my terms, Lily."

"Must we discuss this now? Haven't I suffered enough?"

She shook her head in a futile attempt to clear it. All she could see was Mac's face. She felt his comforting, protective embrace. A shame it was all a game of pretend for him. The day of the fire brought out his true character, and Lily found it appalling.

What else was a game? The story of his impressment, perhaps? Maybe he was a traitor. Maybe he was even betrothed to Miss Eden and all that was a lie too.

How idiotic to take the man at his word. As he'd said, they barely knew each other. He'd been spot on.

"I need time," Lily blurted. "Time to think."

Everett reached into his trouser pocket and produced his timepiece. "I can allow you a couple of hours, certainly. That's only fair."

"I was thinking more along the lines of a couple of months." Years, even.

"No, it's time you decide." Everett glanced around. "I've never cared for the color of this room. It's neither green nor blue." His beady eyes fixed on her. "Your father, bless him, was a man of great indecision. He happily settled for compromise."

"And you think he should have been more puritan—like you?"

"Exactly." He ran his finger across the surface of the sideboard, inspected it, and blew off the make-believe dust. Lily had managed to keep up with the housework. "I've purchased slaves, a cook, and a maid." Again, his gaze adhered to Lily. "Marry me, and you'll want for nothing."

"Except love."

He appeared genuinely hurt. "You still don't think I care for you? Why, I held you in my arms the day you were born. I watched you grow from an adorable little girl into a lovely young lady. I think you were ten years old when I first thought of marrying you."

Lily's stomach twisted. "Ten? I was but a child."

"A precocious, adorable child." His hands clasped behind his back, he ambled to the next piece of furniture. "You thought the world of me."

"You were Papa's friend. I trusted you."

"But you don't now? Not since you met Captain Albright?"

"He has nothing to do with it. It was Aunt Hilda who mistrusted you first, and when you sold off a parcel of land without even the courtesy of an explanation, I felt entirely disrespected, as if my feelings about the matter didn't count." Was every man alike? Mac didn't respect her either. He'd yelled at her and comforted his mules.

Another rumble of thunder, and Lily felt like her head might explode. She placed her palm against her forehead. "I'm afraid I'm in need of a rest."

"First your answer, Lily dear. Marry me, or forget about a rest and start packing. I intend to move into *my* manor shortly."

"And that is how you show me your. . .*love*? Show me that you care?" Lily stomped toward the doorway and Everett caught her wrist.

"Your answer, please."

She halted. "Very well." Shoulders back, she faced him. "I would rather die than marry you, and I will start packing immediately."

Pulling free of Everett's grasp, she ran up the steps. She entered her bedroom and slammed the door behind her. *Infernal oaf!* With one side of his mouth he professed to care, and with the other he evicted her from the only home she'd ever known.

With blinding tears, Lily threw open her wardrobe doors and found her valise. She set it open on her neatly made bed. She'd never felt so alone. No rascally brothers to stand in Mr. Everett's way. No wisdom from Aunt Hilda.

*Oh, Lord, I'm so angry. . .and so very afraid.*

She opened her eyes and blinked back her tears when a movement near the window caught her eye. She crossed the room, intending to discover its identity. There. A shadowy figure moving about the wreckage next door. Mac's barn had been built on a slight incline, which made peering at it from her upper window an easy task. Did the darkly clad form belong to Mac?

She watched sadly as the form disappeared from her vantage point.

Perhaps Mac hadn't left town. Why was she suddenly filled with hope? He'd made it clear he didn't want her.

But shouldn't she demand some answers first? The least Mac could do was listen while she gave him a piece of her mind.

Lily tiptoed down the stairs and rounded the balustrade. Through the hallway then the kitchen, she snuck out the door and sprinted across the meadow. Any snake she encountered had just better watch himself. She was angry enough to bite back!

She slowed at the stone bridge, careful not to slip and topple into the swollen creek from two days of hard rain earlier in the week. Reaching the barnyard, she gasped at the devastation. It pained her to see Mac's cozy cabin reduced to ash. His proud-standing barn, folded into itself beneath the heat of the flames.

"Miss Lily?"

She started and whirled to her right. Mr. Rogan stood there. His sad expression mirrored hers. "I thought you'd left."

"No, I's keepin' my eye on things for Captain Mac."

She dragged out a long sigh. "He's gone then."

"Gone, Miss?"

"Back to Alexandria, I suppose. To his family, whom he didn't want me to meet, probably because he's got a fiancée and he hid the fact from me."

"You's talkin' too fast for me, miss." Mr. Rogan scratched his head. His hair looked as bristly as Mac's beard. "Captain Mac's at the Hawkinses' place. He's doin' lots of thinkin' there."

"Then why hasn't he contacted me?" Lily's throat ached from rising dejection. She felt abandoned by everyone she loved—Oliver, Papa, Aunt Hilda, Jonah and Jed. . .and now Mac.

"He prob'ly knows you love him and figures you'll wait on him for a time."

Was that it? Had she jumped to conclusions?

Lily's gaze fell on the leveled cabin. The only evidence of its existence was the stone chimney. It had cost Mac time, manpower, and money—and a dream. Now it was gone. If it had been *Haus am Bach*, Lily would have been inconsolable also.

As it was, her home had been ripped out from under her.

Fat raindrops began to fall. "I must speak with the captain. It's important." But how could she heap her burden on him now? "Oh, never mind.

Don't give him the message." Perhaps the Kaspers would allow her to stay with them temporarily. She may even be desperate enough to knock on the Clydesdales' door.

A throaty moan wafted from somewhere behind the rubble of the barn. Lily moved in that direction.

Mr. Rogan caught her arm. "No, miss. Don't go there."

"Why?"

"It's a ghost. Me and Marcus been hearing it since the fire."

"Nonsense. The only ghost I believe in is the Holy Ghost."

"Don't go there, miss."

Lily shrugged off the warning and picked her way around the debris. The moans grew louder—from beneath the foundational wall that had collapsed.

She dropped to her knees and rolled away large rocks and pieces of plank which had somehow survived the inferno. The moans continued. Lily rolled another stone away. Then another.

"Please, Mr. Rogan, help me. There's a man pinned under here."

He came to her aid and accomplished with little exertion what Lily had been unable to manage. The injured man's black boots and beige trousers appeared. His fawn-colored waistcoat and black frockcoat. Finally his head. The acrid smell of burned flesh and singed hair rose up and Lily nearly gagged.

Upon closer inspection, she gasped. The man's face was severely burned and his swollen lips barely moved. He strained to breathe. The fact the man had managed to stay alive for forty-eight hours was a tribute to his sturdy constitution.

Mr. Rogan assessed him, then looked at Lily and shook his head as if the man had no hope left.

"Help me. . .Lily."

She drew back. He knew her name?

"He's broken all over, miss," Mr. Rogan said. "Maybe even broke his neck too."

"Lily. . .Lily. . ." The injured man's eyelids fluttered and familiarity gripped her.

"Oliver! Oh, merciful Father!"

"Reach into my p-pocket, Lily. Your papa's will. . .I found it."

"Papa's will?" Hope plumed inside of her. Taking great care not to injure Oliver further, she located the document and pulled it from his pocket. "How. . .where?"

"Silas Everett paid me. . ." Oliver's tight voice trailed off and Lily gave his shoulder a shake.

He cried out in pain.

"There, there. . ." Lily gently pushed his hair off his forehead. Yes, he'd been a rake and a rogue, but she couldn't get herself to withhold even a small measure of comfort.

"He paid me," Oliver said as if divining her thoughts. "Find the money in my coat pocket. Give. . .to. . .my. . .family."

He labored to breathe and Lily felt she had to do something. She set down the document and shot to her feet. "Stay with him, Mr. Rogan. I'll run for help."

She made her way over the dregs of the barn.

"Be careful, miss."

"I will." She walked on fallen planks that snapped beneath her weight. With her next step, she expected her foot to meet the ground, but suddenly she was falling down a dark hole as if the earth swallowed her up.

*Splash.* Icy-cold water enveloped her, stunned her momentarily, but she resurfaced with a gasp and a coughing fit followed. She reached for something to cling to, but her fingers only met stone and brick.

*Papa's well.* Lily had forgotten it even existed.

"Miss Lily!" Mr. Rogan's dark face appeared high above her. "Miss Lily."

"Run for help. Please. The water is so cold, I won't be able to tread for long. And Oliver needs a doctor."

"The man's dead, Miss."

Lily's heart ached for Oliver's parents, who had now lost their son a second time.

"Hang on, miss. I'm goin' to get help straightaway."

Already numbness weighed Lily's limbs. Ironic, if there were to be two upcoming burials. Oliver's. . .and hers. But hadn't she said she'd rather die than marry Everett?

It would seem God had heard and this was His reply.

❤

Mac ran as hard and fast as his legs allowed. He could kick himself for not better marking off that well. He also should have guessed that Lily would come looking for him. He'd planned to see her today and beg her forgiveness. He'd gone back on his promise and hurt her in a fit of anger, although not physically. Still, he'd injured her, all the same. For the better part of the day, he'd suffered through enough of Issie's tongue-lashings. He got the message.

He reached the well, Rogan beside him. He would have brought James, but couldn't take the time to get him from his forge in town. He'd managed to find a coil of thick rope in James's barn, however.

"Lily!" Mac threw broken planks out of his way and lay on his belly to the edge of the well. *Please, God, let her be alive.* "Lily, answer me!"

"I'm here."

"I'm going to throw you a rope." Mac tied a loop in one end. "Slip it over your head and under your arms."

Her coughing spurt signaled that she'd taken in water. "Mac? Help me, please."

She sounded winded. This wasn't going to work.

Mac squeezed his eyes closed momentarily as he searched his mind for an alternative plan. "Rogan. . ."

The man was no longer at his side, but leading one of the mules up from the corral.

"Lookin' like you'd better scale down there and rescue your golden-haired miss. Me and this here mule'll lower you down and pull you back up."

Mac inspected the rope. It would hold his weight. He peeled off his frockcoat and slipped the knotted portion around his hips so he fit like a swing. Rogan harnessed the mule and affixed the rope to its bridle.

"Lily, I'm coming. Hold on."

"I can't. . ."

"Float on your back and sing to me. I'm coming down to get you."

"I'm too tired to sing."

"Come on. Sing, Lily." Mac sat on the edge of the well and gave a nod to Rogan. The rope went taut and Mac began his descent.

"Sing, Lily."

*"The Lord is my shepherd..."* Lily's voice sounded weak. *"I shall not want. He maketh me to lie down in green pastures."* A pause. She gulped a breath.

Mac's swing dropped in another couple of feet.

*"In pastures green he leadeth me beside the waters still."*

The well was as dark as tar with little light shining in from above. "Sing that again, Lily."

Mac descended the last several feet so quickly, he was nearly unseated. His backside hit the water. He reached out his hand. "Lily!" Blast it! Where was she?

His fingers met strands of wet hair. He plunged his hand into the frigid water and grabbed onto a handful of material and pulled for all his life.

Lily resurfaced.

The swing dropped him the rest of the way into the well. "Stop!" He prayed Rogan heard him as he gathered Lily's limp body against him.

She choked and he breathed easier. "I've got her. Pull us up, Rogan. Up!"

The rope jerked. Mac held Lily in his arms and fastened his hands around their lifeline. As they ascended, he positioned his feet on the brick lining of the well, as if walking upward, while Rogan and the mule did the hoisting.

Lily began to cry. Her arms circled him.

"Stay still, my darling. We're almost there."

"I've been so heartless and...foolish."

"You're not the one who has been heartless."

At long last, Mac could see daylight, could hear the rain falling softly. One last, but mighty tug, and he and Lily spilled from the well. Mac released her while the mule dragged him several more feet. His arm scraped over scattered debris.

"Stop!" Mac pulled off the rope and crawled to where Lily lay face up to the gentle rain.

"I was afraid you wouldn't come."

He pulled her to him and stood. The muscles in his arms quivered, but he managed to lift her. "Let's get you somewhere warm and dry."

"Wait. My father's will."

Rogan headed toward the ruins, promising to fetch it and bring it to them next door.

Mac strode toward the stone bridge.

"I'm afraid we're both homeless." Lily dropped her head onto Mac's shoulder.

"Oh?" Mac kept right on walking. "We'll just see about that."

# Chapter Twenty-Nine

o my, um, my chess playing has paid off rather handsomely."

Lily shivered, even though she sat by a warm fire blazing in the parlor's hearth. It had been hours since Mac rescued her from the frigid depths of Papa's well, but she still felt chilled. The doctor said she'd escaped any permanent damage, especially if she didn't catch her death in the next several days. The fact she survived at all strengthened Lily's faith in God— and in Mac.

"Let me get this straight. You won custody of Jonah and Jed and Captain O'Malley's ship too? In a chess match? You?"

"Me." Mac sipped his coffee. "It's the boys I wanted, so I told ol' Madman O'Malley to keep the *Sarabella*. Now he insists I won her fair and square. He knows what a reputation of welching on a bet will do to even the most respected of gamblers." A devious glint entered Mac's dark eyes. "Knowing my seafaring days are over, Prescott has offered to purchase the ship from me. It's already on its way to the West Indies, and I'll split the profits with Albright and Osborn Shipping. Meanwhile, my parents are on their way to Middletown."

"So you can rebuild?"

Mac pushed out his lower lip and gave his shoulders a quick up and down. "Remodel, perhaps." His gaze touched each wall of the room.

"You mean. . .you'll be happy here at *Haus am Bach*?"

"I will. Your happiness means everything to me, Lily. Yes, I could rebuild, but why should I? Everything I want is here."

Tears clouded her vision. "But it's too late. Mr. Everett owns the manor. I saw the deed late this afternoon. His name is on it."

"Could be because he'd stepped in as executor of your father's estate and the boys' guardian." Mac stood and walked to where he'd tossed his overcoat. He retrieved documents from its pocket. "Your father's will. As promised, Rogan delivered it."

Lily took the parchment and unfolded the pages. They smelled like smoke, causing her heart to break for all Mac had lost. . .and for Oliver too.

"How in the world did Oliver get his hands on Papa's will?"

"While the doctor was here, I spoke with the authorities. They speculate that Ashton ransacked my cabin before torching it." Mac reclaimed his chair near Lily's. "My guess is the will was hidden somewhere in your father's writing desk."

"Of course! The secret drawer." Lily hadn't thought to search it. Like the well, she'd forgotten it existed.

"Silas Everett has been taken into custody. If he paid Ashton to start the fire, he's equally as guilty, not to mention partly responsible for Ashton's death."

Sorrow accumulated in her eyes. "What Oliver did was deplorable, but he was trying to help his family survive."

"There are plenty of other ways, all above the law."

"True." Lily focused on Papa's will. "Mac, it states here that I'm to inherit forty thousand pounds and *Haus am Bach*." She almost choked. "Upon my marriage."

"To Everett?"

"To whomever. That is, of course, if Papa didn't gamble his money away."

"We'll check into the matter. However, my guess is the money is there, unless Everett stole it. A formal investigation will be launched."

Lily went back to reading the document. "The land is to be divided among my brothers and me, but not until they reach the age of sixteen." She looked up and frowned. "Everett sent them off because they were in the way of his sordid plans."

"So was I." Mac sipped his coffee, then set the cup and saucer on the side table. "That's why Everett paid Ashton to burn down my barn and cabin. He knew I couldn't afford to rebuild, which meant I wouldn't have anything to offer you. He figured I'd return to Alexandria a failure. He was almost correct."

Mac stood, closed the distance between them, and knelt beside her chair. "I never want you to see me as a failure."

"I never will. I never have."

Mac stroked her cheek. "I know that now."

"I was ready to be the mistress of your log cabin."

He chuckled. "Yes, James told me that."

"I do love you, Mac, and I must confess that I was so angry that I jumped to wild conclusions instead of keeping a cool head."

"So, will you forgive me for barking at you like one of my deckhands?"

"Former deckhands." Lily set her palm on his whiskered cheek. "And, yes, I forgive you."

"Will you marry me? A man named Everett owes me a refund on some property he illegally sold to me."

"I don't care about the money, Mac. I just want to be your wife."

His snug embrace provided the instant warmth Lily's body craved. It melted her heart and sent her spirit soaring. Great burdens of ponderings, doubts, and fears lifted off her shoulders. She knew then that she was right where God intended her to be—

Safe in the arms of her beloved.

# Author's Note

### The Shenandoah Valley

Being a Wisconsin native, I had much to learn about Virginia state history. One of the more interesting facts I came across is that because the southern part of the Shenandoah Valley has a higher elevation than the northern part, the Shenandoah River runs northeast and empties into the Potomac. As a result, when one is traveling north on the Valley Pike, from Woodstock to Winchester, for example, one is going north, *down the valley*. Traveling south, from Winchester to Staunton, is considered going *up the valley*. It's opposite the traditional concept of "down south" and "up north."

### Drinking and Smoking

You'll notice that my male characters, although they are Christians, indulge in a swallow or two of rum wine and ale from time to time. Additionally, they smoke cigars. Many decades after the events of this story, Charles Spurgeon was reported to have said, "Well, dear friends, you know that some men can do to the glory of God what to other men would be sin. And notwithstanding...I intend to smoke a good cigar to the glory of God before I go to bed to-night." While I don't personally condone the practices, I felt it was important that my story be as historically accurate as possible.

### History vs. Reality

While I did much research, I also took great liberties with the town of Middletown in the Shenandoah Valley. I modeled Lily's home after Belle Grove Plantation. It was built in 1797 by Major Isaac Hite and his wife, Nelly Madison Hite (sister of President James Madison). I had the privilege of touring it in 2014, and I felt the history ooze from its very foundation. I also fell in love with the area.

**Andrea Boeshaar** has been married for nearly forty years. She and her husband have three wonderful sons, one beautiful daughter-in-law, and five precious grandchildren. Andrea's publishing career began in 1994. Since then, thirty of her books have gone to press. Additionally, Andrea cofounded ACFW (American Christian Fiction Writers) and served on its advisory board. In 2007, Andrea earned her certification in Christian life coaching and is currently the purveyor of The Writer's ER, a coaching and editing service for writers. For more information, log on to Andrea's website at: www.andreaboeshaar.com. Follow her on Twitter: @AndreaBoeshaar, and find her on Facebook: Andrea Boeshaar Author.